The Hazards of War

Jonathan Paul Isaacs

This is a work of fiction. All of the characters, organizations, and events portrayed in this novel are either products of the author's imagination or are used fictitiously.

THE HAZARDS OF WAR

ISBN-13: 978-1517650087

For Dad

THE HAZARDS OF WAR

Prelude

RAF Sergeant Stephen James Cartwright shivered away in the empty fuselage of the Dakota cargo plane. The thin aluminum skin was no protection at altitude, nor was the sheepskin-lined clothing that covered everything but his eyes. Comfort was defined by rubbing the exposed parts of his face above his oxygen mask to keep his eyebrows from freezing. Cartwright's companion on the other side of the fuselage did the same, with about the same frequency.

"Good God, I've got to take a piss," Simon moaned. "How long do you think it'll take to get us home, now?"

"Why don't you go in the soup can?" Cartwright asked.

"Are you out of your mind? I don't want my equipment to freeze off. There's no way I'm whipping it out this high up. Maybe I'll just go in my trousers, bet that'd feel nice, eh?"

"Until your piss freezes, too. Then you'd be worse off than you are now."

A barely visible furrow creased Simon's forehead above his oxygen mask. "What's a man to do, then? How do they expect us to not turn into icicles back here?" He shifted uncomfortably in his harness. "Who the hell designed this plane?" he added, attempting a joke.

Cartwright also struggled to find some amusement amidst the misery. He rubbed his eyebrows again. At least they were dry. Many bombing runs into Nazi Germany caused the crew to work up such a sweat manning the guns that the frozen perspiration on their skin made for a brutal flight back to England. A specialty mission like this was a cakewalk. Lieutenant Donner had shown up at just the right time.

He and Simon stared at each other. Cartwright watched as his mate apparently decided he couldn't hold it anymore. Simon unstrapped part of his parachute and busily pried his personal hydraulics through multiple layers of flight gear. He must have been bad off in order to take a piss at fifteen thousand feet.

Donner's voice crackled through Cartwright's headset. "Hang on back there, lads, we've got a little company."

"Damn it, can't they wait until I'm done? There's no courtesy left in the world today, Stephen. No courtesy at all."

"Did you expect any less from the Jerries?"

The Dakota started to bank to the left as Cartwright grabbed hold of one of the cargo straps. The night sky would have been pitch black outside. How on Earth had the Germans seen them? That was why the British flew bombing runs at night, to avoid contact, unlike the brute defiance of the American daylight raids. Cartwright wondered if they had been picked up by ground radar like the English had used during the Battle of Britain. Even then, he wondered how good the fighter pilots could be when surrounded by blackness.

Simon sat on the opposite side of the fuselage several feet further down towards the tail. The only light inside the plane was provided by two working bulbs, and the dim light compounded the queasiness Cartwright felt as the plane pitched and rolled. He tried to talk to take his mind off their helplessness.

"Did you use that soup can yet?"

"I don't think my aim is good enough," Simon replied. "Why?"

The plane banked to the right.

"I need something to puke into."

"Just aim away from me, and pray it freezes before it smells."

"I think I'll aim *directly* at you," Cartwright said.

"Then I will be forced to plant my foot in your arse."

The fuselage twisted left and pitched downward. Cartwright felt his stomach rise up into his brain.

"The Old Man seems to be trying to do that for you."

"For both of us," Simon quipped.

The plane continued through evasive maneuvers in the darkness. Cartwright's nerves were starting to fray. On a normal bombing run, the formation would stay on the straight and narrow in order to control the coverage over the target area, even if the flak from the 88's was thick and heavy. Hard evasive flying really wasn't something he was used to, something he hadn't really anticipated when he had volunteered for the mission.

A thunderous *crack* sliced through the air.

The Dakota shuddered violently. Cartwright barely managed to hold onto his cargo strap and not tumble down toward the cockpit. Simon was not so lucky. The other Briton somersaulted through the air into a metal rib with a sickening thud.

"Simon!"

The plane nosed into a freefall. Cartwright clung desperately to the strap as his feet violently dangled about. What the hell had happened?

Donner's voice crackled on the intercom, "The wing's gone! Get out! Get out!"

Oh my God, Cartwright thought. His mind raced through ways to get to the rear hatch. He pulled his weightless body up towards the tail of the plane by grabbing any handhold he could find. Despite the formidable bulk of the Dakota, it kept trying to twist away from his grip as it hurdled out of control towards the Earth. He had to get out, and fast.

After what seemed like an eternity, Cartwright reached the rear hatch and grabbed the release lever. He fought for what little leverage he could manage and popped the hatch away and open from the fuselage. Light from the burning engine danced savagely on the remaining wing, flashing orange and yellow bursts that were quickly swallowed up by the darkness. Cartwright wedged himself in the hatch opening against the blast of cold air and looked back down the plane. Simon's body floated limply in the dead air, and no one had come down from the cockpit—not Donner, not the co-pilot, no one. No one else was anywhere close to bailing out. Were they dead? Should he go back in and try to pull them out?

The dive was so steep that the fuselage was vertical. The whine from the engine was audible even over the rush of air. Time was running out.

Cartwright agonized on what to do. He had known Simon since the beginning of his enlistment. But the Old Man had said to bail out, and that was final—it was the captain's job to manage what could be done to save the crew, not for the crew to second-guess his commands. They weren't supposed to go back into the plane. They were supposed to get out.

Cartwright had thought he was as fatalistic as the other men of the RAF when it came to flying against the Germans, but at this moment of truth he realized he was terrified of dying.

With a twinge of fear and no small amount of regret, he looked one last time back at Simon, drew his lips tight, and hurdled out into the darkness.

1

Soldiers at war often fight the weather as much as the enemy. Today, the weather was winning.

Captain Hans Tiedemann of the Waffen-SS stood in the frigid rain and watched his men try—and fail—to get their truck free. It was a hopeless affair. Each time the Opel seemed like it was about to regain enough traction to move back onto the unpaved road, the tires would invariably slip at the last moment become stuck once again in the quagmire. The soldiers, their camouflage smocks shrugging off lines of water, would bow their heads in frustration and trudge over to try once again. All Tiedemann could do was follow attempt after vain attempt. They were going to be here forever.

"Herr Hauptsturmführer?"

Tiedemann turned and struggled briefly for the name of the lieutenant next to him. Krauss, he thought. Too many people in his *Kompanie* were new, with too little time for them to regroup in southern France. That's what happened when battle groups returned from Russia. Decimation. Scores of replacements. It would take time to learn all of their names. Or maybe Tiedemann shouldn't bother, and it would be easier to forget them when they died.

Krauss was on the short side, a narrow mustache underneath his angular nose and glasses. He was shielding a partially folded map from the rain with the side of his coat. Tiedemann could barely recognize their location through the failing light. Heavy lines from Luxembourg to Avignon represented the roads on which they were supposed to be, but where Krauss was pointing was in the middle of a blank space devoid of any signs of civilization.

"I think we're here, sir," he said as he fingered the map. "Seventy, maybe seventy-five kilometers south of Dijon, heading south. I don't know where we got off of the main road. No one saw any signs that indicated a wrong turn."

"Who was navigating?" Tiedemann asked.

Krauss paused for a moment. "I was, Herr Hauptsturmführer."

Nodding to himself, Tiedemann filed that little tidbit away for later. Krauss came from the General Staff. While Tiedemann was sure the mousy little man was bright, field navigation would be an area for improvement.

Damn it, too many replacements.

Chewing out an officer in a cold November rainstorm wasn't going to help matters. Tiedemann instead wanted to know what could be done to fix their current mess. They had a schedule to keep.

As if reading his thoughts, or perhaps atoning for his sin of poor geography, Krauss offered a possible solution. "Sir, according to my notes, there's a French manor house about a kilometer further down this road. *Domaine des Contis*, a small vineyard. If you would be inclined to stop for the night, we could take shelter there and wait out the rest of the storm."

"We're supposed to be in Perpignan the day after tomorrow," Tiedemann replied. "The Americans are in North Africa as we speak, and if they mean to invade southern France they will not wait on us because you got us lost. We still have some daylight left, even with this blackened sky. I intend to make use of it."

No sooner had the words left his mouth than their problematic Opel lurched forward, showering the soldiers around it in a great splattering of mud. From there the truck quickly fishtailed out of control and slid off the opposite side of the road. Men picked themselves up out of the filth, and even through the heavy rain Tiedemann could see on their faces that the outlook was grim. The truck had overturned into a gully alongside the road. It wasn't going anywhere tonight.

Scheisse.

Tiedemann glanced over at Krauss and their eyes met. There was a moment of silence, then without a word both men looked down in unison at the map.

The house was a large structure that sat on top of a hill and jutted up almost imperceptibly against an angry sky. Tiedemann led a small group of men up a winding path with another lieutenant named Heinrich Springer close at his side. He didn't know much about Springer either, except that he had been in the Hitler Youth and spoke French, and that was enough for the moment. The rest of the men stayed to secure their vehicles roadside for the night.

The stone path was treacherous and kept them exposed to the stinging rain. They were in a fine mood by the time they reached the double doors.

Springer pounded loudly on the wood with his fist.

"Attention! Nous sommes les soldats allemands! Nous vous commandons ouvrir les portes au nom du Führer!"

There was no response. Springer repeated his command to open the door, then grabbed a Mauser rifle from one of his men and punctuated his order with several strokes against the wood. Gradually, faint scrapes and scuffles could be heard from the other side. A few moments later and a door opened to reveal a blonde, middle-aged woman holding a short candle. She was clearly dressed for bed.

"Qui est ce dehors là?"

"Stand de côté au nom du Führer!" shouted Springer.

"Ce qui?" The woman was blocking any passage to the warmth inside.

"Étape de côté, maintenant!" Springer shoved the Mauser at her to leave no mistake about whether or not they were coming in.

"Mouvement? Ah! Ah, non! Robert! Robert!"

The indignation on the woman's face was plain as day, but a soaking Tiedemann didn't care. The people of a conquered land were subject to the will of the conqueror. Passing troops often required food and shelter and most of the French north of the Demarcation Line cooperated—begrudgingly. However, down here in Vichy France, which was presumably still independent, the Germans would have to be a little more forceful. Not that they wouldn't treat everyone decently. France was a cultured country. The Russians received quite a different handling.

The SS troops forced their way into the house. Tiedemann stood in the rear, edging out of the rain as best he could until he was sure his men had secured the area. The doors opened up into a large foyer that revealed corridors on the left and right, with limestone flagstones underfoot that darkened with the water the men brought in. On the grand staircase that faced them, a Frenchman in his late forties was rapidly descending the steps with his palms forward to show he was unarmed. The woman who had answered the door was clearly yelling at him to do something, evident to the Germans in spite of the language barrier.

"Gentlemen, is there something we can do for you?" the Frenchman asked in workable German.

"We require shelter for the night," Springer announced with all the authority of the Reich. "You will provide for our men until the storm ends and the roads become serviceable. Your treatment will be fair if you follow instructions properly and don't force us to throw you out."

"Of course, of course," the man answered in a stammering voice. The horrified reluctance was as plain as day on his face, though he quickly regained his composure. "The six of you are welcome in our home. We are more than happy to greet travelers with a spare bed."

Springer interrupted him. "Six? We have closer to twenty. Officers will be taking over the bedrooms and furniture as required. You and your family may displace to another part of the house as long as you don't cause trouble."

The Frenchman turned white.

The wife saw his reaction and started jabbering at him in incomprehensible bursts. The Frenchman answered in kind, and whatever he said made the woman even more agitated than when she had opened the door to a group of armed men. Springer tried to bark instructions but found himself increasingly ignored as the domestic argument spiraled out of control. The lieutenant's face began to turn red and he reached for the Mauser he had used on the door.

Tiedemann saw what was about to happen and decided it was time he brought their introduction to a close. He stepped through the gauntlet formed by his men and approached the Frenchman.

"What is your name?"

Silence descended upon the room save for the pounding of raindrops outside the open doors.

"Conti, monsieur," said the Frenchman. "Robert Conti."

Tiedemann studied the man for a moment. He was short, well groomed, and clean-shaven. Still quite pale. The brown hair slicked across his head covered a touch of baldness, and his clothes were well tailored with the vague smell of cigarette smoke. Judging by the appearance of the man and his home, it wasn't much of a leap to guess that Conti and his family must have lived well and enjoyed their wealth before the war.

"You say your name is Robert Conti?" Tiedemann asked politely.

"Yes, monsieur."

"You are the Robert Conti of the winery, *Domaine des Contis*?"

"Yes, monsieur."

"Ah. I thought so," Tiedemann said, smiling. "An excellent vineyard. I especially liked your, oh, what was it, *Cadiau* 1934. I used to have several bottles, that is, before the war started. What an outstanding stroke of luck for us to have happened upon your manor."

"*Merci*. We have tried to work very hard at making the best wine possible."

"And you have succeeded, very much so." Tiedemann took a dramatically deep breath. "Monsieur Conti, my men have their own equipment, bedrolls, and provisions. All they need is a roof over their head out of this dreadfully cold rain. Perhaps, if you thought it fitting, they could simply sleep on the floor?"

Conti seemed to regain some of his color at this concession and was now merely off-pale. “Of course, monsieur, if that would be all they need, we could certainly accommodate you. The ground floor would probably work well. Uh, that is, I *think* there would be room for that many men.”

“Oh, I’m sure it will be fine. As far as my officers and I are concerned, however, we would hope for more comfortable accommodations. If that could be arranged, of course.” Tiedemann looked directly into Conti’s eyes. “We wouldn’t want anyone to have to sleep outside in this awful weather.”

The Frenchman started nodding slowly, glancing over at his wife before looking back at Tiedemann. The threat was not lost on him. “Yes, yes, we have a few rooms upstairs that would work well. If there aren’t too many of you. My wife could bring you some linens if you like.”

“That would be splendid. Please ask her if she would do so.” Tiedemann stretched out his arm towards where the woman stood at his left, prompting Conti to begin making the necessary arrangements.

Tiedemann walked back to the open doorway. He could see Obersturmführer Eppler, another one of his lieutenants, leading the rest of the platoon up the path towards him. That was good. But when he turned around it was obvious that Springer was seething. He looked like a dog that had just been yanked back on his leash by his owner.

Conti's wife had already left the room, and Conti himself was calling up the staircase for either servants or more family members to assist. Tiedemann pulled Springer over for a private conversation.

"Speak, lieutenant."

"Sir," Springer gushed, "why don't we just throw them out?"

"Because it's not necessary," Tiedemann said in a private, parental tone. "As you can see, even in war, a certain level of politeness can work wonders. While the French are a conquered people, sometimes they forget. That doesn't mean we don't remind them. But there are better times than when we're dripping wet and about to collapse from fatigue."

"*Jawohl,* Herr Hauptsturmführer!"

"Please continue in assisting our gracious host with his preparations by securing the rest of the manor. Politely."

Tiedemann caught Springer's eye to make sure he understood. Many of his men were hardened warriors, having fought through the horrors of the Russian front where neither side gave any quarter. Unless they were told otherwise, *polite* might simply mean a bullet in the head instead of the stomach.

"*Jawohl!*" Springer yelled again, and immediately began to organize groups of soldiers to search the house.

Tiedemann stood aside to let his men filter in. Their appearance was awful, covered in mud and misery. A night of sleeping indoors was well deserved. They would need it before going back into battle.

And all of it had been arranged without a struggle, using a few simple lies. Tiedemann smiled darkly. While he fancied a quality glass here and there, he had never heard of Conti wines before. If Krauss hadn't briefed him in the car on the way over, it might have taken force to get a roof over their heads after all. Then they would not have had anyone to play servant during their stay.

2

The emergency family meeting took place in the green sitting room. Gabrielle Conti claimed her seat on the edge of the great wooden desk while everyone crowded into what had become her father's refuge. Normally he pondered problems related to winemaking or business. Not so this time.

The entire family was here. Gabrielle watched as her father apprehensively paced back and forth, rubbing his hands together, taking a break only to chain smoke another cigarette with nervous fingers. Gabrielle's mother sat in the padded chair in the opposite corner and held on to young Philippe as if the eight-year-old would be taken away from her. Philippe clearly was more annoyed at their mother's grasp than afraid, and probably was thinking of ways to sneak downstairs and ask the soldiers about their guns. Girard, their old retainer who had been working for the Contis since before Gabrielle was born, was standing with his back against the closed door and appeared particularly fatalistic. There was a hard seriousness in his eyes that seemed to belay a normally jovial face. Girard was built like a soldier, even if his bad foot gave him a limp that had kept him out of the army.

Then there was Gabrielle's grandfather, Marc. The elderly patriarch was glaring disapprovingly at her father from the window. Gabrielle could tell there was going to be another fight. They had never gotten along for as long as Gabrielle could remember. Perhaps that was what happened when a suitor took a man's only daughter away. Gabrielle wondered if Papa would be that jealous when she herself got married.

"You should not be letting the *Boches* stay here," Marc was grumbling. "I cannot believe you gave in so easily. It's disgraceful!"

Here it comes, Gabrielle thought.

"Marc, I tell you we had no choice," her father replied. His voice was already tired. "There is no Unoccupied Zone anymore. If we had resisted, they would have simply thrown us out into the storm and taken over the entire house!"

"They *have* taken over the entire house. And so what if we had to walk to town, even in this weather? At least we wouldn't have to sleep under the same roof as that Nazi filth."

"Keep your voice down," Girard warned. He had his ear pressed to the door, listening.

Her father paced more random patterns across the hardwood floor. The planks were well worn with scuffmarks from many long nights. Sometimes she would join him and sit just as she was now, on the desk with her legs crossed at the ankles, and gaze at him in silent support. This was the room where he would fret about poor harvests or disease in the fields; this was the place he would think about how much money they owed or how much wine they would not sell. This was the worry room.

"We can deal with them for one night," her father said finally. "They were caught in the storm and their trucks were washed out. Yes, that means some inconvenience for us. But it is only for one night."

"And you will accept this?" her grandfather spat.

"*Oui.*"

"What if they find—"

"They're not going to find *anything.*" Papa looked very strangely at her grandfather. "There's nothing here but some old vintners in the French countryside."

The old man grumbled before apparently shifting his argument. "Just them being here is the problem. Robert, you should have lied. You could have said the cellars were flooded from the rain. You could have talked about filth floating up the stairs, about Claudette having some disease, anything to dissuade them from staying here for the night. Now they are billeting their troops here. Next time it will be for more than just one night, it will be for a month. Then two months. And then we will be thrown out altogether. You're letting thugs and criminals take away our home, our security, or our dignity."

"In case you hadn't noticed, Marc, our entire country has had those things taken away."

On and on went their debate. Papa faulted the previous French government as being completely ineffectual, so in many ways the Vichy rule was a much needed change from the machinery that had allowed their country to be overrun with humiliating speed. Even though things were not ideal, it didn't mean they should fight. Active resistance meant that the Germans would tighten down ruthlessly. The only path back to normalcy for a French citizen was to settle in, even if begrudgingly, to life under German influence. That was the way of the pragmatist. Tolerate the occupation. Do as they were told.

Her grandfather felt differently.

"The reason we no longer have freedom, Robert, is because the Vichy government has done precisely what you are doing here. We have let the enemy into our house too freely. An honorable Frenchman would never bow down before an occupying army. It sends the wrong message. You're acting like a filthy collaborator."

"Is that so?" replied her father. "Letting in some men from the rain? That's going to undermine our country? Hardly!"

"That's how it starts. Next, you give some other small concession. Then again, and again, until finally you've become nothing but a lapdog with no sense of patriotism, no sense of pride, no sense of *self*!"

Gabrielle drew a sharp breath. She tried to hold her tongue, but sometimes it had a mind of its own.

"Grandpere—how can you say that to him?"

"Eh?"

"You're always condemning Papa. Always! Aren't family members supposed to stick together?

These Germans barge in waving guns in the air, and you declare that we should have argued with them. That's asinine!"

"Gabrielle, show some respect for your elders!" her mother scolded.

"When it's due, I will. I'm defending my father—*your* husband. Why aren't *you* standing up for him?"

"Gabrielle!"

She switched her attention back to her grandfather.

"This whole argument about letting the soldiers in is ludicrous anyway. It's been storming for days. All that drainage has to go somewhere. It's just fate that all the runoff got channeled onto the road the Germans were using. It's not Papa's fault. It's not anyone's fault. The Germans were going to find us regardless of anything we might do."

"We still have a choice as to how we react."

"Indeed," Gabrielle snarled. "All you do is complain. You say how the wine wasn't bottled right, or how Papa isn't good enough for my mother, or that the grapes were harvested too early. When's the last time you actually *did* anything, Grandpere?"

Grandpere was standing stiffly, an odd expression darkening his eyes. "I've done more than you know, girl."

She dismissed his vagueness as if she was swatting away an insect. "Right now we should be talking about how to get through tonight. From what I saw, those soldiers are pretty much keeping to themselves. I bet they're exhausted. What we really should do is feed them. Fill their bellies with a good, hot meal and put them to sleep. We have vegetables from the garden and some bread from yesterday. Don't give them any provocation so they leave us alone, and that will be the end of it."

Her grandfather scrunched his face up. "Then what about tomorrow morning, when their fatigue is gone and they wake up? If it rains all night, the roads will be just as bad. We'll have a house full of Nazis with nothing to do but cause us trouble and have us cater to their every whim."

"Grandpere—"

"And did you see their collars, girl? Did you even look? The skull and crossbones insignia, the Nordic runes in silver and black? These are no *Wehrmacht* soldiers." The old man lowered his voice to a grave, conspiratorial tone. "These are SS—brutal monsters. They cannot be allowed to stay. We are in great danger with them here. I would not be surprised if they want to kill us all before they leave."

Gabrielle's mother started to cry. She grasped Philippe even tighter and he squirmed uncomfortably.

Shooting an angry look at Marc, her father strode quickly over to her mother and squatted down next to the chair. He took Mama's hands in his, releasing the death grip on their son, and with gentle strokes began to knead her fingers to ease her sobbing. Philippe looked relieved at being free, but their grandfather's words had clearly made him afraid.

"Hush now, my dear, it will be all right," Papa was saying. "Don't listen to him. He's old and bitter and doesn't think before opening his mouth."

"I'm sorry I let them in the door. I didn't realize who they were. I didn't know any better," Mama sobbed. Her graying blonde hair hung in front of her face.

"Shush, sweetheart, it will be all right. It wasn't your fault."

Grandpere wouldn't let up. "How can you say that to her, Robert? Right now, I don't see you doing anything that will make it 'all right'."

It struck Gabrielle as utterly ironic that her family was in this position. They were in the middle of the countryside. *Nobody* ever bothered to come out here. Even the Vichy government left them alone except when it came time to meet the wine quotas, and those mainly affected the larger growers and producers in Burgundy. The Contis held such a small estate that their entire yield would never make a dent in the number of bottles to be sent back to Berlin, and thus the family had managed to often escape notice.

Her grandfather was now trying to enlist Girard for support. The leading questions he asked pushed Gabrielle to her limit. She was only eighteen years old, but she had always been treated by her father as the eldest child, and it was clear he intended for her to one day run the family estate just as he had done. She was as tough and stubborn as anyone else in the room.

"Grandpere, you are not helping with your snide mumbling. Stop sitting there and telling us what trouble we're in. What's done is done. Instead of finding fault, why don't you start being constructive in dealing with it?"

He arched his eyebrows at the challenge. "Well, it may come to that, my little one, since I seem to be the only one with some common sense around here."

"It would be nice to see you actually use it then. Help solve the problem, instead of complaining like one of my boy-chasing girlfriends with stars in her eyes."

Her grandfather's cheeks flushed and he sat back against the window with a stunned expression.

Philippe leaned forward and offered a hopeful suggestion. "Could we ask Stefan for some help with the Germans?"

"Hush! Do *not* make any reference to that man, Philippe!" Robert hissed.

The delivery was so harsh that even Gabrielle flinched, and for a moment she thought that her brother might cry.

A twinge of regret passed over Papa's face. After a deep breath, he clasped his son's shoulder and spoke in a softer tone. "Philippe, you are forbidden to say anything about Stefan. This is very important to all of us. Under no circumstances, ever, are you to refer to or talk about him."

The boy's bright eyes looked at each person in the room before dropping to the floor. "I was just trying to help."

"I know, Philippe. You're a good boy. But in this case, we must be extremely strict. Do you understand?"

"Yes, Papa."

"Good." Papa patted him on the back and gave a savage glare at the old man. Gabrielle could sympathize with her father. It was her grandfather's fault that Stefan was even an issue.

There was an uncomfortable silence, broken only by the splatter of raindrops as they hit the windowpane from the blackness beyond. The tiny hearth was faring poorly against the cold air.

Papa pulled his hand back from Philippe and stroked his thinning hair. They were still no closer to solving their dilemma.

"Robert," Grandpere said. His voice was calmer, more careful.

"*Oui?*"

"You know I only speak the way I do because I care for our family, yes? The Nazis in our house are an extreme danger to all of us. If we're not careful, we're dead. That's why I'm upset. That's why I'm so angry we're in this predicament."

Robert nodded in acknowledgement. "I know, Marc. I know." He sighed deeply. "You know I don't share your views about the Germans. But given the most recent events, it's clear we need to do something. I have to think of something."

"You'd better, Robert. For all of our sakes, you'd better.

3

The master bedroom was tiny.

Tiedemann had hoped for better. A large bed was wedged between a single wardrobe and a limestone fireplace, and there was even less space now that four cots reeking of mothballs had been crammed around the edges. The tall ceiling greedily sucked away any heat that might have made the air tolerable.

As tired as he was, though, and with the early start he hoped for tomorrow, Tiedemann was uninterested in expending energy to pursue improvements in their accommodations. Anything beat sleeping in the field.

Springer didn't seem to agree. "Look at this place. There's dust everywhere. The Conti's sleep here?"

"It beats sleeping in the woods," Krauss said.

"Hardly." The Hitler Youth brushed the blond hair from his eyes. "It's colder than it is outside. Where's the Frenchman? We need him to bring us some blankets."

Krauss still attempted to play the optimist, perhaps because he had gotten them into this situation in the first place. "At least it's dry. That's all that counts in my book."

"Shut up, Krauss," Springer said.

"What if we had some firewood?"

Tiedemann agreed from where he sat heavily on the bed. "Yes. We need a fire." A quick scan didn't reveal any nearby. "Herr Springer, break up one of the cots for kindling. Perhaps that will dispel some of the cold."

The sound of fat raindrops still shattered loudly just on the other side of the ceiling. It took several minutes for the two subordinate officers to dismantle the portable bed and build a small pyramid in the fireplace. Krauss unsuccessfully fumbled with the matchsticks until Springer snatched them away and took over, leaving the smaller man to stand back against the doorway in indignation.

There was a bunch of tromping in the hallway and two more wet Germans entered the room. Johannes Hoffman, another lieutenant, pushed Krauss out of the way as he entered. He was followed by SS-Sturmscharführer Gohler, their master sergeant and senior non-com.

Hoffman wrinkled his forehead. "This is all we've been given? There are only four beds!"

"There used to be five," Springer said. He didn't take his eyes off lighting the fire.

Hoffman stood by the doorway, momentarily stunned. His eyes scanned the room for the odd man out. "Well, Krauss, you'll have to sleep downstairs on the main floor."

"Why should *I* sleep there? Why don't *you*?"

"Because Gohler will need a bitch to keep him warm while he's down there."

Krauss turned red, bristling. Tiedemann had to turn his head to suppress a smile. *General Staff,* he reminded himself. Very different than

Hoffman and Gohler. The latter two were cut from the same cloth: rough, hard, and determined. Plus, they were a matching set. They had both fought in the same unit in Russia against overwhelming odds and unbearable conditions. They had both managed to persevere. Together they formed what Tiedemann hoped he could use as the foundation of his new command structure while they rebuilt their *Kompanie*. The rest of the officers—Krauss, Springer, and lieutenant Wilhelm Eppler—would round out the remainder of his platoon leaders.

He needed every experienced man he could get. *Totenkopf* as a division had been decimated in southern Russia. His own company had fought a ruthless withdrawal from a surrounded position in the Valdai Hills. Many of those men were no longer among the living.

Tiedemann flopped heavily on the Contis' mattress. He tried not to think about how much they would be off schedule if the rain continued. Instead, he let his mind wander to Elise. A mere week ago he had been enjoying her flashing smile and blond curls as they took advantage of his furlough in Berlin. Now, he missed her terribly. They had gone to the opera together, eaten at the best restaurants—the ones unaffected as yet by rationing, thanks to Tiedemann's SS network—and had long talks about what they would do together after all the fighting was over. He had dared to think about the end of the war. And Tiedemann had been able to sleep in a real bed with Elise snuggled across his chest, the warmth of her body radiating through his bare skin in the cold October night.

When he received the invitation to visit Dieter's school, Tiedemann had looked forward to it with the anticipation of any father wanting to see part of his son's life. The room of awestruck nine-year-olds swarmed around the hero from the front lines. Tiedemann did his best to paint them a picture of the heroic SS soldiers fighting bravely in the snow, the vanquished Soviet villains retreating cowardly at the German advance. He watched his son's eyes beam with pride in front of his classmates. Tiedemann was a real life hero to those young boys and girls being indoctrinated into the Nazi way.

Nighttime, of course, brought reality crashing in. Tiedemann had sat on the edge of the bed sobbing, with Elise wrapped over his shoulders cradling him in her arms. He had been unable to think of anything but the men under his command, killed horribly, a thousand miles from home, cold and alone. *Alone.*

There was the squad of men led by Peterson, one of his best sergeants, incinerated by an artillery shell on the outskirts of some nameless Russian town.

There was Corporal Wolff, killed by a sniper when a bullet ripped through his face as he peered around the edge of building.

There was Swedenburg, who had his legs blown off after wandering into a minefield, and Zimmer, who experienced the same after foolishly trying to rescue him.

There was Kohl, who had had his guts blown apart by a mortar shell during a firefight and had lain in the dirt for an hour screaming for his mother before he died.

Tiedemann hated it. He hated all of it. The waste, the dying, the suffering, the life, the *duty*.

Yet, to duty he was bound, for there were no other choices for a German military officer. The Reich demanded obedience. It didn't matter that all he wanted was to be home, with Elise and Dieter, and be a father and husband rather than a commander of men who led them to death. He would soldier on as his duty dictated. But—and this was the promise he had made to himself as he lay in bed with Elise—he would *not* lose his humanity. Someday, all of this would be over, and he needed to keep his soul intact.

In the meantime, the Americans had come.

With the Allied landing in North Africa, the Reich had declared that the whole of France was to be occupied rather than just the northern half. Every German division that had been refitting in the rear was being diverted to the coast for defense. Tiedemann and his replacement officers were no exception, all of them being rushed south with as much speed as was possible to be in place before a potential invasion. There was to be no escape, no reprieve from the lines of battle.

Of course, it seemed fitting that getting to Perpignan on the southern coast of France was not to be easy. They still had their work cut out for them to bring the division up to strength. So many raw recruits. There was nothing worse for a German soldier than to be thrust into a company full of strangers with whom he would have to entrust his life. Gone were the days of regional units—heavy losses had changed all that. The racial guidelines were gone and the Waffen-SS yet struggled to fill the ranks. Tiedemann himself barely knew his own officers.

The last of them, Lieutenant Eppler, appeared suddenly in the doorway. Several dark bottles protruded from his arms folded across his chest.

"What have you got there, Eppler?"

A devilish grin spread across the lieutenant's tan face. "They've opened up their cellars to us. Drinks are on me."

Krauss snapped to attention at the mention of wine and eagerly attempted to pry the bottles from Eppler's grasp. It was almost comic to see the short, balding Krauss overpowering another SS officer who was tall and well-muscled, with sun-bleached hair that fell over a deeply tanned face.

"What did you get? Which years?"

"How should I know, I just grabbed a bunch of them."

"No, no," Krauss said. He scrutinized the labels. "These are just average years. Let me go and I'll get us some good bottles."

"Fine," Eppler shrugged. "We'll just sit here and drink what we've... Christ, could you get a corkscrew while you're down there? And glasses!"

Krauss was already at the end of the hallway. Springer laughed. "How could you forget something like that?"

"Rushed."

"I'll get the glasses for us." A sly smile spread across Springer's face. "I need to find out where that tasty little French girl went anyway. Conti's daughter, I think? She looked lonely at the top of the staircase."

"I'm wet and exhausted. I'll take the alcohol."

Tiedemann cracked a smile as Springer left. He liked Eppler. He was the newest member of his command, an Afrika Korps veteran who had served with distinction until a war wound had sent him back to Germany. Interestingly, following his recovery he didn't return to his unit but instead transferred to the Waffen-SS. It was uncommon, but not an unheard of—the SS paid better. The fact that Eppler was from Bad Tölz probably clinched the change. The town was one of the major training facilities of the SS, and Eppler had undoubtedly been steeped in the SS ideologue long before joining its ranks. Now, assigned to Tiedemann's *Kompanie* a mere two weeks before, he was just in time for the refit. As far as Tiedemann was concerned, the desert warrior's experience would be sorely needed to train the scores of new recruits.

"So," Hoffman said, "are you going to stand there, or are you going to open those bottles?"

"What? How?" Eppler asked.

"Here, give it to me." Hoffman stood from his cot and grabbed one of the bottles of wine. Walking over to a small window, he deftly smashed the glass neck against the windowsill and sent a shower of Burgundy dribbling down the wall. Then, motioning Gohler to toss him the cup from his mess kit, he poured the wine and took a discerning sip.

"Well? How is it?"

"Best thing this side of Berlin. Give me your cups."

Tiedemann watched the wine get passed around. When he took a sip for himself, he found it rather poor. Not that any of that would keep them from consuming it. It was booze.

"Not bad at all," Tiedemann lied. He took another bitter sip. "You must have gotten lucky to pull out these bottles, never mind what Krauss says."

"Thank you. I like to think I'm lucky," Eppler replied. He glanced over at Hoffman, who was lustily emptying the last of the first bottle.

Tiedemann stifled a yawn and studied his subordinate. "So, Eppler, tell me this. What do you think about all of this, getting stuck here, the whole mess?" Every man had different strengths and weaknesses, and he had not yet put together what all of them were with his subordinates.

Eppler filled his cup again and leaned back against the wall in reflection.

"I'm not surprised about the trucks, actually. We had problems like this all the time in Tunisia.

Sand would get in the treads of the rear wheels and then you're done—no traction. Apparently Opels have the same problem with mud."

"So what did you do?" said Hoffman. He threw back another swig of burgundy.

"Dug the sand out of the treads whenever we stopped." Eppler laughed. "We dug the sand out of everything. Our rifles, the antitank guns, you name it, because if we didn't, then we'd find ourselves in a lot of trouble. Nothing would work right. You can have a brilliant commander and able comrades, but if your equipment doesn't work—well, you know how that goes."

"I agree completely," Gohler said. The master sergeant was nodding from across the room, the pale, thin scar that ran from his chin to his left ear shining like a strand of silver. "You have to take care of your weapons. It's the cornerstone for discipline and combat effectiveness."

"How were the men you fought with in Africa?" Tiedemann asked, curious.

Eppler took on a far-away look as he cast his memory back. "Good. They were like brothers to me. I served in the same *Kompanie* for two years, and even though there were a few men that came and went, that core of our group was my family. We sweated through the days together and shivered through the nights together. If one of us had trouble at home, the others were there for you. And the fighting—the Brits are tough. They don't want to give up a single meter of ground. You need brothers that will watch your back when you can't do it yourself. At the end of the day, it didn't matter to us what grand goals the Reich had in store for North Africa. All that kept us together was our loyalty to each other. That was the reason we fought. For each other."

Sadness passed over Eppler's face as he reminisced about his former life, before being wounded, before leaving the Wehrmacht. Suddenly, he snapped back and appeared uncomfortable with what he had said. His eyes glanced over at Tiedemann before dropping to the floor. His face started turning red.

"It's all right, Herr Eppler. Just because we are all SS now doesn't mean we fight for a different cause. The Führer's lofty goals are poor motivation when you're freezing to death in a trench, surrounded by Russian barbarians that live only to kill you. You are exactly correct in naming the reason we are able to hold on. Not ideals. Just each other."

"*Jawohl,*" Eppler replied.

Hoffman laughed. "Except for Springer. For him, I'd wager an ideal is enough."

"I think Herr Springer puts other Hitler Youth to shame."

"That's for sure."

Gohler, who was drinking quietly on the floor, leaned over towards Eppler and began to converse casually with him. The forwardness of the master sergeant clearly caught the junior officer by surprise. Tiedemann laughed to himself. In the army, full of Prussian nobility and the very class-conscious, such an interaction would have been unheard of. It was the norm in the SS. This new lieutenant would have a lot to learn.

Tiedemann was enjoying the gradual warming from the fireplace when Krauss reappeared in the doorway, struggling with a small, bulging sack.

"Now *these* are what we should be drinking. This family has some magnificent years stored in their cellar."

"Excellent! We were almost empty," Hoffman said a little too loudly. "Bring them over here."

Bottles exchanged hands, and while Springer still had not returned with a corkscrew, Hoffman's alternative method of opening them on the windowsill proved sufficient. Wine flowed freely into the mess kit cups as the officers drank it as fast as it came. And for the moment, the raging storm outside became a mere annoyance for the men of the 3d *Kompanie, Totenkopf* Division of the Waffen-SS.

* * *

"*Mein Gott*, my head feels like it's going to explode."

The sound of Springer's voice made Tiedemann open his eyes and stare painfully at the ceiling. The rafters shifted in and out of focus. Springer complained from his cot, muttering obscenities and pleas to the Almighty in equal proportions.

For Tiedemann, the mere thought of talking was too much to stomach. How much had they drunk?

Slowly, deliberately, Tiedemann rolled onto his side and forced himself into a sitting position. His forehead throbbed with every beat of his pulse. He could think of nothing else he'd rather do than lay back down. Discipline won out, however, and Tiedemann clamped his eyes tight as if it would keep his brain from disintegrating. The stale taste of wine filled his mouth and vied for space with a swollen, parched tongue. He was so thirsty.

It took careful movement to look at his pocket watch. Seven o'clock in the morning, far later than normal reveille. The weak light from the window fell upon his comrades in haphazard positions all over the room. Krauss was on the floor, curled up into a ball underneath a raincoat. Eppler sat half-propped up in the corner, cradling an empty bottle of wine in his arms that had poured its contents all over his coat. And Springer, moaning and swearing, lay face down on another cot, clutching his head as if to shield it from mortar fire.

The throbbing in Tiedemann's head gradually turned into footsteps approaching from the hallway outside. He hoped that whoever was making all that noise was bringing a bucket.

Gohler scrambled through the doorway, anxiety on a face normally chiseled from stone.

"Hauptsturmführer!"

Tiedemann flinched from the volume. “Not so loud, please! What is it?”

“It’s Hoffman,” Gohler replied unapologetically. “He’s dead.”

4

The Conti house was built on a hillside, and as a result the wine cellar was partially underground. Getting there required a painful trek to the ground floor, through the kitchen, and down a spiral staircase that groaned under their weight as if pulling itself out of the masonry. Once at the bottom the Germans shuffled single-file along a narrow corridor and past what appeared to be a pantry. Gohler ignored it and took them even further underground until they stopped at an elbow in the corridor. In front of them was a tall arch and a room beyond, while the corridor continued dimly off to their right. Tiedemann's head pounded with every step he took, and when the group stopped, even with the ones he didn't.

"Here's where I found him," Gohler said.

Tiedemann stepped through the arch and into a rectangular room measuring ten meters or more on a side. It was a wine cellar. The walls were obscured by hundreds of bottles stored in rusting metal racks stretching from floor to ceiling. Additional racks extended out into the middle of the room like piers in a harbor. A single row of three electric light bulbs hung down from an arched ceiling to provide some meager illumination. It was far cooler here than back in the house.

Tiedemann followed Gohler to the back corner. Slumped down against the wall was the unmistakable shape of a body. Hoffman.

The lieutenant was propped up into a half-sitting position, his uniform dirty and rumpled as if there had been a struggle. Near his right hand was a broken wine bottle. Tiedemann stood in shock, not believing what he was seeing.

"I was collecting my men to work on the trucks," Gohler began. "I came down here on a whim, thinking I'd take a couple wine bottles for later. I was browsing the racks when I saw Hoffman, dead."

"Where are our soliders? Did they hear anything?" Tiedemann asked. He stared blankly at the scene before him.

"No, Herr Hauptsturmführer. I questioned anyone who pulled sentry duty last night. No one saw any of the French outside of their rooms once they retired for the evening."

Tiedemann closed his eyes. Soldiers were supposed to die in combat, with honor—not be murdered in cold blood somewhere far from the battlefield. Deep sorrow welled up inside him that such a thing could happen.

The feeling lasted only a moment. Fury quickly took its place as Tiedemann turned his mind to their French hosts. How could they possibly think they could get away with something like this? Especially after he had acted so cordially to them upon their arrival last night? It had been a mistake on his part, he now realized. He should have let Springer tear the place apart and throw the whole family out into the cold rain. That was the true role of a conqueror.

Well, now they would pay.

"Springer," Tiedemann said, his voice cold. "Take a squad of men and round up everyone who lives here. Conti, the servants, everyone. Bring them to the great room off the foyer. Line them up and keep them from talking to each other.

"Eppler. You are responsible for securing the manor. I want a report on the layout of the house, key access points, everything. I want to know how the Contis could have done this without waking our men.

"Krauss. Go fetch our things out of that room we slept in and take them back to our vehicles. Except for weapons. Every SS man carries his weapon.

"This family will pay for such an outrageous act. But I am reserving special treatment for the actual murderer. We need to find out which of these villains is responsible. Now, go!"

"*Jawohl!*" The three lieutenants barked in crisp unison before scrambling back upstairs. Gohler, who remained behind without an assignment, watched Tiedemann expectantly. Like a properly trained German soldier, he stood at their post until instructed otherwise.

Tiedemann stepped back to the arch, turned, and silently studied the room. Only discipline kept him from flying off the handle. He was incredibly angry, but he had learned long ago in combat that one could not succumb to emotion in the middle of a fight. It led to bad—fatal—decisions. And there was something—a bare tickle of an errant thought deep in the back of his mind—that was bothering him about this scene.

Why would the killer have been so careless as to not even hide the body?

"Herr Gohler, is this exactly how you found him? Did you touch or move him at all?" Tiedemann walked back and knelt down near the body.

"I tilted his head to the side when I took his pulse. That's how I knew he was dead. But that is all I touched."

Tiedemann examined Hoffman closely. There were scratches on his face mixed with the stubble on his cheeks. His tunic was ripped open at the top of his chest, the black collar and Death's Head emblems of the *Totenkopf* insignia sticking out stiffly as if it had been yanked open.

A struggle. Hoffman had not died without a fight.

Looking down at the broken bottle, Tiedemann studied the jagged edges and noticed for the first time that there was broken glass *everywhere*. It was more than what seemed like could have come from a single bottle. Wine, and possibly blood, had dried all over the packed earthen floor. If Hoffman and the killer had been grappling, it was likely that two people slamming each other into the wine racks would have knocked bottles to the ground. That meant that whoever had done this was most likely a man. Who else would be strong enough to fight with an SS officer?

"Herr Hauptsturmführer," Gohler asked. "Can you see how he was killed?"

Good question, Tiedemann thought. He wasn't sure. There didn't appear to be any stab wounds, and a quick search through Hoffman's clothes revealed a noted lack of bullet holes. With as thick as the walls were down here, it was questionable whether or not a gunshot would even be heard by anyone upstairs.

Tiedemann pulled Hoffman's upper body toward him and lay him flat on the floor. A bloody patch of matted hair was on the back of Hoffman's head.

"Here. He was clubbed, it looks like. Something heavy. A wine bottle, perhaps?"

"That would explain the broken glass."

"Not all of it," Tiedemann corrected. "There's too much."

Quickly, a thought came to Tiedemann. "It looks to me that Hoffman tried to defend himself with this broken bottle. Maybe he got in a few cuts on his attacker. That would make it much easier to identify him, yes?"

"Agreed. Maybe we'll get lucky."

"Luckier than Hoffman."

Tiedemann stood up. Gohler remained kneeling and quietly uttered what sounded like some kind of prayer over the dead body. After a curiously long minute he finished and also stood, his head hung in dejection. Tiedemann noticed the dampness in the man's eyes.

"Herr Gohler, how long have you known Hoffman?"

"A long time, Herr Hauptsturmführer. Since May of '41, when we were both camp guards at Bad Tölz. He was the only commanding officer I've had."

A year-and-a-half. That was practically a lifetime in the military of a nation at conflict with the rest of the world.

"I'm sorry, Gohler."

The Sturmscharführer nodded absently, his eyes filled with the faraway look that men got from war.

If there was ever a time that a man needed to be given something to do, this was one of them.

Tiedemann put his hand firmly on the sergeant's shoulder and spoke in a low voice. "Go upstairs and help round up the swine who did this." He was sure that there would be plenty of motivation to do a good job.

"*Jawohl*!" Gohler snapped, turning sharply as he exited.

Tiedemann made one last visual sweep across the room. He was turning to leave when a metallic glint caught his eye from the edge of one of the wine racks. He bent down and picked up the shiny object that they had almost missed.

A plain, tarnished ring nearly lost among the earth and rusted metal. A wedding band.

"Not fair to a wife to lose a husband like this," Tiedemann muttered to himself, feeling the ring that adorned his own finger. His own was far too loose after many months in the field, eating poor rations on an irregular schedule. The wedding band practically fell off every time Tiedemann washed his hands. If Hoffman's had been just as loose, a wild blow could easily have flung it across the room.

Taking the ring, Tiedemann squatted down and tried to put it back on the corpse's finger. Oddly, the ring wouldn't fit. Tiedemann squatted back and thought. He realized that because of Hoffman's sitting position, his hands must have swollen up from the blood that had pooled in the lower portion of his body. Sadly, reluctantly, Tiedemann abandoned the effort and slipped the ring into his own pocket. He would be sure that it was sent back to Hoffman's wife along with his other personal belongings.

He stood up to leave. Tiedemann felt his lips drawing tight in restrained anger. When he found out which one of the Contis couldn't account for their whereabouts the prior evening—the cold-blooded murderer who was responsible for this senseless crime—that person would pay dearly.

It was time to see what those traitorous French had to say.

5

The first blow sent Papa to the floor.

Forced to watch, Gabrielle could barely hold herself together. Papa writhed on the floor while the blond officer repeatedly kicked him in the ribs. Then the German followed by another vicious jab to Papa's face. Now her father was curled into a little ball—coughing, struggling, not doing a very good job of protecting himself. Gabrielle thought she was going to be sick.

The officer paced back and forth around Papa's crumpled body. Gabrielle thought she had heard one of the other men call him Springer. He could be the Devil himself for the amount of malevolence that was radiating from him. He finally stopped, his boots ominously close to her father's head.

"Do not speak to each other again!" Springer barked in French. "No one talks! No one moves! No one looks around!"

"Hände hoch," another soldier commanded, waving his rifle. Hands up. Gabrielle winced as her father slowly lifted his arms, the agony clear as day on his face. She continued to stare transfixed as he painfully threaded his fingers behind his head.

Springer had wheeled back on her. "I said, no looking around!" he shouted, spittle flinging from his lips.

Gabrielle snapped her eyes back to the wall. They were all arranged in the Great Room—Grandpere, Mama, Girard, and even little Philippe—resting on their knees and facing away from each other along two of the walls. Springer was lurking behind them. Just the thought of him there, ready to strike unseen and without warning, was terrifying. But strangely, Gabrielle found herself more angry than afraid. *How dare they threaten them!* What she would give to sock that *Boche* in the mouth. What was all of this nonsense about, anyway? She had watched the Germans' arrival last night from the top of the stairs. Springer had been embarrassed after being told to stand down by the captain. Now his resentment appeared to be bubbling through with renewed force. To Gabrielle it seemed obvious that he had it out for them; he wanted to show them who the boss was.

The tension was palpable. Gabrielle could feel a trickle of sweat thread its way down the center of her back. Her fists involuntarily clenched each time Springer's steps paused behind her.

After several minutes she heard a new arrival from the foyer. This one had slow, deliberate footsteps in a much different cadence than the boot tromping of the soldiers ransacking the house earlier. Gabrielle stole a glance to see the German captain walking imperiously into the Great Room. He strode over to the large stone hearth and turned to look down upon them in their kneeling positions. She remembered him vividly from the night before. He was tall, with black hair and a piercing set of eyes that reflected a calculating mind behind them.

Minutes passed. The captain studied the Contis in unnerving silence. From her position at the end of the lineup, Gabrielle could just make out his profile.

Finally the captain motioned to Springer and said something in unintelligible German. Perhaps they would finally find out what was going on.

"One of our men was murdered last night," Springer translated.

Gabrielle felt the blood drain from her face.

"I intend to find out which of you is responsible," the German captain continued, with the words turned into French as soon as he spoke them. "Normally I would interrogate you individually, without sharing my motivation. I would make each of you account for your whereabouts. It is more difficult to hide the relevant facts when you are not privy to the intentions of the questioner.

"However, I am telling you upfront for two reasons. One, you are a small group and you already know something is amiss—no sense in trying to catch you off guard. More importantly, the body of my officer was not hidden. It was simply left lying on the ground without any care taken to conceal his death. This indicates to me that perhaps it was an accident. Perhaps somehow, for some reason, Herr Hoffman was killed through understandable, though not necessarily acceptable, circumstances. Unfortunate things often happen despite our best intentions."

The captain began to pace in front of the fireplace, his words coming out as if he were speaking rhetorically rather than to his prisoners. "So. My question is this. Which one of you is responsible for Herr Hoffman's death? As a soldier, I must know. And I will find out, one way or another. But first, I am giving whoever did this the chance to speak out. Come forth with honor and dignity. If you are the culprit, tell me now and save us the painful alternative of extracting the truth by force. I am an understanding man. Accidents happen. I will take into account any extenuating circumstances. And I would be inclined to act leniently if the person who did this speaks out, in return for such a gesture of good faith."

Listening to the speech made it obvious that the Nazis weren't going to let the death of one of their own go unpunished. But what would they do? Grandpere had reveled in his stories of SS cruelty last night, scaring all of them to death. Many were rumors, but they all rung with a degree of truth that gave pause. Beatings of French villagers for showing petty defiance. Men shot for anti-German graffiti. Twenty-five French men and women, randomly selected, lined up against a brick wall, and shot in reprisal for the alleged murder of an off-duty German soldier.

Of course, that was the way her grandfather was—alarmist and dramatic. Gabrielle could only guess as to whether any of those accounts were really true. If she listened to her ears, she had to admit that the captain's words sounded rather reasonable. Wasn't this the same man who reined in Springer the previous night? Wasn't he a man of culture who appreciated fine wines and had acted with courtesy towards her father? Hadn't he told his men to sleep on the floor rather than toss Gabrielle and her family out into the storm?

Surely this was all just some kind of mistake. The captain had to know that. And glancing at the way the captain was now standing, with an earnest face and lips drawn tight, he seemed to be the sort to keep his word. He had proven the night before that he was a civilized man.

But when she caught a glimpse of those icy blue eyes, a little voice in the back of Gabrielle's head pleaded with her to not say a word.

For what seemed like forever, the captain watched. Gabrielle felt her apprehension grow as no one spoke up. Keeping your mouth shut had been the unwritten rule of her schoolyard, and those principles seemed best to apply here. Silence seemed far safer than a member of her family laying their head on the chopping block, with a stranger's word being all that stood between life and death.

"I am disappointed."

The German started his pacing again. The boot steps echoed ominously on the wooden floorboards.

"So. If no one will accept responsibility for his or her role in this crime, so be it. We will be forced to do this the hard way. I assure you the process will not be pleasant, nor will the outcome. But that is your choice, not mine. I have made my offering. You have refused it. Obersturmführer!"

Springer stopped translating into French and snapped to. The captain continued talking in German but now in a much harsher tone. Gabrielle couldn't begin to follow all the guttural commands. It sounded very military.

"*Jawohl*, Herr Hauptsturmführer," Springer replied at last, and started pointing to the soldiers around the room to carry out unknown orders.

"Excuse me, monsieur."

Gabrielle turned her head in shock and stared at her grandfather.

What was he doing? He had spent the entire night before lambasting her father, and now he was going to talk to the Germans?

The captain motioned for Springer to come back and translate. He looked down at the old man. "*Ja*?"

"Monsieur, if I may... I'm sorry, I don't even know your name."

The captain stared at the old man as Springer translated. After a long pause he finally spoke. "Tiedemann."

"Ah. Monsieur Tiedemann. My name is Marc Rimbault. If I may speak for my family, I can tell you that none of us has committed any violence against you or your men. This is the first that anyone here has even heard of your loss. And we have no reason to act in such a way, as we all realize that you are merely passing through our vicinity on your way to do more important things. I admit it is unfortunate that you have lost one of your men. But why, pray tell, do you think that any one of us is to blame?"

Tiedemann regarded the old man with narrowed eyes. Then he spoke to Springer. The blond officer smiled darkly.

"He says, he will be glad to discuss with you why he thinks that. Privately."

Two soldiers grabbed Grandpere roughly by the shoulders and hauled him to his feet.

Oh, God. Gabrielle felt the goose bumps crawl out in full force.

There was a sudden, loud crash in the kitchen. Gabrielle barely noticed the ensuing commotion until Tiedemann himself became distracted by the noise. The German took a step back and looked inquisitively toward what sounded like men shuffling and stomping.

A soldier with a black submachine gun appeared in the entry way to the Great Room. He was clearly agitated.

"Obersturmführer, können Sie mit uns kommen, bitte? Ich glaube, wir haben einen Spion gefunden," the soldier told Springer. He waved his head

towards the kitchen and stole repeated glances at the prisoners.

Gabrielle took advantage of the distraction and looked over at her father. She didn't know what the soldier had said, but Papa had turned his eyes towards Grandpere and they were sharing a grim look.

Tiedemann tucked his thumbs into his belt and turned back to her grandfather. His expression was a mixture of smugness and distaste.

Gabrielle felt a terrible fear knot her stomach into a tiny ball.

"Yes indeed," Springer translated. "You ask me why I think one of you is to blame? Let us see if there's a reason to think so."

6

Cartwright held his breath and tried to stay still in the darkness. If his legs hadn't been cramping up he wouldn't have dared move, for during the past hour he had heard nothing but boot steps coming and going from outside his tiny hiding space. But hours of sitting motionlessly had twisted his muscles into knots. As the discomfort passed the point of being tolerable, he straightened his leg out until it extended right into a heavy iron frying pan, the *only* frying pan, and knocked it off of its shelf with a loud clank.

He didn't think anyone had noticed. The mansion was large and relatively empty. The soldiers combing through it had a lot of space to spread out and otherwise get lost in the daily noises of living. Surely that would drown out his little mistake.

An entire minute passed by, and at last Cartwright allowed himself the luxury of taking a normal breath in the confines of the cabinet.

A low voice somewhere nearby spoke in German.

Cartwright's heart started racing in mad contrast to the stillness he forced upon his body. More voices now, followed by shuffling feet that sounded far too close to be anything but deliberate searching. All because of the damned pan.

He wasn't even supposed to be hiding in the kitchen. He had spent most of the night in the rafters above, in a small cubbyhole sandwiched between floors that he had been told was used for hiding valuables and, in this case, shot-down Englishmen. That was the concealment into which Girard had shoveled him, under the loose floorboards of the green bedroom.

The cubbyhole had to absolutely be the smallest, most inhospitable hole in all of southern France. *This place is hidden*, they had said. *This place is safe*. Maybe, as long as the rats didn't chew his ears off as he dozed against the rough timber. Even the roaches refused to remain with him there. But they had been in a rush when the Germans arrived. Talk about being unlucky. Marc had said they had not had any contact south of the demarcation line in the two weeks since Germany had annexed Vichy France. Even then, the winery would have been small enough to escape most casual notice. The family was surely caught off guard when Germans actually appeared on the front doorstep.

And then, there was the final twist that had led him to his current predicament. The hiding place happened to be right over the kitchen, and there was a gap of just over a foot between the edge of the little wooden platform and the wall that revealed the inside of the large kitchen cupboard built into the masonry. It was the cabinet where the pots, pans, tins, and cans were stored for cooking, and it had proved too much of a temptation to a starving airman to not see if he could slip down to the floor below and scrounge some food. So Cartwright had squeezed himself through the gap, landed softly, gorged on some fruit preserves, then discovered much to his dismay that he could not climb back up to the cubbyhole above.

Now, jackboots clattered loudly in the kitchen. It was two or three men from the sound of it. Hushed voices spoke in strange words before being followed by a long pause.

Cartwright's breathing had slowed to a bare minimum, but he was sure his heart was beating loudly enough to be heard by everyone in the house. The footsteps started again, spreading out across the room, and were followed by the sounds of cabinet doors opening and closing. The Germans were searching for the noise.

Then they found him.

Blinding light crashed into the cabinet as a young German soldier, eighteen or nineteen at the most, swung open the door and peered at Cartwright. Their eyes locked for a moment, both men unsure of what they were seeing or what to do next. Then panic washed over the boy's face as he stepped back, gave out a yell and raised the barrel of his Mauser.

The unnerving sight of the muzzle pointed right at him was all it took. Cartwright yelled, thrusting his hands out in front of him as if it would protect him from metal ripping through his body. "Don't shoot! Please, don't shoot!"

"*Heraus! Komm heraus!*"

Cartwright remained frozen with his hands outstretched. The last thing he wanted to do was to make any sudden, threatening moves. That would be a quick way to eat a bullet. But despite his docile behavior, the soldier only became more agitated.

"*Kanst Du nicht hören? Komm heraus! Jetzt!*"

Two more Germans with rifles quickly came into view, their alarmed faces squarely outlined by black steel helmets. One of the men, older and with hard eyes that must have seen years of combat, growled roughly as he reached down into the cabinet and grabbed Cartwright's collar. Instantly Cartwright was flung through the air onto the hard stone floor, landing face-down with a thud that would have jarred his teeth loose if he hadn't been clenching them so hard. A knee between his shoulder blades pinned him while the soldiers checked him for weapons. Of course they wouldn't find any. At least, aside from the frying pan.

Additional footsteps filled the kitchen. There wasn't any way Cartwright could turn his head to see the new arrivals, though he had a good view of the dust underneath the kitchen cabinets.

A lively discussion between his captors quickly started. Cartwright listened to the German words without comprehension. He was sure it was colorful; after all, it wasn't every day that someone made the discovery of a grown man cowering amongst kitchenware. He noticed the word *Spion* seemed to be thrown around quite a bit. That made the hair on Cartwright's neck stand up. *Spion* sounded a little too much like *spy*, and it didn't take much imagination to think of what enemy soldiers probably did to spies.

"*Steh auf, Du Spion*!"

Before Cartwright knew it he had been hauled upright and thrust back against the cabinet. A particularly disagreeable hinge poked into his left shoulder blade.

The barrels of four rifles were now pointed straight at him, daring him to make a wrong move and making it exceedingly difficult to maintain his balance without inviting a bullet. A fifth soldier, an officer, stood to the side and studied Cartwright with an indiscernible expression on his face. He had a very deep tan and looked curiously at this new prisoner with weathered eyes.

"*Wie heissen Sie, Spion? Was tuen Sie hier*?"

"I-I'm sorry, I don't speak German."

A puzzled look filled the officer's face at the sound of hearing English.

Cartwright quickly found himself thinking that he had made a mistake. The German's lips twisted into a snarl before he roughly grabbed Cartwright by the lapels and hauled him up to the tips of his toes. "*English? Sie sprechen English? Du bist ein englischer Spion! Sie verstecken sich hier nach Ihnen töteten unseren Kameraden. Was tuen Sie hier, eh? Was, eh?*"

Cartwright stammered out the only words he could think of for a reply to the German jibber-jabber. "Stephen Cartwright. Royal Air Force. W-7-8-2-4."

The German looked like he was ready to tear him apart. Clearly that was not the right answer.

Cartwright was thrown to the ground. The Kraut delivered a savage kick to his stomach, expelling any breath that he had managed to suck in while he had been frozen solid in fear. Another kick followed and the Briton felt like he was going to vomit.

"*Halt, bitte.*"

There was silence for a moment before Cartwright dared to open his eyes. When he did, there was a pair of highly-polished jackboots standing right in front of his face. Christ, these blokes came in from a muddy rainstorm and this one had time to clean his boots? Turning his head slowly upward introduced him to a very tall man also wearing the uniform of an officer. The soldiers around him hauled Cartwright to his feet and held him while the new German inspected his prisoner.

Cartwright gave the German an equal amount of attention. His height, in combination with jet black hair and piercing blue eyes, made for a striking figure that held the air of a patrician upbringing, something that Cartwright could spot easily after a long career in the class-conscious RAF. It was also difficult to miss the skull's head and SS insignias on the officer's collar—or the pistol strapped to his waist.

Chills ran down the back of Cartwright's spine, chills that weren't caused by the sweat clinging to his clothes.

"*Sprechen Sie Deutsch*?" the Kraut commander asked. His voice was calm, patient.

A tiny response was able to work its way up from beaten lungs to Cartwright's cracked lips. "No."

The first officer, the one with the deep tan, stepped up to the elbow of his commander and quietly whispered in his ear. While the words were foreign it was pretty clear what his vote was as to what should be done with this British interloper. The fear in Cartwright's stomach once again fought for attention against the rapidly churning thoughts in his mind that desperately wanted to avoid being executed on the spot.

Raising a hand, the SS commander silenced his deputy. Icy eyes slid over Cartwright's rumpled uniform to the flight insignia on his lapels. The German nodded slowly to himself as he worked out what was going on.

"*Luftwaffe*?"

That was a word Cartwright did know. Yes, he was a member of the air force. He nodded to make sure the commander knew he was correct.

An errant thought made Cartwright shudder. Only a day before, he had almost accepted Robert's offer of clean clothes to replace his dank and torn uniform. Had he done so, he would have lost his flight pins—and the only proof that he was something other than a spy.

If he had changed clothes he surely now would have been dead.

The German officer barked orders at his men and Cartwright found himself being dragged out of the room. Where they were taking him was anyone's guess, but at least it seemed like there might be at least some sort of temporary reprieve from a nasty end.

7

They went right to the spiral staircase at the back of the kitchen. Two soldiers held each of Cartwright's arms until they began to descend single-file, where the subsequent manhandling caused the airman's feet to miss at least every other step. At the bottom the entourage turned right and stumbled its way past the pantry, through a corridor of exposed brick, and to the ancient archway of the wine cellar. The next thing he knew, Cartwright was flying through the air and landed headfirst into something metallic and unyielding.

The German officer strode into the room behind him. He issued a stream of orders that Cartwright couldn't understand, but the two soldiers grabbed him yet again and forced him up into a sitting position. Then they stepped back and raised their rifles. A deathly quiet filled the cellar as everyone stared at him. A wave of panic hit Cartwright. This had to be some kind of firing squad. Was this to be the end of it all, underground in a cold, dank hole?

But they didn't shoot. Seconds dragged into minutes. Cartwright's mind raced through all the things that might be about to happen. Were they going to interrogate him? How? He didn't speak German. Was he to be tortured? To what end? Why had they taken him to the wine cellar of all places? His head was throbbing from where it had struck the edge of one of the wine racks, and it felt like there was a trickle of something—blood, sweat—running down his scalp. The pack of Nazis was watching him closely. The captain in particular was disturbing. Studying every move Cartwright made like a night owl ready to swoop down on a field mouse, the German stood motionlessly and simply observed.

Footsteps sounded in the corridor outside. A small man entered wearing round glasses and carrying a black leather notebook against the gray of his uniform. Cartwright thought he looked like a rat, with a sharp, pointed nose and thin moustache that could have doubled as whiskers. He mentally dubbed him The Rat.

The Rat and the captain conversed briefly in German before refocusing their attention back on Cartwright. Where was all this going? Were they going to kill him, or lock him up as a prisoner of war?

"What is your name?" the Rat asked in accented English. He flipped open his little notebook and prepared a pencil to write.

I'll be damned, Cartwright thought. A bilingual rat. Well, the little animal deserved a treat, then. "Stephen Cartwright. Royal Air Force. W-7-8-2-4."

The Rat recorded the information. "Herr Cartwright, what are you doing here in France?"

Cartwright's training on how to act if captured behind enemy lines took hold. He remained defiantly quiet.

"Did you not understand me? I'll ask again. What are you, a member of the Royal Air Force, doing here on the ground in France?"

Silence.

The Rat looked tight-lipped to his commander. All it took was a single head nod from the captain and another German, a solider with a soft cap and a thin, silvery scar on his face, strode over to Cartwright and slugged him right in his sternum.

Oxygen fled. Constricting pain. Cartwright tried to breathe, to gulp air like a fish out of water and prevent his insides from collapsing, but the thug who had landed the first blow added a second, then a third. His misery became something indescribably greater as little flecks of light danced around his vision.

Then, the beating stopped. It took Cartwright half a minute to force a breath, which he did with little grace and much spittle. A spasm of violent coughing doubled him over with a finishing touch.

"Now, Herr Cartwright," the Rat began again. "You have a choice. You may either answer my questions or we let Herr Gohler try to convince you otherwise. Am I clear?"

A cough and a nod.

"Good. I want to know what you are doing in France. Tell us how you came to be here at *Domaine des Contis*?"

Cartwright struggled to draw in enough oxygen to speak, all the while damning himself for being too weak to withstand a little physical punishment. If anything, he worried that he would not be able to regain his breath fast enough to talk. Cartwright felt a sudden pang of shame. He knew his lack of breeding was showing through. An RAF officer would never have allowed his dignity to be assaulted so, even if captured behind enemy lines, but an enlisted man such as himself had little recourse other than to take what was given to him. And what was being offered—the promise of a long, thorough beating—left Cartwright little choice in the matter.

"We were shot down," Cartwright gasped. "I was the tail gunner flying a night raid and we were shot down on the way to our target. I managed to bail out. I don't know about the others."

"What was your bombing target?"

Cartwright eyed the Rat nervously. He didn't like the idea of answering specifics. More often than not, doing so tended to get one into deeper trouble.

"Herr Cartwright? I asked you a question. You don't want Herr Gohler to persuade you to loosen your tongue again, do you? What was your bombing target?"

"Stuttgart."

"I see. Did you have a large number of planes in your formation?"

"Sure, but I couldn't tell you how many. Like I said, I was the tail gunner."

The Rat slowly wrote in his notebook. "Your accent is... different. Where are you from?"

"Birmingham."

"Where again?"

"Bur-ming-*um*."

"Ah." The Rat scribbled the new information in his little notebook, although Cartwright could tell by looking at him that the goon had no idea where Birmingham was. "Where did your plane crash? Surely it must be near here."

"I don't know, exactly. Like I said, it was at night, and God only knows which direction. When I hit the ground I stayed hidden until morning. Then I scouted around a bit until I found a dirt road. I followed the road and it led me here. End of story."

"How many days ago was this?"

Cartwright took a deep breath. His lungs were aching, a reminder for him to not seem too evasive. "Not sure, really. Time's been a bit of a blur since it happened. Three days, maybe four? Could have been a week ago for all I know."

"All right. Then when did you arrive here at the mansion?" the Rat asked.

"Day before yesterday."

"And what have you done here since then?"

Cartwright crinkled his forehead. What?

"Herr Cartwright, I asked you a question."

"I know you did, I just didn't understand it."

"I was quite specific. What have you done here at the mansion since you arrived?"

Cartwright considered the query for a moment. "I don't know. Haven't paid that much attention. Ate. Slept. Thought about how to get back home. Hid from you lot. That's everything."

"And what about last night? Which of those things were you doing when we arrived?"

"Well, let me see. That would be hiding, then."

The pencil stopped moving behind the little notebook. "No, you weren't. Why would you be hiding upon our arrival? You didn't know who we were. The Contis were certainly taken by surprise. I want to know exactly what you were doing just before we walked in the front door."

"The few seconds before you barged in I was in the kitchen. Eating. When your comrade started barking out orders in the front foyer, I dove into one of the cabinets to get out of sight as soon as possible. That's where I stayed until morning."

"You stayed cramped up in that cabinet from our arrival until we found you less than half an hour ago?"

"That's what I'm saying," Cartwright replied.

The Rat wrote in his notebook, though the little man's demeanor made it clear he didn't believe him.

"I should tell you," the Rat replied, "that our interrogation will not be confined to your answers alone. We will be asking all of the Contis similar questions. If your story does not corroborate with what they tell us, the result will be very... painful to you. Fatal, perhaps.

"So I'll ask you again, one last time. Are you sure that the entire time our party has been present at the manor, you have remained in the kitchen?"

"Yes."

"You're lying."

"No, I'm not."

"You *are*, and we'll see if Sturmscharführer Gohler needs some exercise. Tell the truth now and save yourself a lot of pain. Save the Contis a lot of pain."

"I'm not lying," Cartwright insisted. His voice broke. He desperately hoped that his fear would not be interpreted as dishonesty.

"Why are you all marked up? The scrapes on your knuckles there, and your face. What is that from?"

Cartwright looked down at his hands and realized that they were shaking. He did his best to lay them flat against his legs and steady them. "Must have been from that tree that I parachuted into. Branches and twigs will do a number on you when you can't see where you're trying to land in the middle of the night."

"You're lying!" the Rat shouted.

"Why do you think I'm lying?" Cartwright shouted back.

The Rat started pacing back and forth across the cellar. His round glasses were slipping down his nose as his hands flailed about, though his elbows may as well have been bolted to his hips given the zero motion they produced. The whole thing would have been comical if not for the armed men standing all around.

"Because I know the truth!" the man screamed in a squeaky, breaking voice. "You have no idea how much evidence we have. You were prowling around last night, weren't you? You were sneaking around and came down here to the cellar last night!"

"I don't know what you're talking about." Cartwright fought to speak steadily.

"Damn you, man, confess!"

"Herr Krauss." The calm, patrician voice of the German captain fell over the wine cellar.

The Rat rapidly composed himself, looking slightly embarrassed at his outburst. What had made him so emotional, Cartwright wondered?

The RAF sergeant glanced about the other members of his audience while the two Germans talked. The soldiers with the rifles seemed edgy, frustrated, and that was a dangerous thing when fingers were on triggers. Gohler, the thug with the scar, had a cold expression that seemed borderline psychotic. It made Cartwright's chest ache just thinking of the beating mere minutes before.

Cartwright glanced over at the captain. The tall German returned his gaze as he listened to his subordinate. Even now he was being studied. How much did they know? How much did they *think* they knew? He wasn't sure what facts the Nazis had been able to put together in this short amount of time, but the Rat's questions certainly indicated some manner of deliberate probing. That in and of itself did not bode well for a captured prisoner of war.

After a long pause, the captain gave several sentences of orders to the assembled crowd. There was a chorus of *jawohls* and then he, the

Rat, and all the other Germans filtered out of the cellar. Only Gohler and one other soldier remained. Gohler began to walk toward him.

A brief wave of panic struck. Cartwright cringed, but the fear changed into apprehension when the stout German walked past him. Gohler went to a corner and seemed to be studying one of the wine racks that extended out from the wall. After a moment he called over to his comrade.

The other soldier, presumably a private, jabbed his rifle muzzle at Cartwright and motioned over to Gohler. Time to move, apparently. Cartwright started to stand up.

He barely got off the ground when the first sucker punch came. A set up. Lightning-fast boot kicks landed in his ribs, crumpling him to the ground. Cartwright pulled into a little ball, desperately trying to shield his head and torso, but the blows still came. Then rough hands dragged him along the earthen floor over to the corner.

Gohler delivered another fist across Cartwright's jaw, making him see stars. Then the German stopped. The thuggish sergeant hovered malevolently over him like Death itself, breathing heavy, contemplating whether to dispense more pain. But instead, mercifully, he took a step back and abruptly marched out of the cellar.

The remaining German soldier, lowering his rifle on the far side of the cellar, leaned against the wall as he settled in for guard duty.

Cartwright lay in the fetal position and bled. When he finally tried to move, waves of pain flooded his body and he lost his bearings more than once. His arms felt like they were filled with lead. It hurt to breathe. It took a few minutes for him to will himself into upright position against a nearby wine rack. Once sitting, Cartwright rubbed his chin and checked to see if all of his teeth were still there.

Eventually he moved on from his immediate physical condition to survey the overall situation. He was now a prisoner. The Germans had placed him in a corner of the cellar where the wine racks made a sort of holding pen, with obstructions on three sides and a direct line of sight to the guard. He was cold and uncomfortable in this awful place, clearly a deliberate move on his captors' part to stress him even more. And the abrupt exit of the captain could only mean one thing. They were going to interrogate the French and see what they might know about their English house guest.

Cartwright sat in pain, afraid to move. God alone knew how he was going to get out of this getup.

If he stayed alive.

8

Tiedemann barked out orders as he led the entourage of soldiers back upstairs. He stopped in the kitchen to consider what he had heard. Thoughts muddled through his aching, hung-over mind and he needed to get them straight.

He was sure Cartwright was lying.

His reaction was all wrong. Tiedemann had purposely let the Englishman sit on the ground unmolested while they were waiting for Krauss. He would have expected the prisoner's eyes to wander all over the unfamiliar room: *Where am I? What's going to happen to me? Is there a way to escape?* But instead, Cartwright hadn't shown any disorientation at all, instead pretty much locking his gaze on the Germans. The lack of interest was so pronounced that it was almost as if Cartwright was *avoiding* looking at anything.

So that meant that Cartwright had been in the wine cellar before. Was it while he was committing a murder?

There was a big part that didn't make sense, though. Tiedemann thought that if anyone would have hidden a body after a struggle, it would have been a downed airman who was trying to remain unnoticed. Instead, Hoffman's body had been left in the open for anyone to see. That part certainly didn't add up. And despite Krauss's insistence, he had a hard time imagining why Cartwright would have risked moving recklessly through the house while enemy soldiers were all about.

Tiedemann's nature was to act with precision. He did not want to slaughter this whole family in a fit of retribution. He wanted to exact revenge on the killer. He wanted to *know* who had done it.

So, before he came to any conclusions, he needed more information first—information he intended to get from the Contis. Even now, the shock of being caught would be wearing off as his prisoners sat in their stress positions in the Great Room. Tiedemann had to get back to questioning the French, before they regained their wits and concocted alibies.

Of all the suspects, the men were at the top of the list in their likelihood of being the guilty party. Tiedemann closed his eyes and tried to associate the faces, names, and impressions that he had been able to gather.

Cartwright, of course. He was an enemy soldier behind the lines and trying to avoid capture.

The old man, Marc Rimbault. He seemed too smart for his own good after trying to make a deal in the Great Room.

Robert Conti and the retainer, Girard Laurent. Both were possibilities, even though their motives were less clear.

Then there were the women and the young boy.

Conti's wife Claudette seemed the hysterical type. If she had been scared enough, could she have lashed out with a lucky blow and caused Hoffman's death?

Tiedemann didn't know much about Gabrielle Conti, the teenage girl. She had avoided the soldiers. But she was very pretty. Had the soldiers avoided her?

The Conti son, Philippe, was no older than nine or ten and normally not a logical suspect. But what if he had been involved somehow? Young boys were often adventurous. Perhaps he had triggered a chain of unintended consequences.

God, my head hurts.

The only way Tiedemann was going to get anywhere was to go through the process, question each one of them, and look for inconsistencies. He prayed he would find some. This wasn't Russia. They were in France, an old and cultured country as civilized as any other. Tiedemann didn't want to resort to torture to gain a confession, nor did he want to have a mass execution.

Gohler climbed up the staircase behind him, scowling.

"Perfect timing," Tiedemann said.

"Sir?"

"We are going to begin our fact gathering. You are in charge of managing the prisoners. I want each of the Contis taken to a different part of the house. Keep them separate and under guard. I don't want them to see each other or to be able to communicate in any way. I also don't want them to know in what order they are being interrogated.

Bring each to me so that I may question them one at a time."

When the Germans marched back into the Great Room, the Conti family members were still in kneeling positions along the walls. Gohler gave instructions to separate the prisoners while Tiedemann entered the adjoining library. The walls were lined with half-empty bookshelves, and there was a table onto which Tiedemann threw his cap. Yes, this would work well, Tiedemann thought. He dragged an old leather chair into the partial shadows of the corner. That is where he would sit. Springer and Kraus cleared the furniture from the middle of the room so that it was empty, with just an old area rug covering the wooden floor.

Tiedemann took his position in the battered chair, to the side. "Bring in the grandfather, Rimbault."

The old man was hauled in roughly and forced to kneel on the floor. Tiedemann sat to the side, partially obscured by the angle and the shadows, but still with a clear view of body language and facial expression. All he saw so far was grim resignation.

"Herr Springer, tell our friend I would like to return to our conversation. What were we talking about? Ah, yes. *Motive.*"

Springer paced menacingly as he translated.

"You neglected to tell us that you were hiding a British airman in your house. We should execute you on the spot for such a crime."

No reaction. The old man stared into space, with any inclination to make a deal packed up and folded away.

"Herr Cartwright had some very interesting things to say about you and your family."

There was a subtle change in the Frenchman's pallor at the mention of the Englishman's name. Tiedemann had known there was more behind this than met the eye. Interesting.

"I am going to ask you some questions now. And I trust that you will reply only with the truth. Because later, when we question your granddaughter, if her answers were to differ from your own... that would have to mean she was lying, yes? That would be unfortunate. I can't think of anything my men hate worse than a pretty young girl who lies. They would undoubtedly need to teach her a lesson. Am I being clear, Herr Rimbault?"

The old man finally turned his head to look at the captain. He understood. Tiedemann noted that there was little, if any, fear to be found in the defiant Frenchman's face. Only smoldering anger.

"Springer, soften him up."

Springer punched him in the cheek. Rimbault ricocheted into the hardwood floor before the German hauled him back up and shouted at him to remain still.

"Good," Tiedemann said. "Let's begin then. Why don't you tell us what's going on here?"

Rimbault spoke, and Springer translated. "He says he doesn't understand, that there's nothing going on."

"Again, Springer."

The blond officer kicked the old man in the kidneys. Rimbault doubled over in pain. Tiedemann held his hand up to stop—best to start small. More encouragement could come later, perhaps on one of the others while Rimbault was forced to watch.

"One of my officers is dead, and there's an enemy airman hiding out in your home? Come now, Herr Rimbault, there most certainly are things going on, and that's just the surface of it. Why don't you tell us what your involvement has been? Start with the flyer."

The old man grunted as he struggled to sit upright. "The Englishman wandered onto our doorstep several nights ago. He'd been shot down and was in miserable shape. So we took him in, fed him, clothed him, gave him shelter from the cold. And then you arrived."

"Several nights ago? How many?"

The old man hesitated, as if unsure his answer might reveal a lie told by someone else. "I'm not positive. I think it might have been the night before last, but I'm not positive," he hedged.

"What sort of plane did he fly?"

"I don't know."

"How many of his companions survived the plane crash?"

Rimbault betrayed a smug look. "You seem to know more than I. None of my family speaks any English."

Springer punched him in the ear this time. It was a full minute before the old man was able to regain his composure.

"I'd remember your manners, Herr Rimbault, lest you forget to whom you're talking," Tiedemann said. "If we don't get what we need from you, we will continue next with your granddaughter."

A cough was the only reply.

"How many companions?"

"I—I don't know. No idea if he even had any. Don't... don't know what sort of plane he flew. We've seen only him." Rimbault's voice was ragged now.

"How many nights ago did he arrive?"

"I told you, maybe two, I think. I'm not sure," the old man wheezed.

"And where did you keep him all of this time so that he wouldn't be found?"

"We're in the middle of the country, monsieur. No one comes here. There wasn't any need to hide him anywhere until you arrived with your patrol."

"So when we arrived, where did you hide him? Down in the wine cellar, perhaps?"

It was a leading question on purpose. Tiedemann saw the old man's eyes glance over to the left—just for a moment. This was an old trick he had learned from an interrogator on the Eastern Front. Watch where a person's eyes looked as they recalled answers to questions they were asked. The eyes betrayed the mechanics of how human memory worked. Looking to the left meant that the brain was retrieving visual information from something actually seen. Eyes to the right meant the prisoner was summoning up what something *would* have looked like, because there was no actual memory.

"Why, I don't know."

A lie. The old man's eyes indicated he had seen Cartwright in the cellar. Something to build upon.

"The kitchen, Herr Rimbault, the kitchen," Tiedemann said. "That is where we found him. Weren't you paying attention when all that noise drifted through the hallway? You hid him in the kitchen."

"Yes. You found him in the kitchen," the old man said, his eyes glancing to the right. His words were too deliberate. Interesting, Tiedemann thought. Rimbault had to imagine what hiding the Englishman in the kitchen had looked like. Cartwright had been placed somewhere else prior to his discovery.

"So how did Cartwright come to be hidden there, Herr Rimbault? Did you put him there?"

"No. I did not make the decision."

"Who did?"

Pause. "My son-in-law, most likely, but I am not sure."

"How are you not sure?"

"I'm sure you can imagine that things were a bit chaotic when you knocked on our door."

Tiedemann tilted his head to the side. "Why the kitchen at all, do you suppose? You have a wine cellar underground. Why did you choose a room that was so close to where we billeted our men?"

"I don't know."

"Well, that doesn't make sense." Tiedemann folded his arms and stared at the Frenchman, pausing for a moment. "I don't like liars. Will your granddaughter know more? Perhaps she will tell us that he was hidden somewhere else, that he was in the kitchen when we found him because of some other reason?"

"She will not know anything," the old man snarled. "The only one who might have decided where the Briton would be kept is Robert."

"*Deciding* where he would be kept is different from *knowing* where he was kept."

The Frenchman remained silent.

Tiedemann decided to move on from his circular, repetitive questions. "So, your son-in-law? Robert? Yes, then. Tell me, did you spend any time with your son-in-law last night?"

"Of course."

"Where?"

"There is a small bedroom upstairs where we usually discuss matters."

"And while you were in this room, with my soldiers walking about in your home, did you by any chance discuss how you were going to keep a hidden British flyer safely out of view from a platoon of SS soldiers?"

"I'm sure it came up," Rimbault said sarcastically.

It was becoming apparent that he had some hostility toward the Germans. Perhaps that was important.

"Your son-in-law seems like a very intelligent man. Do you think he is smart?"

"Yes, I would say he is."

"Then I don't understand what's going on here. It doesn't seem very smart to move someone's hiding place from the cellar to the kitchen when there are so many troops about, does it?"

Rimbault stiffened. "We weren't hiding him in the cellar."

"Really? Then who *were* you hiding in the cellar?"

Tiedemann waited for Rimbault to show some physiological sign of a mistake. There was something going on, for sure. Was there another airman somewhere?

Tiedemann stroked his chin and lit a cigarette while he lounged in the leather chair. He thought through what else he had heard during his barrage of seemingly random questions. Making mention of the cellar had been completely hypothetical, simply a piece of bait to draw out more information. It was quite clear that the old man's eyes betrayed a visual memory when Tiedemann mentioned the Briton being down there. That potentially placed both men at the crime scene, although the time of occurrence had yet to be determined.

"Springer. Again."

The blond lieutenant threw several more punches into the old man's side. After a minute Tiedemann stopped him. Left on his own, Springer would just try to beat the truth out of their prisoner. But physical punishment worked best with gaps to recover.

"You seem quite certain that Cartwright was not hiding in the cellar," Tiedemann continued. "Quite certain indeed for someone who professes to not know where he was kept at all."

"I am merely guessing, monsieur. You yourself said that the he was found in the kitchen."

Tiedemann changed the subject. "You were together with Robert in this bedroom you speak of. When?"

"Early last night."

Of course he would say it was early. Later in the night would cause too much suspicion. "How early?"

The Frenchman closed his eyes as he tried to remember. "I don't know the exact time. After you had retired for the evening, but before you had fallen asleep. We were together for a while."

Tiedemann didn't buy it. He needed to build the mental bridge as to how the old man could have seen the Briton in the cellar, and at what time.

"Why should I believe you?"

"One of your officers saw us."

Tiedemann's eyebrows arched. That was the last thing that he expected to hear as he tried to spring a trap on the Frenchman's story.

"Who?"

Springer asked the question and looked surprised at the response. Then the junior officer turned to Tiedemann. "He says it was me."

Tiedemann stared. "Well?"

Springer hesitated. "I don't know, sir. It could have been. Honestly, I don't remember much after the third bottle of wine."

Tiedemann cursed and shook his head. The lingering hangover reminded him to be still.

"Why does he think it was you?"

Springer asked the question in French and related the reply. "He says that his son-in-law and he were arguing with the door ajar and that I 'poked my blond head in to see what the commotion was about.' The old man then told me that they were having a private discussion and closed the door on me."

"*Tell* me you remember it, Springer." Exasperation was bubbling up.

Springer was turning a little red. "I'm sorry, sir, I don't. But I do remember wandering all over this house at some point looking for the stairs to the cellar, so it could have happened."

Tiedemann frowned.

"All right. Keep translating."

"Herr Rimbault, how long did your discussion take place with your son?"

"An hour, perhaps."

"And then what did you do?"

"I went to sleep with the rest of my family."

"What were you arguing about when Herr Springer introduced himself through your doorway?"

"All sorts of things. You."

"And what to do with us? How to take revenge?"

"No! Why would we do such a thing? You were going to be leaving today, when the rain let up. To try and hurt you or your men would be more than foolish. We have nothing to gain."

"If it was intentional, yes. If it was an accident, that's something different. Are you saying my man's murder was an accident?"

"No, I'm not saying anything. I don't know anything about your officer's death. I assure you, none of us do."

"But was the Englishman in the cellar last night?"

The old man's eyes unmistakably darted to the left once again. Tiedemann knew he was lying by omission when he kept silent.

Tiedemann held his finger on his lip and thought some more. Did the old man's alibi hold water? Granted, no one knew the exact time that Springer must have walked in on the two Frenchmen, but at least they had an initial placement of their location early in the evening. And it was away from the cellar. And judging from the old man's eyes he was sure that the airman had been underground at some point, which allowed the easy presumption that the Englishman had been responsible for Hoffman's murder. But there were still pieces missing. The timing seemed wrong.

"Herr Springer. Do you think any of our soldiers would have seen the old man if he had gone to the wine cellar?"

The lieutenant thought for a moment. "I would expect so, Herr Hauptsturmführer. Gohler had men on guard the entire night."

Tiedemann nodded. There was more here than met the eye, but he would come back and revisit the inconsistencies. He needed to test the information from the others. Then perhaps he could make sense of it all.

"Very well. This has been quite interesting. Herr Krauss, you have been taking notes, yes?"

"*Jawohl.*"

"Good. Herr Springer, please get Herr Gohler and have him put the old man under guard in one of the bedrooms. Don't let the other prisoners see him. They'll be more on edge if they don't know what's happening to each other."

"Which room, Herr Hauptsturmführer?"

"I don't care. Upstairs, the first one you see. Whatever."

"*Jawohl.*"

As Gohler arrived and then departed with the prisoner in tow, Tiedemann turned to Krauss.

"Bring in the young girl next. Rimbault seems very protective of her. Let's find out what sort of person she is."

9

Gabrielle let out a cry of pain as she was hauled upright by her hair. She instinctively clawed and scratched to protect herself, but it was no use. Another solider pinned her arms to her sides and she was made to walk toward the library, kicking in protest.

When she was at last thrown to the floor at the feet of Captain Tiedemann, Gabrielle was strangely furious. Sure, she was scared of what the Germans might do to them, but this last bit of treatment was simply unconscionable. Gabrielle turned her head angrily to the man that had carried her in and let loose a stream of insults that would have made her grandfather blush.

There was dead silence in the room.

Gabrielle kneeled, sat back on her heels, and smoothed her skirt. She lifted her chin defiantly and stared at her captors. There was Tiedemann, sitting with an unreadable face in her father's reading chair. There was another Nazi officer with round glasses and a mustache who was peeking at her over his notebook. And there was Springer, who had a raised eyebrow and bemused smirk. Gabrielle glared at him the longest; she knew Springer spoke French and would have understood what she had said.

"*Interessant*," Tiedemann said to no one in particular.

A short conversation transpired between Tiedemann and Springer.

"That is quite a show of defiance, Fraulein," Springer finally said. "Should we conclude that we have found the murderer already?"

Alarm bells rang in Gabrielle's head. It was hard to swallow her pride. It was that much worse that Springer was quite obviously enjoying himself dominating a pretty French girl. She had met that type before. But for survival's sake alone, a meeker tone seemed to be the prudent thing to put on. Gabrielle managed to look sullenly at the floor in what she hoped was an acceptable show of subjugation. Inside, she was fuming.

She heard the captain speak in German before Springer translated. "So, Fraulein Conti. Tell us about last night."

"What do you want to know?" she answered.

"That is for you to tell us."

Gabrielle sniffed incredulously at such vague direction. "What?"

Springer stiffened. "Don't annoy me, Fraulein. It is not something you want to do."

Gabrielle struggled to find a meek nod.

"I am asking you to tell us about last night," the German continued. "Why don't you start with what you did after we arrived at your home?"

That seemed simple enough. "Once your men came inside the house, my father told me to collect extra linens and take them to their bedroom. So I did."

"Extra linens?"

"Bed sheets. For the cots for your men, since that's where I was told you were going to be sleeping."

Springer translated for his captain, who thought for a moment and then spoke in a voice too low for Gabrielle to hear.

"Did you bring the cots as well?" said Springer.

"What?"

"You brought the sheets and bed linens. Did you bring the cots to the master bedroom as well? They were there waiting for us when we went upstairs."

It seemed like an odd question. "No."

"Who did?"

Gabrielle paused for a moment. "Girard."

Springer conferred with Tiedemann, then turned back to her. "The one with the limp? Not a very nice thing to make him carry such unwieldy things up the stairs."

"He is our hired worker," she replied simply.

More discussion amongst the Germans. The officer with the round glasses was busily writing into his notebook. Gabrielle shifted uneasily at the level of attention they seemed to be giving such simple comments.

"Very well," Springer said eventually. "Then what did you do?"

"I was told to go to the sitting room and wait. I stayed there until my father got the rest of the family together to discuss our situation."

"And what situation was that?"

Gabrielle looked Springer right in the eyes. "You're joking."

"Not at all," the German replied.

Her temper started to bubble again. "You beat down our door at gunpoint. You threaten my mother and father and then take over our house. And you ask what our situation is?"

As boorish and rude as Springer was, he actually flinched at Gabrielle's verbal lashing. She couldn't resist following up. "Any problem we may have had about your presence here has been completely validated that you've imprisoned us, and *beat us*, in this strange interrogation you're undertaking. We haven't done *anything*! You've terrorized us from the beginning and now you are treating us like the fault is *ours*? How dare you!" Her voice was rising now, and a little tickle in the back of her brain was flashing danger, but she couldn't stop. "We are out here minding our own business, just trying to make a living making wine so that we can afford to eat while your government takes more and more things away from us. Then you come here and take our home and our freedom away, even after we let you stay to get out of the storm. And the way you repay us is by taking us prisoners and threatening us. *Mon Dieu!* And you have the nerve to ask me what I mean when I say we were discussing our situa—"

Springer punched her.

At first, Gabrielle didn't know what had happened. Her brain tried to rationalize how it was that her head was flat against the wood floor, and flecks of light danced in front of her eyes as if to mock her for her insolence. Gradually she realized that she was being brought back upright by several sets of hands. She was still woozy and the Germans had to hold her steady.

Springer's voice was busily chattering with the other German officers. Gabrielle gradually came to her senses. Her cheek ached. Part of her couldn't believe what had just happened. The rest of her couldn't make sense of anything else.

After a lively conversation with Tiedemann, Springer at last turned back to her and addressed her again in French.

"You'd best mind your attitude before I have to hit you for real. Now, you say your family was in the sitting room. Who specifically was there?"

Back to it—just like that? Still stunned, Gabrielle gave a straightforward answer. "Myself and Papa. My mother, grandfather, and brother. And Girard."

"Was the British airman there as well?"

What did he say?

Gabrielle turned in shock towards Springer. Had they found Stefan? They had not brought him to the Great Room. And surely her grandfather had not betrayed his presence; after all, it was at his insistence that they take him in to begin with. Yet somehow the Germans knew about the Englishman and that he was on the premises.

Despite the sting in her jaw, Gabrielle focused on Springer's eyes and spoke very carefully. "There was no British airman in our sitting room."

Springer smiled. "No, of course not. He was hiding in the cellar."

Gabrielle stayed silent. To her surprise, so did the Germans. When she glanced over at Tiedemann he was watching her like a hawk, but somehow the captain seemed disappointed in her answer. After what seemed like forever, he spoke again to Springer.

"How many times did you go down to the cellar to see him last night?"

"I never went to the cellar last night."

Springer leaned forward. "Are you sure?"

"Quite."

"That Englishman is surely a dangerous spy, Fraulein. Herr Tiedemann wants to know what sort of contact you've had with him."

There was a lie on the tip of her tongue, one that would maintain that she didn't know to whom they were referring. But Gabrielle realized that it would be pointless. The *boches* had obviously either discovered or captured Stefan. Denying his existence was not a good strategy. So she quickly searched for a minimal answer.

"I've only barely seen him. My father shuttled me off to tend to chores when he arrived and I have not been involved."

"How long ago did he arrive?"

"The night before last, I think, but I can't remember exactly."

"He has been here two days and you have had no contact with him? I don't believe you."

"It hasn't been as much time as that," Gabrielle replied. "It was late at night when he came here. Then I was busy with the usual work around here. You arrived yesterday. I've been too busy helping my mother to get involved with anything else."

Springer translated for Tiedemann and the third officer with the glasses scribbled in his notebook. Gabrielle hoped she wasn't saying anything that would contradict someone else in her family. How could the soldiers have found out about Stefan? He had been hidden so well. The nook underneath the floorboards in the green bedroom was far too difficult to find without help. Gabrielle hoped to God that someone like her mother or Philippe hadn't been beaten to force some kind of confession. The thought of any of them being hurt made her stomach turn.

Tiedemann unexpectedly barked an order in German and a soldier came into the room. Springer pointed to Gabrielle and gave some instructions that she didn't understand, but it appeared that her interrogation was over when the soldier grabbed her roughly and started hauling her out of the room.

"Wait! Stop!" Gabrielle cried out. Her stomach was doing flip flops.

Everything was happening too quickly. It was as if she was being pushed inexorably towards a cliff, where the drop off to her doom was clearly in place, but she couldn't comprehend why she was being pushed, or whether it was for real or just a misunderstanding. All she knew was that she had no control over her own safety, and it was terrifying.

"Where are you taking me? What about my family? We haven't done anything to you. Why are you treating us like this?"

Then the Germans were out of sight. Gabrielle was pulled like a sack of potatoes through one of the corridors to an old storage room and thrust through the open door. She stumbled right into an end table and knocked it over, taking herself along with it. The door slammed closed behind her. Aching, she sat in the middle of the floor, alone with the throbbing pain in her cheek.

What was going to happen to her and her family?

* * *

"That's a feisty one," Springer admired. "Did you see how she smoldered when I punched her?"

Krauss nodded in agreement. "Her temper certainly suggests that she could have killed someone."

"Oh, yes, I bet she could have. So much attitude. How sweet would it be to take her down a notch or two?"

"No, no," Tiedemann replied, stroking his chin. "She doesn't strike me as the type. I find her attitude more youthful impetuousness than malice. What is she, sixteen? The girl has spirit, but that doesn't make her a threat—particularly when she crumples on the ground from one simple blow."

"But you can't rule her out, can you?" said Springer.

Tiedemann thought. "No. At least, not yet. But other things don't line up either. First of all, she gave very clear indications that she had not been to the cellar at all last night."

"She could have been lying."

Tiedemann shook his head. "The eyes, Springer, it's all in the eyes. She showed no recognition whatsoever. And honestly, I'm not surprised. If I were her father, I wouldn't let her out of my sight lest a German soldier get too interested."

Springer's eyes had a dangerous glint in them. "Wise man."

"But," Krauss squeaked in, "just because the girl didn't go down to the wine cellar, that doesn't mean Cartwright hadn't been down there."

"She showed no knowledge of him hiding there," Tiedemann replied. "And that's the crux of it, Krauss. We have to build the story from the fragments of their interrogations. There are lots of things that could have happened. I want to trap them in their lies."

"Do you believe her? That she didn't know where he was hiding?"

"I suspect that *everyone* knew. In fact, their coordination was probably vital in hiding him."

Krauss grumbled. "She certainly didn't provide much of an alibi for any of the Frenchmen. Conti, Rimbault, and the servant."

"No, she didn't," Tiedemann agreed. "In fact, I'm more suspicious of them than ever. We've heard Rimbault's version of last night. Let's move on to Conti."

10

While they waited for the next prisoner to be brought in, Tiedemann paced the room in an attempt to take his mind off the throbbing hangover. It had been a long time since he had had one this bad. He remembered earlier that year sitting at a café with eight other officers, back before they had been deployed east. They had thrown back the cognac as if it were water and got rowdier by the hour as inhibitions fled. He remembered an intricately beautiful mirror behind the bar, probably a hundred years old, with an ornate brass frame that stretched to the top of the two story ceiling and projected out from the wall. Dietrich, one of Tiedemann's lieutenants, had decided through some thought process that could only be guessed at that it made sense to try and climb it. He hurdled onto the back bar over the protests of the barkeep and succeeded in scaling about one meter before the brass frame bent, allowing the entire pane of glass to slip out and shatter on the floor. Tiedemann and his men roared out in laughter of course, and there were so many glass shards afterwards that the café seemed like it surely had been bombed.

Tiedemann wanted to smile. But the cold reality that Dietrich and the others were dead on some dry steppe in northern Russia quickly stole the humor.

The soldiers who fought under him were brothers united in a cause. They no longer had homes other than the battlefield, family other than each other, nor hope other than the promise of a victory that seemed forever on the horizon. All they had was each other, and the confidence that they would be there when the time called for it.

That was why Tiedemann had to find out who killed Hoffman.

Robert Conti was brought in and ignobly dumped on the floor. Springer instructed a soldier to remain as a guard while Tiedemann reviewed Krauss's notes from the other interrogations. There had to be a connection somewhere between Cartwright, the cellar, and Hoffman.

"Herr Conti, we have some questions for you." Tiedemann addressed their prisoner directly, in German. "Your answers will determine whether the members of your family live or die. Do you understand?"

Conti was silent.

Remembering the reaction that Conti's father-in-law had, Tiedemann tried to use Gabrielle for some leverage. "Particularly your daughter, I think. She had some interesting things to say."

The Frenchman tried his best to look dismissive of the comment, but Tiedemann saw his complexion growing pale. Physiological signs were so hard to disguise. He much preferred solving matters this way, intellectually, rather than how they did in Russia. At times it was all that he had to remind himself he was a human being.

"Very well, then. Let's start with your houseguest. How long has Herr Cartwright been here?"

"Two nights. He wandered in from the fields and so we took him in out of kindness." Conti glanced at Tiedemann. "It's hard to simply turn someone away when they're in need."

Tiedemann dismissed the jab. Conti's response was too prepared, as if he had expected the question. Not good. That meant the investigation was starting to drag, and his prisoners were finding time to think up alibis and alternative facts.

"Where did you hide him upon our arrival?"

"In the cellar."

Finally. With a glance at Krauss, Tiedemann pressed on. "Why there?"

"Because it was far from the front door. We were pressed for time when you arrived."

"Who took him there?"

Conti fumbled slightly before answering. "I told him to go there and he went on his own."

"Very interesting," Tiedemann said mockingly. "When I first saw you, you were coming down the grand staircase into the foyer. My men have searched the house thoroughly and have found no other staircases to the upper level. So tell me, how is it that you expected Cartwright to get to the cellar, past us, when both of you were upstairs and we were standing right next to the only way to get there?"

The Frenchman did not reply.

"I'm waiting."

"We... had arranged beforehand that that was where he was to hide, should he need to."

Tiedemann stepped back and barked an order. Springer took a rifle from the soldier at the door and swung it solidly into the Frenchman's ribs. Conti sprawled out across the floor. A few moments later he contracted into the fetal position, and his lungs finally allowed him to gulp enough air to release an agonizing sob.

"I do not like liars, Herr Conti. That is one blow. Lie to me again and your daughter will receive one in addition to yourself. Am I clear?"

"Yes," Conti sputtered from the floor.

"Now, where was Cartwright hiding when we arrived?"

Conti gasped. "Please. I told you what I know. I thought he was in the cellar."

Tiedemann could not get a good view of the prisoner's eyes, so he continued with questions instead. "Then why is it we found him in the kitchen?"

"I-I don't know. Please, please. He must have gone there on his own. I don't know why."

"So, somehow, this airman, this *enemy soldier*, was able to move around undetected in your house while we prepared to sleep for the night. Is that what you are telling me?"

"Yes, I suppose so. I can't tell you where he did and didn't go."

Tiedemann thought these answers came a little too easily. Had Conti already decided who a suitable scapegoat might be? Had he offered up Cartwright because it might spare the members of his family?

"You know, of course, that the body of our comrade was found in the cellar, yes?"

Conti turned even paler, if that was possible. He stared straight ahead while Tiedemann remained silent. Eventually Conti's anxiety caused him to steal furtive glances around the room, terrified to see what was coming next.

Tiedemann walked around in front of him and knelt down several feet away.

"Herr Conti, the problem I have is this. Cartwright was *not* found hiding in the cellar, and there's no way he could have gotten back and forth without being seen by my men. That is not where I think he was hiding. Tell me, who was it that opened up the wine stores to my men?"

"What do you mean?"

"We drank some wine last night, at your invitation. Which of you took my officer down to the wine cellar and invited us to drink?"

Conti looked up at him and mumbled.

"What?"

"I said, I did."

"Why?"

There was a strange confidence in Conti's eyes. "God's truth, I wanted your stay to be a hospitable one, so I thought some wine would be appropriate. You looked road weary, exhausted."

"Were you trying to get us drunk?"

"*Non, monsieur*."

"Were you trying to get us off guard?"

"No! I mean, I thought you might want to relax after fighting the storm, and a little wine can go a long way. It is our specialty, after all."

Tiedemann kept to himself any comment about the quality of the Conti specialty. "Who else knew you had opened your cellars to us?"

"My father-in-law."

Tiedemann paused and looked over at each of his officers. Springer was oblivious and was apparently choosing the location on Conti's body for his next kick, but Krauss returned his gaze with an interested look. Perhaps some things were finally starting to make sense.

"Tell me, was Herr Rimbault happy with our arrival here?"

"My father-in-law is not... fond of Germany."

"Indeed. One has but to spend two minutes with him to see little other than abject hatred."

Conti looked increasingly uncomfortable. "Sir, hatred is a very strong word. He is simply reeling from the collapse of our nation. He is only frustrated that we took you in after we already have lost so much as Frenchmen."

"I disagree," Tiedemann countered. "I think he is a crafty, spiteful man that had plenty of motivation to raise a hand against us. Tell me, what were you and he arguing about last night?"

"Arguing? I-I don't understand."

"You were having a verbal fight with Rimbault. Herr Springer here even saw it before your father-in-law closed the door on him."

"Sir, that was not an argument, that was simply a discussion about the wine cellars. Marc did not like the idea of giving our best stores to you while you were here, since that is what we need to sell in order to survive. He thought we should keep—"

"So, a French nationalist with a hostile attitude who discovers that German soldiers, potentially off guard and slightly inebriated, are going to the cellar to steal his wine. Pretty strong motivation for a murder, wouldn't you say?"

"No, wait, you misconstrued what I said—"

"Herr Conti, who killed my officer?"

There was a slight pause. "Oh, God. I don't know. Please believe me, I don't know. We didn't mean for anything bad to happen. I don't know."

"Well, I think I do. We have heard enough for now. Springer, take him out."

"Herr Tiedemann," Conti pleaded, "please, you have the wrong impression. No one here has raised a hand against you. Please!"

Springer and the soldier standing guard went over and picked up the prisoner. Conti's body contorted in pain as they hauled him out, and Tiedemann was left with the bespectacled lieutenant Krauss. The two men said nothing for several moments as they reflected on what they had heard.

"So, Krauss. Do you think Rimbault is guilty? That a deep hatred pushes him over the edge when a couple Germans pop open a few shitty-tasting wine bottles?"

Krauss shook his head. "It seems to me that there are still quite a few pieces missing."

"More than a few," Tiedemann agreed. "For the life of me I don't know why anyone would risk retaliation. Conti is correct. Why wouldn't they just leave us alone?" He stroked his chin. "And why wouldn't they hide the body?"

"Perhaps Rimbault is crazy? With his loathing for us overpowering any sort of normal restraint?"

Tiedemann thought about that possibility. "Perhaps. But unlikely. I think we have a bit more work to do before we finger our criminal."

"Of course."

"I need some time for my mind to sort through the facts. Bring in the area maps and let's lay them on the table. Maybe reviewing our route back to Perpignan will help my subconscious work things out."

"*Jawohl.* Anything else, Herr Hauptsturmführer?"

"Send Springer to the cellar to check on the airman. See if he thinks Cartwright could have been hiding down there. Maybe we missed something. I can't rule out the Briton's role in Hoffman's death yet."

Tiedemann's stomach growled.

"And get something to eat, for God's sake, before we all pass out from hunger."

11

Gabrielle had not eaten a single thing so far that day, so it was a bit of a shock when she was ushered into the kitchen to prepare food.

At first she thought it might be a Godsend. A gruff German had retrieved her from one of the bedrooms and brought her downstairs to join her mother. Unfortunately, once they realized the quantity of food they were supposed to prepare, it was apparent they weren't being asked to feed themselves.

There was a lot to do. Mama sliced the bread while two soldiers marched Gabrielle to the pantry at the bottom of the spiral staircase. She had to all but empty out the family food stores to get enough for so many soldiers. Then Gabrielle had to stifle her resentment as they chopped turnips, potatoes, and carrots and threw them in the pot. A little lamb haunch went in for some substance and the pot was set to simmer.

Food was so hard to come by these days. It wasn't right that someone else was going to eat what the Contis needed to survive. Why couldn't the soldiers consume what they brought with them?

Mama was a ball of anxiety. Gabrielle was glad she had inherited her temperament from her father. She tried to give her mother's arm a squeeze here and there to reassure her.

"It will be all right, Mama. We will get through this."

"I'm so scared!" Mama whispered back. Her wrinkled eyes looked as if they could start spilling tears any moment.

"Mama, don't cry now. Don't let them see you do that. Focus on the kitchen work."

Yes—so thankful that her nerve came from her father. This family wasn't big enough for two women who couldn't keep it together.

The stew warmed and Gabrielle and her mother tried to look busy while they waited. They would take turns moving things across the counter and shuffling up the unused ends of vegetables so that the soldiers would think they were still working. After a half hour, one of them—a tall, sandy-haired boy who would have been cute if not for the hard look in his eyes—barked something in German as he pointed to the pot. He obviously wanted to know when it would be ready.

"Gabrielle, what do we tell them? It won't be finished for an hour," Mama said. It took time for a stew to come together.

"They seem to want it now, Mama. We'll have to give it to them. It's not going to be us eating it."

"What *will* we eat?" her mother whispered.

Gabrielle's stomach echoed the sentiment. "Not everything I cut up went into the pot. Here. Take these potatoes and put them under your apron when the guards aren't looking."

"They're raw."

"They're food. Take them."

After more insistence from the guard, Gabrielle signaled that the soup was "done" for whatever that meant. The soldiers had a brief conversation before one of them jerked his head and motioned for her to follow him.

Gabrielle knew she didn't have a choice. With a lingering glance toward her mother, she stepped forward until the German roughly took her elbow and guided her to the far end of the kitchen. The German directed her through hand gestures and unintelligible orders to fill a basket with bread. Next he had her fill a smaller pot with stew. Lastly, she was forced to sling the basket over her arm and carry the soup pot out of the kitchen, using a towel to insulate her hands from the heat. On the way out she saw the other soldier making her mother do the exact same thing. Apparently they were also to be the wait staff in addition to the chefs.

The sandy-haired soldier looked like he was perhaps Gabrielle's age. He led her through several corridors until they arrived at the front landing, where another German was conversing with the sergeant with the scar on his jaw. So, they were guarding the front door. Gabrielle longingly wondered what would happen if she made a break for it. The fantasy did not last long as her eyes slid over to the machine pistol that the soldier carried over his shoulder.

Her escort pointed at the basket she was carrying and again spoke words that she didn't understand. Nonetheless, it was clear what she was supposed to do. She put the pot of soup on the floor and took two bowls out of the basket for the Germans to use. The sergeant snatched one from her and helped himself, followed by the other guard. Gabrielle closed her eyes at such a lack of manners. She felt like she was feeding farm animals.

The boy German snatched at her elbow to lead her to the next stop. Gabrielle angrily pulled out of his grasp and cursed at him. He glared at her. For a moment, panic balled up in her stomach as she thought back to Springer. Gabrielle prayed she hadn't made a terrible mistake. The thought of being beaten again frightened her, and while this German was still a boy, he was a soldier too.

Luckily the tension was broken when the sergeant reached for another slice of bread. The boy stepped back, and Gabrielle took advantage of the moment to put on a display of meekness as she picked up her basket. It seemed to work. Her German handler pointed down the corridor. Gabrielle took a breath of relief and retrieved the soup pot.

The pair left the foyer and passed through the Great Room. Gabrielle shuddered at the thought of how they had been lined up earlier that morning. No one was there now, and she didn't know if that was a good thing or a bad thing. They kept moving and traced their way through the halls to a back bedroom. A guard holding a rifle stood outside the door, and he smiled broadly when he understood why they were there. He loosened his rifle strap and swung it over his shoulder so that he could use both hands to get at the food.

Gabrielle wondered why this soldier was all the way over here away from the other Germans. Was he guarding someone? It had to be—they had broken everyone up from the Great Room and moved them to separate places. Who could it be? Her father? Philippe? Gabrielle was dying for some affirmation that everyone else was all right and, while they were enduring an unfair and barbaric invasion of their home life, she knew they could all get through it if they just kept their heads.

She realized with a start that her sandy-haired escort was watching her intently. As if reading her mind, he nodded his head toward the bedroom door. Was that an invitation to look inside?

Gabrielle eyed him uncertainly. His eyes were so... *weary*. He must have seen some action already. But yet the offer was there. Why? She thought back to moments before, when she had pulled her elbow away. This young man had not retaliated.

She studied his face. He must understand, she decided. He still saw her as a human being. Some humanity was still present that could acknowledged how Gabrielle felt at her world being turned upside down by a home invasion. Despite it all, she was still a person in his eyes.

Taking a step forward, Gabrielle pushed down on the door latch and cracked the door open.

Girard was crumpled on the floor in a pile of torn clothes. The well-groomed graying hair that adorned his head was matted and unkempt, and his face was swollen with cuts and bruises. But the worst of it was the look in his eyes as he stared at the opening door. There was fear there, pure and simple, at who might be coming in to deal with him. If it hadn't been for the shock, tears would have certainly welled up in Gabrielle's eyes.

The German escort abruptly shut the door. *Enough*, he signaled. Time for them to continue their circuit.

Gabrielle's temper started to smolder again. Poor Girard. How could they have done that to him? Didn't they understand that her family had nothing to do with this soldier's death? A bunch of drunken buffoons sauntering around their home—with guns, no less. Why couldn't they accept that perhaps this man had an accident of some sort?

The obvious answer came to her as they walked. The Germans had beaten Girard because they could. Their egos, their sense of superiority, their conditioning would all drive them to find the enemy. Any enemy. For the first time, she wondered if maybe everything wouldn't turn out all right.

A few more stops and they returned down the servants' corridor back to the kitchen. She refilled her soup pot and wished Mama was back with her. The thought of Girard and what might be in store for the rest of them kept echoing in her head. He had been in her family's employment for ever since she could remember. He lived with them and had practically helped raise Gabrielle and Philippe. She hoped that he was really not that badly injured. Moreover, she hoped to God that Mama didn't see anyone who had been beaten like that. Her mother would not be able to cope.

When the pot was topped off, the German soldier motioned her over to the spiral staircase.

Gabrielle froze, feeling fear creeping into her stomach. Why would her escort want her to go into the cellar with him?

"*Komm, Fräulein,*" he insisted.

Gabrielle took a deep breath and stepped forward. They proceeded single file down the rickety staircase into the cool air of the underground. The main corridor had originally been a natural passage that her paternal grandfather, Papa's father, had widened and finished out as a convenient way to get to the underground cave. That giant, naturally-occurring cavern was where they stored all of the wine barrels during the fermentation process. But that was further underground. The German nodded again for her to walk ahead, and Gabrielle had to assume they were instead headed toward the Conti's personal wine cellar where they stored finished bottles.

She was right. It took only a minute before they were at the brick arch and the racks of bottles beyond. Another soldier stood guard here, also young, but with dark hair and a harsh scowl that made him look ugly. Gabrielle's jaw tightened when she saw Springer standing next to him.

"Well, well, what have we here?" The blond officer had a bored, disinterested look that quickly evaporated. It reminded Gabrielle of what a lion might look like when it spotted a potential prey.

"Food," she said. She glared at him, refusing to break eye contact.

"Most generous. Are you handling our stay well enough?"

Gabrielle blinked at the oddity of his manners. Springer's voice was disarmingly friendly. Was this the same man that had so savagely beaten her during her interrogation? He was smiling at her.

"I'm... alright." She stood there in the doorway, holding her basket.

"Forgive me for my behavior earlier," Springer continued. "Sometimes things get a little carried away during interrogations. I'm used to questioning Russians, not members of a peaceful French family. How is your face? I hope I did not leave a mark on you?"

"It's fine."

"Very well." Springer tipped the edge of the basket with his finger and examined how much bread was left. "Excellent, just enough. Let's dispense what we have here, shall we?"

The soup was poured and the bread loaf broken into several chunks divided between the guard, Gabrielle's escort, and Springer. Springer offered a remaining piece of bread to Gabrielle. Cautiously, she took it from his hand. With no apparent repercussions, ravenous hunger overtook her and she greedily stuffed the bread into her mouth. Who knew when she would get another opportunity?

A raspy cough off to her right caught Gabrielle's attention. She turned and her eyes fell upon a huddled figured sitting on the floor. She gasped, inadvertently choking on some of the breadcrumbs still in her mouth.

It was Stefan.

She had to look twice to make sure. Girard had looked bad, but there weren't words for what had been done to the Englishman. Stefan had his back against the far wall, forearms on his knees, hunched over in obvious pain. Cuts littered his swollen, dirty cheeks. His clothing was soiled and torn far beyond the state it had been the night before. The Germans had beaten him solidly.

Stefan's eyes were looking intently at her. *Danger.*

Gabrielle stared back blankly, a jumble of thoughts in her head. She had not had much direct contact with the Englishman. Her father and grandfather had kept him sequestered since he had stumbled into their home almost a week ago—although ever since then, they had all had it drilled into their heads that if anyone found out about him, he had only been there "two nights." During the day, the three of them plus Girard were nowhere to be found. In the evenings, the men all congregated in the Great Room while Mama, Gabrielle, and Philippe tended to the house.

Nonetheless, Gabrielle had spied on him. She was intensely curious about this handsome, foreign soldier who had appeared randomly out of the night. He had noticed, too. A lingering glance or a nod and smile had come her way at least once a day. They didn't need to speak the same language to have a basic level of communication.

Stefan's eyes suddenly grew wide and he threw his hands up over his head.

Gabrielle jumped aside in a panic. Then the laughter hit her ears, and she watched Springer make another menacing lunge at their prisoner. Stefan flinched again as he threw his hands protectively over his head. The Englishman looked just like her father had when he had been beaten for talking in the Great Room.

Gabrielle had her own chance to flinch when Springer grabbed her by the elbow.

"Ah, my dear, don't worry about him," he said. His voice was light and jovial. "We'll protect you. Those British, they're just animals. Don't know the first thing about hygiene, either, do they? Look at this one, all covered in dirt and blood. Can't say I like it. Smells, too. It must be easy to get knocked around a bit down here underground."

Springer clearly got a laugh out of his own wit. He spoke in German to his companions and got more snickers before turning back to her. "Now, let's help you finish your rounds so that you can get back, shall we? We don't want you to be late. I'll take over as your escort. There's only one more stop anyway, so it shouldn't take long. Come, yes?"

There wasn't much of a choice. She gave a last lingering look towards Stephen's beaten face. He was staring at her again, the same message of warning in his eyes.

The blond German led her out of the wine cellar, but instead of going back toward the kitchen he turned her down the corridor that connected to the wine cave.

"Where are we going?" Gabrielle demanded with some alarm.

"There's only one more soldier on duty, and he's this way," Springer replied. "Come on, let's go."

Gabrielle thought back to the previous night. She had seen Springer prowling in search of alcohol. Had they found something in the wine cave worth guarding? Was there really a soldier posted back this way?

They walked for some ten meters or so before the corridor opened up into the dim vastness of the barrel cave. Filling the space before them were rows of oaken barrels, round ends and fat middles held tight by bands of dark iron that were stacked two or three high in solid wooden stands. The casks formed the walls of a virtual labyrinth in which it would be easy to get lost. *Or hide*, Gabrielle thought. It was an enormous, empty, isolated place, poorly lit by sporadic electric lights that hung in solitude every ten or twenty meters. Springer continued to guide her around this corner and that as they made their way to the last German.

At last, Springer slowed his steps and used Gabrielle's arm to turn her around slightly. "Quite romantic down here, isn't it? I've always admired winemaking. There's so much culture and tradition associated with it that it almost delineates where civilization begins and ends. Wouldn't you agree?"

"I wouldn't know about that."

The hairs on Gabrielle's neck stood on end. Glancing sideways at Springer, she tried to keep walking and prayed that she had nothing to worry about. Please, she thought, please let this guard be just up ahead so that she could deliver the food and get back to her mother.

Springer grabbed her elbow solidly and kept her from moving away.

"Shouldn't we almost be at your soldier's post?" Gabrielle pleaded. "It's easy to get lost… *hello? Where are you, sir*?"

"That's not necessary," Springer drawled.

"No, please—"

"You needn't be afraid of me, my dear. You're well protected in the hands of *Der Führer's* army."

Springer's other hand gently stroked Gabrielle's back, and she jumped. That made the German laugh. "For goodness' sakes! Relax, my dear. Everything will be all right. Don't you believe me?"

Gabrielle looked at her feet and said a silent prayer. She knew she was attractive girl. That wasn't helping matters at the moment. She was standing with a monster who had beaten her father and family. She stayed silent and waited, still hoping that they if she just kept quiet, Springer would shrug his shoulders, give up, and resume their task of feeding the last guard.

Please, let there be a last guard.

The SS officer moved inappropriately closer to her. Gabrielle took a step back and found herself blocked by a wall of wine barrels. Panic started building in her stomach as the German leaned over to kiss her. There was nowhere for her to go. She froze, trapped, her lips drawn tightly together while Springer pushed his mouth against hers.

"Now that wasn't much of an embrace, was it?" the German said. "There would be more passion between us if I were kissing stone. Let's try that again, my pretty French maid. It's fine. You don't have to worry about showing a little life, you know."

Despite his soft words, Springer grabbed Gabrielle roughly by the arms and pinned her against the barrel. He forced a kiss on her again. This time, Gabrielle actively struggled. She dropped the soup pot and tried to push his hands off of her, tried to turn her chin away. But the soldier was too strong. Their mouths smashed together and Gabrielle responded with the only thing she could think of to defend herself. She bit him.

Springer jerked back in surprise, with a small gash of bright red welling up on his bottom lip.

Gabrielle tried to make a break for it, thinking she might be able to lose him in the maze of wine barrels stacked in the cavern. But the German's grip did not loosen. There was a moment of silent tension between the two of them and the barrels. Springer stared at her with a dumbfounded look on his face.

Oh, God, Gabrielle thought, *what is he going to do to me?* The realization of being utterly helpless closed in on her and she was sure that she was going to vomit.

Then, of all the things the imposing Nazi officer could have done, Springer laughed.

"Excellent! I like the spirited ones," he said as he wiped his lip with the back of his hand. "Absolutely excellent. This will be much better than I thought."

Gabrielle didn't see the fist coming. Springer slugged her hard in the stomach, knocking the wind out of her and making her collapse to the ground. Then he grabbed a fistful of her hair and hoisted her back upright. Springer threw her back against the barrel to kiss her again, and Gabrielle felt a shooting pain through her own bottom lip. It took a moment to realize he had bitten her back; she could taste the saltiness of her blood flowing past her tongue. Then another backhand and she was off her feet. She lay in a daze with her face against the hard, stony floor.

Springer stood towering over her. He had loosened his tunic and was undoing the front of his trousers.

"Don't worry, little Gabrielle. The first time is always a little rough, but I haven't met a girl yet who hasn't wanted to come back for more. Trust me. You'll like this."

12

Cartwright shoved his hands into his armpits to keep his fingers warm. The air in the cellar was bloody cold. He understood from Robert that wine bottles were supposed to be stored at twelve degrees Centigrade, and that didn't seem like it should be so bad, but the prolonged coolness and lack of any activity had sapped most the temperature from his body. Cartwright shivered in his misery as he stole furtive glances at his guard's heavy overcoat.

The German watching over him was another piece of ornamental decoration detracting from the cozy atmosphere. The soldier had the mean, battle-worn stare of someone who had seen combat in difficult circumstances. Cartwright knew that look well.

Being under fire in the sky was horrific. One could only sit and wait as enemy fighters closed in with the sole intent of ripping a plane to shreds. Machine gun fire would disintegrate whole parts of the fuselage, while exploding flak randomly gutted anyone inside. Sturdily constructed bombers became fireballs before rolling belly-up into a death spiral. There was nowhere to hide in the sky. Nowhere to run. Sometimes the Messerschmitts would zoom by so closely that Cartwright could see the pilots' facial expressions.

Regardless of whether one fought on the ground or in the sky, the net result was the same.

Death. Cartwright wondered if that was the end in store for him now.

Thinking about Conti's daughter didn't help. Cartwright had never really been introduced to her—not surprising, given how busy he and the men of her family had been since that first night. He didn't even know her name. The girl had kept her distance while they worked, with only an occasional peek from around the odd corner. He didn't blame her for being shy. How else would one act at the sight of a tired, dirty stranger who only spoke English and whose few possessions included a compass and revolver?

But one thing was for sure: she was gorgeous. Long brown hair and beautiful dark eyes. Surely she made heads turn whenever she walked down the street. That was the worrisome part. Cartwright saw how that bastard Springer looked at her before he escorted her out of the wine cellar. It didn't take a genius to recognize the character and intentions of such a man.

He hoped that she was okay. In the meantime, he had to contend with the current company. The SS guard stood like a statue near the arch entry, his hands resting on the MP40 mac
hanging from his shoulder.

Cartwright had long since
trying to plot escape, so h
away some of the time. Fo
labels of the wine bottles
him. The bottles were
was little variation in

didn't matter, of course. Cartwright didn't know French. His commoner roots meant limited exposure to the luxury of a classical education. He simply imagined as best he could what some of the words must have meant. It didn't take a genius to know that *Vin* meant vine. *Raisin* appeared a lot, although Cartwright knew for a fact that wine was made from grapes, not raisins, and he couldn't for the life of him figure out what a raisin would have to do with the process. *Terre* sounded like terror, not a very pleasant image for such a nice winery. *Vendange*. Must mean vendetta? *Pain* was mentioned every now and then.

Cartwright squinted as he tried to make sense of the yellowing labels. Pain, terror, vendettas. Granted, he didn't know much about the wine making process, but it all seemed rather brutal. Why would anyone carry on such a grudge against a harmless bunch of grapes? Perhaps the French wine industry had some sort of seedy, violent history he didn't know about.

He went through some more bottles and gradually realized the SS guard was watching intently him. Cartwright tried not to think about the machine pistol. He moved his arms a little slower, was a bit more careful in pulling bottles out of the rack and replacing them—anything he could do to not appear threatening. How ironic that he was practically lying on the floor, beaten to [illegible] yet *he* was the one struggling to appear

The guard took a step forward. Cartwright froze.

Amazingly, the guard walked over to a different wine rack and started examining bottles himself. Cartwright was dumbfounded. He was not about to have the *shite* kicked out of him? The Englishman stared in silence as the Hun gently lifted a dusty specimen from Conti's finest vintages off of its cradle. The soldier's face took on a youthful wonder as he studied the bottle. When he finally put down the bottle it was only to pick up a second one.

It would have been a perfect—*perfect*—bonding moment except for the fact that the wine rack the Hun had decided to investigate was right next to *the wrong wall in the cellar.* The wall that had newer construction than the rest. The one where the masonry didn't quite match. The wall would spell disaster for all of them if examined too closely.

Cartwright pretended to also study more wine, but in reality was observing what his keeper was doing. He needed to distract him. Luckily, the opportunity was an obvious one. Two men from different sides in the war, united through a common boredom.

"Hallo," Cartwright said.

The guard glanced over as if surprised his prisoner could talk. His boyish face drifted off into nothing for a moment, considering. When he looked back, Cartwright knew that he had connected. The guard gave him a small nod.

"My name's Stephen. What's yours?"

Silence from the German as he stood holding a wine bottle.

"Steee-vennnnn," Cartwright tried again, pointing to his chest. "Stephen. Now. What's your name?"

The German seemed to understand what was being asked but acted unsure of whether he should say anything. He was a soldier first and foremost. One did not fraternize with prisoners. After a moment, however, boredom appeared to win out.

"Ich heisse Erich."

"Erik? Good to meet you. I noticed that you're looking at these bottles. Here, here's a good year that might interest you." Cartwright took the bottle he was holding and rolled it along the floor towards the German.

Erich watched the bottle as it came to a stop at his feet. He paused, then cautiously bent over to pick it up and compare it to the wine he was holding. Glancing between the two labels made him smile. Cartwright grimaced when he saw that the bottles were the same.

"Well, there we are. We both must have good taste."

The German considered the two bottles for a moment, then turned and walked to the arched doorway. He opened a small pack with his belongings and carefully stowed the wine away for safekeeping. There were obviously few comforts for an infantryman marching across Europe. Alcohol was prized highly by all.

Cartwright felt an unease in his stomach. He hoped he wasn't around when the German drank it and discovered how terrible it was. The good stuff was off in the oak barrels in the wine cave. All of these bottles? Well, there were reasons it tasted like piss.

Erich finished stowing his gear and stood back up to face Cartwright. He was obviously pleased with himself for being so opportunistic. So much the better, Cartwright thought. He preferred a captor who was in a good mood.

"Of all the places to be held prisoner," Cartwright began with a smile, "I suppose there are worse places than one that is filled with booze. Wouldn't you say?"

The German returned a small smile. Reaching into a pocket in his tunic, he pulled out a package of cigarettes and offered the end to Cartwright. The Englishman took two after a careful glance to make sure it would be allowed. Erich produced a lighter and got both of them started in puffing away.

Cartwright kept talking in between drags. "Although I must say, this place is quite a mess. Lots of broken glass everywhere. I wonder what sort of ruckus caused it?"

He spoke slowly and studied Erich for any sort of clue from his question. German and English had enough similar words that he might get lucky and hit upon some common understanding. But Erich just stared at him.

"Can you tell me why I was brought all the way down here? There are plenty of other places to hold me captive. The house upstairs is much nicer. Why the cellar?"

Erich went back to leaning against the wall near the archway, his hands back to resting on his weapon. The slight smile was gone. The questions weren't working. Was it the subject matter? Or just the language barrier?

Cartwright changed tack. "So how long have you been in the SS?"

A blank look.

"Right. Since birth, I bet. Old Adolf probably spoon-fed you with a mess kit. You don't speak English, do you?"

Another blank look. He was getting nowhere.

The stone wall of the cellar was only a few feet behind Cartwright. He slowly scooted himself past the wine rack until he could use it for back support. His muscles were tight and it felt good to use them even for such a small purpose. Thankfully, Erich didn't seem to mind the repositioning. He simply watched and smoked.

"Whew, that's better," Cartwright said. "Not the most comfortable accommodations. Before you lot got here, I actually had a nice, warm bed to sleep in, do you know that? Even better than the barracks in England. Not that I'm complaining about the cellar here. It beats a hole in the ground like you're probably used to, I'm sure."

The German continued to silently study him. He did seem more relaxed and at ease than he had been earlier. That had to be worth something.

"So why are you giving the Conti's here such trouble? I suppose you stopped here to get out of the rain, but the weather seems like it's cleared up a bit. Why are you staying around?"

Still no comprehension. Cartwright gave up. The language barrier existed here as much as it had when Cartwright first arrived at the winery. No one understood anything he said—except Robert, to a small extent, and the German officer Cartwright had mentally tagged as The Rat. Otherwise he was a stranger in a foreign land, and utterly alone. It didn't matter whether the tongue of choice was French or German.

"Well, Erich, would you like to learn some English then? We have nothing better to do to pass the time. Can you *speaken-English*?"

The German didn't reply, but Cartwright could see that he had his attention. The Briton pointed to his eyes one at a time and said, "Eyes."

Erich watched closely.

"Ears," Cartwright continued. "Head."

Erich cleared his throat. "*Kopf*," he replied.

Cartwright smiled broadly. Monotony was winning over discipline. "Yes, that's it. *Kopf* means head. I think."

A couple more. "Feet."

"*Füsse.*"

"Hands."

"*Hände.*"

"Very good, old chap. Let's make it interesting." Cartwright picked up a wine bottle. "I put the wine in my hand." He pointed alternately to the two main objects in the sentence. "Wine. Hand."

Erich nodded. *"Ich nehme die Weinflasche in meine hände."*

"Well done. We'll make an honorary Brit out of you yet." *And then maybe you'll be able to help me get out of here—even if you don't realize it.*

The two men went through other simple words and phrases. Cartwright was enjoying himself when boot steps sounded from out in the corridor. The two men clammed up instantly, but when the sergeant with the scar strode into the cellar with Erich's relief guard, it was obvious he knew something was going on.

"Was geschieht hier, Ackerman?" Gohler yelled.

Erich immediately stood at attention and shouted something short and unintelligible in reply. His eyes were focused off into space despite the fact that Gohler was inches from his face.

The sergeant looked outraged. What followed was an exchange that was utterly incomprehensible to Cartwright. It adhered to a defined pattern between the two men of what appeared to be harsh question, excuse, rebuke, and apology. Then it repeated. Even a skilled translator would have been likely hard pressed to follow the German slang and profanity. Cartwright tried to crawl into the smallest ball his body had ever attempted, as if it would make him invisible.

When he was finished, Gohler yelled a final command and Erich disappeared into the corridor. Then the sergeant glared at Cartwright.

Uh oh.

"Geben Sie mir Ihr Gewehr," he said to the new guard.

Without hesitation, the soldier handed his rifle to the sergeant.

"Hold on, there, old boy." Cartwright wanted to squirm his way into the darkest corner possible.

Gohler began walking purposefully towards him. The scar on the sergeant's face made it seem as if he was grinning a wicked smile.

"Herr Cartwright, Ich verstehe, dass Sie meinen Soldaten unterrichtet haben, Englisch zu sprechen. Möglicherweise ist es jetzt Zeit für etwas Deutsch."

Although the words were foreign, somehow the Englishman knew exactly what they meant. The sergeant understood what the two of them had been doing, that Cartwright had been trying to teach the soldier a few basic English phrases.

Now it was time to learn some German.

The stock of the rifle crashed into Cartwright's arm, then his side, then his stomach. Pain rushed in in waves.

13

Tiedemann was in a foul mood. He was starving. Where was the food he had ordered to be made?

The entire squad was getting even further behind schedule as they wasted time in this mire of a crime investigation. He wondered if he would be reprimanded. They should be putting more energy into righting the overturned truck back on the road. But the hangover was the worst of it. Silently Tiedemann damned himself yet again for drinking so much of that awful Burgundy. He would stick to schnapps next time.

Gohler waited patiently by the door of the study. The sergeant had just finished giving his report about the Englishman and his antics in the cellar below. Tiedemann found it mildly interesting that the flyer was trying to communicate with a soldier performing a tedious guard assignment. But he suspected that it was little more than that. He didn't buy Gohler's interpretation that Cartwright was a spy, though whether the Englishman was their murderer remained to be seen.

"So, Herr Gohler, did your little interrogation prove whether Cartwright speaks German or not?"

"No, Herr Hauptsturmführer. I spent a half hour working him over. He doesn't seem to understand anything but English. I must add, however, that I'm certain the Englishman is hiding something from us. Perhaps something more than trivial."

"And you base this assertion on... what?"

Gohler stiffened. "Sir. I do have rather extensive experience with questioning prisoners. We had ample opportunity on the Eastern Front when we were dealing with partisans and informers. You start to develop a certain sensitivity to underlying motivations. I can read people, and that Tommy is worried about something other than his own skin."

The rain was resuming outside, and fat drops of water began to splatter against the window pane. More bad luck.

Tiedemann thought for a moment before deciding there were enough people already trying to interpret the prisoners' answers. "Thank you for reporting what you saw, Herr Gohler. I will take it from here. There's something else I need you to work on, now, beyond managing the prisoners."

"Of course, Herr Hauptsturmführer."

"We need our vehicles back on the road so that we can get out of here. Get that truck upright."

Gohler stiffened slightly at the abrupt dismissal of his interrogation. But soldiers of the Reich did nothing if not obey orders. "Sir! With your permission, we can accomplish that objective more quickly with more men. The Opel is stuck fast and quite heavy."

"What do you suggest?"

"Let's consolidate the guards and put the prisoners into the same rooms. That will let me put more men on truck detail."

Tiedemann frowned, triggering a massive hangover throb. He needed food. He needed water. He needed *closure*. Who had killed Hoffman? He really didn't want to slaughter this whole family and move on just to stay on a time table. His German upbringing was more precise than that.

"Fine, whatever. Get it done."

"*Jawohl.*"

A flash of lightning from the window intruded into the room as Gohler exited. Only Krauss was left with him now.

"So, our Birmingham Englishman is now a special agent who speaks German? I think Herr Gohler must have drunk more than the rest of us last night," Krauss needled. He fidgeted with his spectacles.

"That's enough, Krauss." Tiedemann slumped into the chair next to the window. He wasn't about to have his subordinates riding each other, particularly when one of them was a bookish mole of a man who had seen little, if any, combat. "Gohler and Hoffman had quite a bit of service history together. I'm not saying that he's imagining things, but if he is, it should be excused to some extent. He's had a rough time."

"Of course, sir," Krauss replied with what barely passed as sincerity.

"Watch your tone, Herr Obersturmführer."

Krauss stiffened and saluted. *"Heil Hitler!"*

Tiedemann rubbed his throbbing forehead and stared outside. There was a lot of shaping up that would have to take place amongst his soldiers and officer corps once they reached their destination. Krauss's behavior was a prime example.

As a combat division, *Totenkopf* had performed moderately well in the frozen steppes of Russia. They had broken out of an encircled position after months of horrific weather and heavy casualties. But the steep losses in men and materiel meant there was a severe need for replacements. Getting good men was always a hurdle, but *Totenkopf's* particular history provided a challenge for Tiedemann in his quest to rebuild his company.

Partly as a by-product of the stunning speed at which Germany had been able to subdue its enemies thus far, there was a continual need for a police force to fill the power vacuum left in newly occupied lands as the front-line military advanced. Just because a line on a map suggested that Poland or Czechoslovakia now belonged to the Reich did not mean that the citizens were somehow magically converted into loyal subjects. That was where the mainstream SS came in. The SS was responsible for occupying a new territory and arresting intellectuals, Jews, political and religious leaders, or any other influential or meddlesome persons who could stir up trouble by opposing the Nazi ideology. The *Totenkopfverbände,* or Death's Head troops, had a particularly specific role in running most of the concentration camps that were set up in these areas to hold the dissidents.

However, the demand for replacements necessitated that parts of the SS be brought forward into field divisions. These units were designated as the Waffen-SS. Along with *Das Reich*, *Liebstandarte Adolf Hitler*, and others, *Totenkopf* was one of the named divisions that saw front-line combat, and true to its namesake many of its men came from the *Totenkopfverbände* camp guards. Unfortunately, this was a problem for a field commander like Tiedemann. At best, the fact that his troops had once been prison guards meant that their fighting skills were poor. There was a performance penalty for a lack of discipline and steady drilling. At worst, they could be petty and brutal monsters used to a life of easy power. It was Tiedemann's job to build the *esprit de corps* and combat toughness his men would need in order to become an effective combat group. And while he felt he had a good corps of officers to replace the ones he had lost in Russia, the subconscious behaviors that surfaced from time to time served as a reminder that there was still work to be done.

But that was just the way it was. Tiedemann didn't subscribe to the most extreme ideologies of the SS, but he had to make it work nonetheless. It was an ongoing, continual effort.

The rain had really picked up outside. Tiedemann's attention drifted out into the view of the vineyard. It was quite pretty, with the hazy rows of grape leaves having turned yellow and red amongst the wet mist. The dark sky somehow seemed to accent the colors. A stray part of Tiedemann's mind wondered if human remains would provide good fertilizer for a vineyard.

Damn it all.

He didn't want to resort to a mass execution. This was not Russia. These were civilized French citizens he was dealing with. It was not right that Tiedemann and his men should have to use indiscriminate force to exact revenge. Or was it that he had become sick of death, sick of killing? How different he felt from even a month ago, where he would have no sooner ordered the death of Soviet guerrillas than a wounded dog in the street. That mentality seemed so inappropriate here in the Burgundy wine region. He wasn't cut out for this. Tiedemann was a front-line man, where the enemy was clearly defined and fought according to the rules of engagement.

With renewed purpose, Tiedemann forced his mind back to the murder. He had to figure this out, even if everything he knew was circumstantial. What *did* he know?

Marc Rimbault certainly knew that German soldiers would be taking wine from the cellar, and he was hostile enough to suggest that he might actually act on that knowledge if he wanted to exact some twisted revenge on a lone SS man.

Robert Conti seemed a bit less likely as suspect, but he had also been exposed as a liar during his interrogation, which meant that the odds increased significantly around whether he was holding back other clues.

Cartwright, originally the most promising suspect, seemed quite oblivious to anything other than being a prisoner of war. Tiedemann couldn't pick up on what it was that Gohler thought he saw. Either the Englishman was a fine actor, or else he was innocent of everything except being in the wrong place at the wrong time, in the wrong army.

Girard, the servant whom Springer had beaten severely in a fit of frustration, had a crippled foot and didn't seem physically capable of winning any sort of physical struggle.

The rest simply didn't make sense as legitimate suspects. Conti's wife kept breaking into hysterics. She had to be out. What about the girl, Gabrielle? She was pretty, and certainly defiant enough if there had been any unwanted attention. Had she been accosted, fought back, and gotten in a lucky mortal blow? Philippe, the little boy, would be incapable of a melee with a grown man. But what if there had been some sort of accident? His weakness could be a reason that the body had not been hidden.

Why didn't the murderer hide the body?

Tiedemann sighed. He didn't think he could get away with another full day of delay.

"Sir," Krauss said as if reading his thoughts, "I know this interruption in our travel is unacceptable. Would it perhaps be better if we turned over this investigation to the SD? I believe they have a field office just a short courier's ride away in Dijon."

Tiedemann frowned. There was no way he was going to turn this over to the secret service arm of the SS and deal with the embarrassment of one of his men being killed while the rest were drunk and off guard.

"Krauss, you've been taking all the notes as we talk to the prisoners. Have *you* not been able to draw anything from them as to who the murderer is?"

"Of course, sir," Krauss squeaked eagerly. He looked delighted at this invitation. "The best approach, I believe, is to make an independent assessment of how Herr Hoffman was killed, develop the likely scenarios, and then look for supporting evidence to narrow the field. The evidence can be either physical or drawn verbally from the suspects' stories, of course."

For a full minute there was massive paper flipping from the little notebook Krauss carried with him. Tiedemann's shoulders sank. This conniving little man was the antithesis of a warrior, with his narrow shoulders, excessively groomed moustache, and diminutive presence. It was amazing such men could get into the combat divisions. The need for replacements must be significant.

"Ah, here we are. These are some scenarios I have already worked up from my notes. May I read them to you, sir?"

"Yes."

"Case one. Marc Rimbault detests the Reich so much that he opportunistically exacted vengeance upon Hoffman."

"Obvious," Tiedemann muttered. "But why would Rimbault not have hidden the body?"

"Perhaps he was trying to send us a message of his contempt."

"And put his family in danger? I can't rationalize that yet. What else?"

"Case two, Herr Hoffman was murdered by Robert Conti protecting his daughter."

A variation on the self-defense of a pretty girl. "Go on."

"Gabrielle is quite fetching, and virtually every man in the ranks is talking about her. I understand from the other officers that Hoffman was quite the womanizer who boasted frequently of his exploits. What if he had gone after her? Robert Conti could have happened upon a drunk Hoffman forcing himself upon the girl and smashed his head in with a nearby bottle. Quite an understandable reaction, though duty would demand that Hoffman's death still be repaid in kind, of course."

Tiedemann stood up and stretched. The idea was circumstantial, but certainly logical. He walked over to the small table where he had placed Hoffman's personal effects. There were the usual items one would expect to find from a soldier in the field. A compass and map. A battered wristwatch. Identity disks. His *Soldbuch*, which upon cursory review revealed records of his pay going back six months. Keys to something known only to Hoffman. A weathered, creased photograph of a very pretty woman, though whether it was of Hoffman's wife back home or a girlfriend in the field, Tiedemann now wasn't sure. Many soldiers had both. Hoffman also had what appeared to be a love letter to go with it, but Tiedemann left it folded up. Reading was the last thing he felt like doing. Aside from a few coins, there was nothing else.

Tiedemann fingered the photo as he examined it.

"Looks like Hoffman had good taste in women," he said finally. "And yes, the Conti daughter is certainly attractive. But I am not convinced that leads to rape, especially when he has someone like *this* back home." Tiedemann thumped the photo with his finger. "What are your other possibilities?"

"Case three. Hoffman discovered the Englishman hiding in the cellar and was attacked and killed as a result."

"I don't think Cartwright hid in the cellar," Tiedemann said. "I watched his eyes when he spoke of being in the kitchen since our arrival. I believe him."

"But it makes sense, sir. I know you are keying off physiological clues, but let's review the logic of the argument. Cartwright says he hid in the kitchen. But if you were trying to avoid the enemy, wouldn't you go to the most remote place you could find? Wouldn't you do anything to avoid accidental detection?"

"What if he didn't have time to move?"

"The staircase leading to the cellar is right there in the kitchen. He could move back and hide underground with a minimal amount of increased effort."

Tiedemann scratched his chin uncertainly.

Krauss looked through his notes. "Do not forget that Robert Conti contradicted Cartwright's statement. Conti says they hid him in the cellar."

"He was guessing. He backed off considerably when put under duress."

"But logically," Krauss pressed, "it makes more sense that the Englishman hid further away from where we were."

"Then how did he come to be found in the kitchen cupboard?"

"Perhaps he was *leaving* the cellar."

Leaving the cellar.

Perhaps. But why? Running from the scene of a crime? Why not run the other way, to the big underground wine cave far away from the enemy?

"Tell me, sir," Krauss said as he flipped violently through his notepad. "What do you think about Cartwright being here in the first place?"

"I think the Tommies should have had a better pilot."

"I, uh... yes, sir." Krauss didn't seem capable of appreciating the dry wit. "Nonetheless... I think surely he must have been the one that killed Hoffman."

Something about that conclusion felt too wrong, too obvious. Tiedemann needed to think. And he needed to give his subordinate something to do so that he wasn't incessantly hovering nearby, creating a nagging and constant distraction.

"Krauss, I need to write a letter to Hoffman's next of kin explaining about his death. I want it done as soon as possible, particularly since he was killed behind the lines rather than in battle. Draft it for me, please. Address it to his wife, and finish it by the end of today so that I may familiarize myself with it."

The look of distaste on Krauss's face was plain as day. "Herr Hauptsturmführer, with all due respect, do we not have more important matters at hand? We still have an investigation to carry out."

"Then I suggest you make haste in drafting the letter. Have Gohler work on it with you, he and Hoffman served together and were good friends."

"I... of course, sir," Krauss said, defeated. "Request permission to be dismissed."

"Only if you find out what is holding up my food. I'm going to start randomly shooting people if I don't have a meal here in the next ten minutes."

Once Krauss had left the room, Tiedemann pulled Hoffman's wedding ring out his pocket and rubbed the edges with his fingers. Its pale gold was battered and worn, having seen many months in the harsh elements of the battlefield. Briefly he considered tossing it into the pile of Hoffman's other personal effects. That was the official, procedural thing to do. But for some reason Tiedemann resisted. If the ring was included with the letter Krauss was drafting, Tiedemann thought it would get back to Germany much quicker than the rest of Hoffman's belongings, not to mention the fact that a gold ring included in the official parcel ran the risk of not still being in there by the time it reached its destination.

Tiedemann put the ring back in his pocket. He would include it with the letter to the man's family and trust that that would be enough. It was all that he could do.

Another soldier, loyal to the Reich, gone. At barely twenty-two years of age.

Tiedemann stood up. He *had* to single out the murderer. Even though he was surrounded by death on the battlefield, even though he never let himself get too close to the soldiers he served with—this time Tiedemann had to know who killed Hoffman. This was not war. This was murder. And maybe, just maybe, identifying the perpetrator would help Tiedemann continue to believe that there was a difference between the two.

14

Finally, food arrived. Tiedemann was seething. His head and stomach were killing him, and if he didn't pass out he'd probably start shooting.

"This stew is cold, Springer! What the hell were those two women doing in the kitchen?"

"I'm sorry, Herr Hauptsturmführer. Apparently there was a mix up as to which of the two prisoners was supposed to bring food here to the study. I will have Herr Gohler discipline the men involved."

"Never mind, just—damn it all. Give it to me!" Tiedemann nearly tore the basket off Gabrielle's arm and took out the scraps of bread. The fool girl was trembling. Tiedemann chewed on the tough crust and considered her behavior. Gabrielle remained silent was staring holes into the floor. Quite a difference from when they had questioned her earlier that morning, where she had been all attitude and defiance. She was clearly afraid, more so than before. Why?

Tiedemann glanced at Springer. His lieutenant had a satisfied smirk on his face and was watching haughtily from nearby. Something had happened between them. Tiedemann didn't know that he cared what it was, but he approved of the change in demeanor and wondered if it would provide leverage for getting more information. Perhaps she had simply come to realize how much she and her family were in trouble.

"Don't you have something to do, Herr Springer?"

"*Jawohl!*" the lieutenant snapped. But before Springer led the young *fräulein* back out of the room, he handed Tiedemann a small, folded envelope. "Herr Hauptsturmführer, I found this on the girl's person as we were making rounds. You may want to take a look at it."

"What is it?"

"I'm not sure what it's all about, sir. It's, uh... a love letter of sorts." Springer's expression betrayed his amusement. "In German."

"This is hers?"

"Yes, sir."

A French girl with a German boyfriend. Perhaps there was hope for her soul after all.

"Very well. I'll take a look after I'm done eating." He tossed it on the table with his other work. Then he turned to the girl and, with his head cocked to the side, narrowed his eyes in thoughtfulness. "And I thought your father was the only one who understood what we were saying all this time. Very interesting."

Gabrielle lifted her head to steal a glance at Tiedemann but quickly resumed her meek posture. It was clear she was listening, though.

Very interesting indeed.

His stomach rumbled.

"Thank you, Herr Obersturmführer. Dismissed."

The rain was coming down harder by the time Tiedemann finished eating. Bread crumbs lay scattered across the table next to a chipped bowl that had been emptied as quickly as it had been brought. The stew hadn't been particularly tasty, just some vegetables and turnips with some bits or meat in a broth, but any change from the food German soldiers received in the field was a victory. And the bread... anything the bread did to soak up the leftover alcohol in his system was a Godsend.

It was amazing how much better he felt after just a little bit of a meal. Turning back to the hand-scrawled notes spread alongside his dishes, Tiedemann reconsidered everything they had learned to this point about the murder.

Everything was circumstantial. While they had mused on motivations, timing, and locations, there was nothing that provided a definitive indicator of guilt. The Cartwright, Marc Rimbault, and Robert Conti were still the prime suspects, with Cartwright in the lead. None of the suspects had any marks from a struggle except for possibly Cartwright, who had been battered and bruised when he was discovered in the kitchen. Those marks could have been from his parachute jump as the Englishman claimed. Or they could have been from hand-to-hand combat with broken wine bottles in the cellar. Hard to tell.

Scratching his head absent-mindedly, Tiedemann glanced over at the letter Springer had discovered. On a whim, he opened the envelope and pulled out the paper inside. The stationary was very worn, as if it had been folded open and closed many times. The upper left corner of the paper had a jagged triangle torn off and missing. An unsent letter that Gabrielle had never mailed?

With a half-hearted effort, Tiedemann began to read.

12 April 1942

W—

It is difficult for me to write these words. We have been together for so long, yet we have also been apart to the point that our relationship has lost meaning. If anything, you taught me that we must be true to ourselves if we are to be able to suffer through this world.

I am leaving you. I have found someone else that is not away fighting a far off, distant war. Someone who can give me the attention and time that I need as a companion, and more of the love that I once had with you that is now gone. I am in love with him. He is in love with me. I need to feel that companionship, that warmth of touch when someone holds you, that bonding of minds and souls, and he gives that to me. We are going to get married. I have already filed the papers for a divorce between you and I, and I ask that you accept the inevitable and capitulate.

I know that it is not your fault that you are not here. I still respect you and what it is that you are doing. But there are certain undeniable needs in a woman's life, and love is paramount. I care for you, but I do not love you anymore. And I must be true to myself. Please understand.

G

Tiedemann rubbed his forehead. *How odd.*

Did Robert Conti know that his only daughter was already married? Tiedemann managed a sarcastic smile at the thought of a secret wedding to a conquering soldier, though it was unfortunate that it seemed to be ending. Perhaps she was upgrading to someone in the SS.

In any event, the letter seemed irrelevant in the respect that it was dated some months ago and was still in her possession. A letter never sent may as well not have been written. The wear and tear suggested a good deal of ambivalence about it. But in what way could he use it?

Tiedemann tossed the paper on the table and leaned back in the one chair still in the Conti library. It was of a great size, with faded red upholstery and sporadic rivets of tarnished brass that held it together over flimsy padding. To the German officer it seemed one of the most comfortable pieces of furniture in which he could remember sitting.

The rest of the room appeared to have been splendid as well—once. Half-empty bookshelves smelling heavily of dust lined the south wall from floor to ceiling, while wallpaper patterned with a rich red and gold covered the remaining walls. All of it was faded except for the rectangles where great paintings and other works of art must have once hung. Many of the books had likely been burned for heat since oil was horded by the great German war machine. Aside from Tiedemann's chair, the only remaining piece of furniture was a large, oaken table that had contained deep gouges on the surface.

Such was the price of war. Tiedemann dared not dream of the day when combat would be over and the Reich reigned supreme. The more likely outcome would be that he and his men would die at the front lines long before. But if he did survive, against whatever odds, Tiedemann could picture himself retiring to the countryside and living in a chateau much like this one. In peace and away from the killing.

A knock on the door gave Tiedemann a start. He briefly considered pulling his boots back on, assuming his feet would allow it after four days of travel across France. Lethargy and a full stomach made it too challenging to move.

"Enter."

Obersturmführer Eppler appeared in the doorway, his deeply tanned face an ever-present reminder of his not-so-distant service in North Africa. He had changed out of his uniform with the wine stain around the armpit and was now wearing a new tunic that was merely drenched from the rain outside.

"Herr Hauptsturmführer, we've discovered something that you need to see."

"What?"

"Another building here on the grounds. A storage building. But it has a tunnel that goes underground to the wine cellar."

Tiedemann leaned forward. Was this a clue that would point more clearly at one of their suspects?

He reached over to his boots with borrowed vigor and pulled them on his feet. Then he grabbed his rain gear and followed his lieutenant out the door.

The rain was falling hard again from a dark and angry sky. Tiedemann and Eppler hugged the walls of the house for shelter as they trudged around to the back of the grounds. They ended up in a large rectangular courtyard, with cobblestones separated by tufts of grass paving the broad ground in front of them. A large barn squatted some fifty meters from the main house on the other side of the courtyard. Tiedemann kept his head down and did not observe much beyond the splashes of water from his boots as they sprinted across.

The barn structure was built from bare stone that did wonders to keep out the weather, although an occasional burst of wind would gust through the wide open doors and chill to the bone. The interior was an open layout and one could dimly see the underside of the roof some six meters above cloaked in shadow. Tiny glass windows sat high on the walls and allowed in weak rays of light. At ground level, four huge, wooden vats sat massively at one end of the room, ostensibly used for the storage of fermenting grapes, and there was a large cabinet with glass doors that contained chemistry equipment for monitoring the process. Rows of oak barrels and empty bottles formed a tidy arrangement a few meters from the far wall.

Two German soldiers whom Eppler had left behind snapped to attention as Tiedemann surveyed the building. Tiedemann ignored them. When they had first entered the wine growing regions on the way to Perpignan, Krauss had talked incessantly about the art of wine production. It drove most of the officers to the brink of insanity. Tiedemann now wished he had listened more.

The facilities here were unfamiliar, and Tiedemann could only remember bits and pieces about what some of the equipment was for. There was a great wooden trellis, for example, that was supported horizontally over the vats. Krauss had elaborated on how French winemakers would grab the horizontal bars with their hands and hang themselves down into the vats, using their own bodies to stir the grape juice to promote more homogenous fermentation of the must. The huge amounts of carbon dioxide produced from the chemical reaction of the yeast and sugars presented a continuous danger to those that undertook this activity, and there was always the possibility that the person would pass out and drown in the vat.

Tiedemann shook his head. Only the French could love wine so much that they would risk their lives during its creation. A German would have invented a machine to take care of it.

He wandered over to the oak barrels. Eight of them sat horizontally in a long metal rack that Tiedemann was sure could be melted down to make a lot of bullets. Several small wooden crates also occupied the ground nearby, each filled with corked wine bottles and handfuls of straw for shipping. Tiedemann lifted one of the bottles. To his surprise, the contents did not move.

"This bottle is filled with something solid."

Eppler moved close and picked up another. The two men compared the bottles. Each had an identical label and heft. A gentle shake confirmed that whatever was inside was not wine.

"Open this, please," Tiedemann said.

Eppler produced a utility knife and laid it edge up against one of the barrels. He raised the bottle in his other hand and smashed the neck against the blade.

Tiedemann smelled it immediately.

"God—that stench!" Eppler spat. "These are the worst winemakers in France!"

"No," Tiedemann said. He took the bottle from Eppler's hands and allowed for a careful sniff. "That's ammonia you smell."

"Ammonia?" Eppler was clearly puzzled. "For cleaning the wine vats?"

"I don't know." Tiedemann wasn't sure why a cleaning agent would be in solid form. He would have to come back to this. "Show me this tunnel you found."

Eppler immediately wheeled on one of the guards. "Where is Hermann?"

"He went back down the ramp to secure the bottom."

Eppler jerked his head to the side and led Tiedemann behind the row of wine barrels. In the ground was a long, rectangular opening, with sturdy wooden planks forming an incline from the barn floor down into the depths below. Tiedemann walked to the end of the rectangle and squatted down to see if he could view the bottom. The ramp sloped down at a shallow angle, reached an intermediate platform, then turned one-hundred-eighty degrees and continued its descent. There was a dim yellow light that seemed to filter up through the darkness.

"Herr Hermann? Are you there?" Eppler shouted.

The light grew stronger as footsteps approached. An older SS soldier holding a flashlight appeared at the bottom of the ramp, nearly twenty meters beneath the ground. "*Jawohl*?"

"Where does this go, Herr Eppler?" Tiedemann said.

"This ramp extends underground into a very large cave that contains hundreds of wine barrels. It's the same cave that's further down the corridor from the wine cellar beneath the house. That means there are two ways into the cellar—one from the kitchen, the other from outside. Someone could have entered the cellar unseen by our guards."

Tiedemann scratched his chin again. Could one of the Conti men have climbed out a window, darted unseen across the courtyard, and made their way down to the cellar from the outside of the house?

More importantly, would there be a reason they would do such a thing?

Why?

"Show me what's down there."

The two soldiers in the barn remained behind as Eppler and Tiedemann descended below ground. They met up with Hermann and continued down the second ramp until they reached a small vestibule embedded into the limestone rock. It was quite dim; the sporadic placing of electric light bulbs hanging from the ceiling was laughably insufficient. But Tiedemann could distinctly make out rows upon rows of barrels stretching into the blackness. Some of the rows were stacked three high, effectively building a mazelike labyrinth in which it would be easy to hide.

"Has this area been secured?" Tiedemann asked.

"Yes, sir. We made an initial sweep of the cave and found no one, and there are two more guards posted at the far end near the cellar. The barrels fill about half the cave. The rest is largely open, empty space. There are odds and ends stored about—unused bottles and so forth."

"Lead the way, Eppler."

Eppler took the flashlight from Hermann and walked carefully into the main cave. The air was cool and it was difficult to see, and not just because of the poor light. The stacks of barrels were oppressive. Wooden casks were arranged in long rows and were set upon sturdy wooden timbers that acted as supports and guides for their storage. Every twenty or so meters there would be a break in the aisle for a cross path that could be used to traverse laterally across the cave. Tiedemann fought the feeling of being ambushed and had to resist unfastening the snap on the holster that held his Luger.

Eppler turned left past the end of yet another row of barrels and led the party to a small corridor exposed in the limestone wall. There appeared to be light coming from the far end.

"Schimpff! Peterson! We're coming through to your end," Eppler barked.

A distant *Jawohl* was the reply from the guards at the far end of the corridor.

Eppler led the way, followed by Tiedemann, and Hermann bringing up the rear. The corridor was tight, not even a meter wide and with a low ceiling. It took about a minute for the group of men to reach the end with the guards. Tiedemann very quickly found himself in another dimly-lit hallway. This time, he recognized the broken plaster and exposed brick of the corridor outside the wine cellar where Hoffman had been killed.

"Interesting," Tiedemann had to admit. Another way to the scene of the crime.

But there were always other possibilities. Tiedemann cleared his throat of the cold, wet air. "It could have worked in reverse, could it have not? Someone could have hidden down here, been surprised by an unsuspecting Hoffman, committed the murder, and then joined the family upstairs as well."

Eppler looked puzzled for a moment before the understanding sunk in. "Someone like the Englishman?"

Tiedemann shrugged before turning to Shimpff. "You. Go find Obersturmführer Springer and bring him down here. He needs to see this as well."

As the soldier hurried off, Tiedemann had Peterson and Hermann assume guard duty at this end of the corridor and nodded for Eppler to walk with him the short distance down the hall to the wine cellar. Tiedemann spoke in a low tone so that the words were only available to Eppler's ears.

"What do you make of all this, Eppler?"

The lieutenant frowned his deeply tanned face. "Sir?"

"I'm asking for your opinion. Yes, I know that's not something the *Wehrmacht* does, but it's what I do. Tell me what you think these findings mean."

"It means anyone here could have escaped the scene of the crime."

"Quite a hike, though, from the cellar to the barn, and then to the house?"

"Yes, sir."

"Who do you think would be up for it?"

Eppler thought. "Robert Conti. Or the Englishman."

"I think Cartwright. The servant has a gimp leg, and I don't see the women measuring up. Plus the Frenchmen have an alibi of sorts. Even though he doesn't remember it well, Springer saw Conti and Rimbault arguing inside late into the night."

"A good conclusion. You have the motive and the means with that man."

For the first time in what seemed like ages, Tiedemann smiled. "We're getting there, Herr Eppler. The pieces are starting to fall into place. But I can't decide why Cartwright would have been so sloppy with the murder. Wouldn't you hide a dead body?"

"Perhaps," Eppler said, speaking slowly. "But it is my opinion, sir, that you can't explain all things all the time. Who's to say why people behave the way they do." His eyes glimmered with a strange intensity.

"True."

"All I ask, sir, is for permission to participate in the punishment of the guilty party. This has become a personal matter for me."

An unexpected comment. "How so?"

"I found out the other day from Gohler that Hoffman had a duty station at the work camp in Bad Tölz back in '41. That's my hometown. I did not know him personally, but I am sure that we must have had friends in common, and I had been looking forward to comparing notes with him." Eppler took a sad, deep breath. "That chance is gone forever now."

"I didn't know that." Tiedemann could scarcely believe Eppler's bad luck. "I'm sorry."

"Thank you, Herr Hauptsturmführer." The glimmer in his eyes returned for a moment. "This war has taken so much away from me. From all of us. I will be glad when it's over."

"As will I, Herr Eppler, as will I."

15

Gabrielle marched sullenly up the grand staircase, her thoughts a distant and detached muddle. She was barely aware of her feet moving as Springer prodded her down one of the second floor hallways. They stopped in front of a guard with whom Springer conversed in German before he gave her a slap on her bottom. The new soldier took her by the elbow and started to lead her toward a bedroom door. Gabrielle's skin turned cold and she felt like she might vomit. *Not again. Please, God, not again.*

They reached the bedroom. The guard turned the handle and pushed her into the center of the room. The next thing she knew, her father was there next to her and had his arm around her shoulder.

"Gabrielle, sweetheart! Are you all right?"

"Papa?"

"Yes, my dear, yes. It is me."

Slowly, Gabrielle turned to look at her father. His face seemed so familiar and yet she had difficulty in feeling any emotion. She did the only thing that came to mind and stared at him with dull eyes.

Papa was holding her awkwardly with his right arm. She sank against his chest and squeezed him as if she couldn't believe that she was real. He winced, then she heard him start to sob. For a brief moment, the sudden warmth and security of the embrace brought tears to her cheeks. She was almost able to relax, to let go and start to become a human being again... but at that instant she felt her own father stiffen. He was staring at the door. Gabrielle turned head away from Papa's chest to look.

Springer was watching her.

His eyes were far from polite as they went over her body. She absently met his gaze and he gave her a small smirk that made her skin crawl. After a few more agonizing moments, he finally wheeled around and pulled the door shut behind him.

"Gabrielle!" Papa whispered sharply as soon as they were alone. "Look at me. Are you injured? Did they hurt you? Tell me."

She gave a small nod in response to his question but could not bring herself to look at him. Her father seemed uncertain as to what to do. After a moment of indecision he hobbled back to his feet and led her back to the lone chair in the room. He sat her down and kneeled by her side.

"Gabrielle, tell me where they took you. Tell me what they did to you. Can you do that?"

She looked back at him blankly. The numbness was still there. It was as if the past hours had only been a dream, and Gabrielle had difficulty finding the words or thoughts around what had happened.

"*Gabrielle.* Can you speak?"

A moment passed before she finally managed, "*Oui.*" She thought her voice sounded tiny and weak.

Papa breathed just a bit easier. "Please, girl, tell me what they did with you."

It was difficult to focus. Gabrielle couldn't think of where to begin; her memory was a jumble of events with seemingly no chronological order. She scrunched her eyes shut and forced herself to pay attention. She thought back to earlier in the day. She had woken up, gotten out of bed after a fitful night's sleep, then dressed. Been dragged to the Great Room. Questioned and beaten, then locked up in a bedroom by herself. Her recollection was starting to come back.

"The Germans. They took Mama and me to the kitchen. We were told to cook for the Germans. We had to empty the pantry in order to have enough to work with. They ate everything, Papa, everything."

"That's all right, my dear. Just relax. We'll find food somewhere else after the Germans leave." Papa draped his arm across her knees and sighed, as if he could only hope that they would be so lucky. "Tell me more."

"One of the soldiers escorted me around the house to the soldiers that couldn't leave their posts. I had to carry the stewpot and a basket of bread. It was very heavy. I didn't understand why they wanted me to carry it instead of just one of them doing it."

"Did you see mama or Philippe? Girard?"

"I saw Stefan."

Her father stiffened. "Where?"

"In the cellar," Gabrielle replied. Her voice sounded to her like someone else was using it to speak. Her mind felt sterile. Was she dreaming all of this? It had to be a dream.

"How did he look? Is he alive?"

"Yes. He was sitting in the corner, all beaten up. I was looking at him as the soldiers ate. There was blood all over his face and clothes. He looked like he was in a lot of pain."

"But he's still alive?"

"Yes."

"Then that's something, at least," her father said. "They're still keeping everyone alive. Different than the Russians. They still see us as human beings."

Gabrielle let out an inadvertent sob. Then another, and suddenly a deep well of emotion started to gush out. The detachment was gone. The sound of her father's voice, his attempts at comforting her, his warm grasp, it was all too much. She didn't feel tough any more. She felt like a child, a defenseless child at the hands of these terrible men who had taken over her family's home. She started bawling. Papa brought her close and she struggled to hide her face in her hands. They stayed there for a while together, Gabrielle in the chair and her father kneeling beside her.

A long time went by before the crying stopped. Gabrielle felt as if she had run out of tears. Her throat was sore and her nose had run so badly that she had used up her father's entire handkerchief.

The welcome detachment was coming back, but this time it was being fueled by exhaustion.

Papa tried to touch her face. She jerked back. It felt too much like what had happened in the cellar.

"Gabrielle," her father said softly.

She shook her head violently.

"Tell me. Just... tell me."

It was clear her father suspected. That just made Gabrielle feel even worse. The injustice, the shame of it all. She wanted to run away. How could she tell Papa? He idolized her, and she didn't want him to ever think that she had been treated that way. Her lips twisted around in revulsion at the thought of putting to words what had been done to her.

"*Herr Springer.* In the cellar. He was watching Stefan, but then he saw me and said he'd take me to the last soldier. He led me away down the hall. He t-took me t-to... h-he t-took me t-to..."

Gabrielle dropped her eyes to the floor. Papa reached toward her cheek again but she pushed his hands back. She took a deep breath and tried to steel her resolve.

"Springer took me to the barrel cave. He raped me, Papa."

The room was deathly silent. Her father was still on his knees, pale, staring coldly at her face. His jaw was clenched tight, but she could still see the quiver in his cheeks from the strain of how hard he must have been biting down. How ashamed he must be, his darling daughter, debased and violated like an animal in the dirt of an underground hole. The only thing that kept Gabrielle from crying even more was that she had no more tears.

Slowly, Papa put his hand gently on the back of her neck, and pulled their heads together until their foreheads touched.

"Sweetheart. I'm sorry. I'm so, so sorry this happened to you. If only I could have protected you. My poor, sweet little Gabrielle."

"I'm sorry, Papa. I tried to fight back, I tried," Gabrielle blurted out. She found herself clinging tightly to his shirt. She had to turn her head sideways to still breathe.

"Hush, my dear. It's not your fault. There's nothing you could have done differently. It's not your fault."

Gabrielle held on to him for a few minutes. After a while her father asked, "So, then Springer brought you back up here to jeer at us?"

"No," Gabrielle said softly. "When he was... done with me... he took me to see the Germann captain. Tiedemann. They talked about me for a while. It was strange, though, Papa. The captain spoke to me directly right before we were dismissed. He just walked right up to me and spoke to me in German. He looked right at me with those pale blue eyes as if he fully expected me to understand what he was saying. And I had no idea. Why would he address me like that, Papa? It was so frightening. I thought they would kill me right there."

"I don't know, sweetheart. I don't know."

Gabrielle sniffled some more. "Anyway, Springer sent me back to the kitchen to make sure all of his men had been fed. Mama was gone, but it was only a few more minutes before Springer took me back here, to you."

"He took you himself, did he?"

"Yes. It was strange, when I was carrying the soup around it seemed like there were soldiers everywhere. But aside from the ones with Tiedemann, it's like they've all disappeared."

Her father said nothing, but started to draw her into an embrace like he used to do when she was a little girl. That was long ago, when she was not so independent. Gabrielle put her arms out to stop him. Their eyes met and she saw that he was disappointed, but understood. She felt silently ashamed. But after being restrained against the packed dirt of the cave floor, there was a limit to how much she could let herself be held right now.

The thought made her feel even more disgusted with herself. Here she was, pushing her own father away when she needed him more than ever.

Gabrielle forced herself to reach into her pockets. "Look, Papa. "I brought some bread for you. Don't let the guard know, I think the Germans mean to keep you hungry. But I had a chance to grab some when we were making lunch for the soldiers."

Her father took the bread. But there was a distracted look on his face that clearly indicated his thoughts were elsewhere.

"Papa? What are you thinking about?"

He took her hands in his and spoke with a low voice.

"These Germans were on their way to the coast when they got sidelined here. If they aren't sitting around the house anymore, it could mean they're getting ready to pull out."

"That's good. Isn't it?"

"This death of the German officer is still unresolved in their minds. If Tiedemann and his men are packing up to leave, it can mean one of only two things. It could be they've given up their investigation because of their timetables. If that's the case, they might just line us all up and shoot us and be done with it."

"Oh, my God." Gabrielle bit on her knuckle. "What else could it mean?"

"It could be that they've found something we don't want them to find. That would be far, far worse."

"Worse? What are you talking about? Papa, I don't understand."

Papa started to stand. Gabrielle saw him rise into an awkward and huddled form, with a severe hunch over to his side. His left arm was drawn tightly against his abdomen. He walked painfully to the door and listened for a moment to verify their privacy, then turned back and shuffled to the chair. Her father's face was very dark.

"Papa. You're hurt."

"No more than anyone else."

Gabrielle didn't believe it for a second. The way her father stood—perhaps all of his ribs were broken, or just some, but the strong and vibrant man she so looked up to appeared anything but. He appeared weak. And it was heartbreaking.

His eyes, however, still held the hard-headedness she shared as his daughter.

"Sweetheart," he started. "There are... things that you don't know. Things your grandfather and I have kept secret from you. We wanted to protect you. We didn't want to pollute your innocence." He blanched on that last word, and Gabrielle felt another pang of shame.

"What secrets? Tell me, Papa. You know you can trust me."

"I know I can, Gabrielle. I'm not worried about trust. I'm worried about lives—many more than our own."

Her father's jaw clenched, as if some monumental decision had just been made in his mind.

"We can't ride this out anymore, Gabrielle. I fear the life as we've known it is gone forever. We've got to get out of here."

"Let me help, Papa." Gabrielle was surprised at the strength in her own voice. But she was determined, now more than ever, to not be a victim.

Papa smiled grimly and studied her with sadness in his eyes, as if he had given up on something important to his soul.

"Then listen to me carefully. We're running out of time and there will be no room for mistakes."

"*Oui.*"

Her father swallowed. "First thing. In the far front-right bedroom, you know, the empty one where your Uncle Yves used to stay when he came to visit, before the war? There's a red blanket in the armoire. Or at least there was. You know the one I'm talking about?"

"Yes—the faded one with the patch in the corner."

"That's the one. You need to get to that bedroom. Find a way to hang that blanket outside the window as if to dry."

Gabrielle managed to look up at her father's face. "But it's raining."

"That doesn't matter, sweetheart. Just hang it out. Pinch it shut with the window so that it doesn't fall. Don't let the Germans see you do this. This is very, very important, Gabrielle. We need to get this done as fast as possible. Do you think you can make it happen?"

"I'll find a way somehow." She thought for a moment. "The *Boches* have let me play servant all morning. Maybe I can get it to last a little longer."

"That's my girl. Next, I need you to—"

"Why, Papa?"

"What?"

"Of all the things we could do to flee, why are you asking me to hang an old blanket out in the rain? What does that accomplish?"

“It is something your grandfather arranged a long time ago. It’s a signal.”

“A signal for what?

Papa clenched his teeth grimly. “To send help.”

16

Gohler couldn't believe what he was hearing. "He wants me to report up to the house?"

"Yes, sir," the soldier said. The intermittent rain was falling again and dripped off the rim of his helmet. "He was quite clear."

The first sergeant glared at the muddy road where the Opel was still stuck. Eight mud-caked soldiers had just finished tying lengths of rope between the capsized truck and Herr Tiedemann's staff car. At least they weren't in Russia. Everything would be frozen.

Still, this was utter nonsense. Krauss was fast becoming the most disliked officer in the entire *Kompanie*. It somehow stood to reason that he would pull Gohler off one of their top priorities so that he could help with some stupid administrative task. But an order was an order. If there was fallout to be had, he would let it come from Herr Tiedemann.

"Willinger!" Gohler shouted. If he was leaving, he had to put someone else in charge.

A stocky trooper with close-set eyes perked up from the flooded ditch. He carefully trotted over until he stood soaking in front of Gohler. "*Jawohl*, Herr Sturmscharführer?"

Gohler waved his hand at the rest of the soldiers congregating near the truck. "You're in charge, and you've got practically all the spare manpower there is. Get that bitch out of the ditch. I've got to go deal with Krauss."

"*Jawohl,*" Willinger replied, looking relieved that he wasn't being told to report to the lieutenant instead.

The trudge up to the manor was slow going. Sheets of water slid downhill over the saturated ground that could not possibly absorb any more moisture. Once inside the front door he wiped his boots on the coarse rug—a force of habit—then shook the water off of his parka. He still left a trail of muddy footprints to the library. Krauss was standing in the far corner and eagerly snooping through shelves of hardbound books that stretched from floor to ceiling. He was totally oblivious to everything around him, including the maps that lay out on the large oak table. They were all but forgotten now. So much for their navigator.

Gohler put a fist to his mouth and coughed to get his attention.

Krauss looked up, surprised. "You're wet."

"Yes, Herr Obersturmführer. It's raining."

The man's eyes narrowed behind his round-rimmed glasses. "I know it's raining. What were you doing out in it?"

"If you recall, Herr Tiedemann instructed us to get the trucks back on the road."

Krauss looked around nervously, as if the Hautpsturmführer were about to walk in at any moment. Quickly he regained his composure. "Ah, very well. Any success?"

"Not yet, Herr Obersturmführer."

"Just as well, then. I have another assignment for you." Krauss theatrically rubbed his hands together. "Herr Tiedemann wants you to draft a letter home to Hoffman's wife for him to send his regrets. Of course, he may need to edit some of it to get the feel right for the letter to be from him, so we want time for an additional draft. You'll need to… why do you have that look on your face?"

Gohler blinked. He hadn't realized that he was frowning. "The Hauptsturmführer wants to send a letter to Hoffman's wife?"

"Yes." He paused. "What?"

"I'm sorry, sir, I'm surprised by the request."

"You're surprised? That your commanding officer wants your help in offering condolences? You were a friend of his."

"Permission to speak, Herr Obersturmführer."

"Go on."

"Hoffman and his wife were getting divorced."

"Why?"

"He was quite the ladies' man. Frau Hoffman didn't much appreciate that he couldn't keep it in his pants."

"Really," Krauss said. He struggled through this new information before circling back to beginning. "The man is dead, Herr Gohler. You don't think his wife would want to know? Cheating isn't on the same level as death in most couples' lives."

"For most people, yes," Gohler agreed. "But not for Sabine Hoffman."

"Please explain."

Gohler sighed. Why did he have to explain his friend's personal life to this idiot?

"Hoffman and I have known each other since we were kids. We're both from Bad Tölz and we both served in Russia. We were both enlisted men, too, before he got a field promotion. I know his family practically better than my own. So I can speak with certainty about the state of Hoffman's marriage after years of him chasing skirts. Frau Hoffman will probably throw a celebration if we send her a letter like you're suggesting."

Krauss stifled a yawn and looked irritated. Gohler frowned even more. What a disgusting excuse for an officer this man was. It was clear he didn't really care about Hoffman or his family. He only wanted to dish off an uninteresting task given to him so that he could get back to the books.

"Look, Gohler." The lieutenant straightened his collar. "I'll let those comments pass because Hoffman was a friend of yours. But you're going to write his wife a letter because Tiedemann said so. That's the end of it."

"*Jawohl.*"

"Here," Krauss said as he fished a photograph out of his pocket. "Maybe this will smooth things over. Include this picture of her that Tiedemann found in Hoffman's *Soldbuch*."

The photo was a snapshot—of someone else.

"That's not Sabine."

"Who?" Krauss asked. He had returned to his perusal of the bookshelves.

"Sabine. This isn't her. I don't know who this is."

"It was in his *Soldbuch*. That's not his wife?"

"No, Herr Obersturmführer."

The round-rimmed glasses framed an even frostier look from the small man. "Then I guess you shouldn't include it after all."

Gohler returned the glare. "*Jawohl*, Herr Obersturmführer."

"Now," Krauss replied, searching hesitantly around the room until his eyes fell on the large table. "You'll excuse me, Sturmscharführer, but I need to get back to these maps. Someone has to have our route plotted back on the main roads."

"Yes, sir, I saw that you were quite busy with that when I disturbed you."

"Yes, I wa—thank you, Herr Gohler. Dismissed."

As he left the room, Gohler looked down and examined the photograph. It was a portrait of a woman, a very pretty one at that, with blond hair and a slight smile that made her all the more sultry. Flipping the photo over revealed an inscription.

Johannes, I will love you forever. Greta.

Strange, Gohler thought.

Hoffmann had been like a brother. They went all the way back to guarding the concentration camps, back when *Totenkopf* was more about mopping up newly conquered lands than being a front-line fighting force. But in all that time, Gohler had never heard Hoffman talk about a girl named Greta. And for someone that frequently bragged about his exploits with women, such an omission was unusual.

17

Tiedemann's stomach was still growling, so he and Eppler left the cellar and went back to the kitchen. There wasn't much there. How did these French survive? His soldiers ate like locusts but Tiedemann had a hard time believing that there wasn't more food stored away. All he could find was a small jar of fruit preserves in the corner of a cabinet. He ate it straight from the jar, using his finger as a spoon.

Springer had joined them and was standing atop the spiral staircase in the kitchen corner. Every few moments he would deliberately shift his weight and cause the structure to squeak and creak. At any moment it seemed the iron might pull right out of the mountings. It was a huge amount of noise regardless.

"Listen to that," Springer said. "What a piece of crap. We should just pull it out and ship it back to Germany for scrap."

Tiedemann examined the staircase as he dipped his finger into more preserves. It was filthy now, the mud from multiple jackboots having coated each of the steps.

"Look at all the mud," he said.

Eppler cocked his head to the side. "It doesn't have to be clean to melt it down, does it?"

Tiedemann shook his head. "No—that's not what I'm saying. The steps are covered in footprints. Mud. It's been constantly raining.

Look at our boots. Yours, mine—they're *schmutzig*. Dirty. You can see where we've been walking."

"*Ja*," Springer agreed. He pointed to his own boots. "Mine are far cleaner than yours since I've been inside all day."

"So what does that mean?" Eppler asked.

"It means we can test our theory. If the murderer—Cartwright—entered the wine cellar from the outside, through the barrel cave, his shoes should be filthy like ours. Yes?"

Comprehension dawned on Springer's face. "That would seem to line things up."

Tiedemann looked expectantly at Springer. "Well?"

"Sir?"

"Go look!" Tiedemann ran his index finger around the bottom of the jar, casually scraping out the last of the fruit.

"*Jawohl!*"

Springer barely had time to move before Krauss barged into the kitchen. His face was ruddy and he was panting like a dog.

"Excuse me, Herr Hauptsturmführer. It's all wrong, what he's been saying. It took me a while but I've finally figured it out."

"Figured out what, Krauss?"

"The flight path doesn't make sense," Krauss said. "Stuttgart is too far."

The faces of three German officers returned identical blank looks.

"What are you babbling about?" Springer demanded. "What flight path?"

The small man's chest kept heaving. God help them when he has to run across the battlefield, Tiedemann thought.

"Springer, I gave you a task. I suggest you get going."

"*Jawohl*," the blond lieutenant said. He disappeared down the staircase on the way to the wine cellar.

Tiedemann turned back to Krauss. "Begin again please. I'm not following."

"I'm sorry, sir." Krauss took a few more moments to catch his breath. "There's a huge hole in the Englishman's story. He's lying."

"Lying about what?"

"About his bombing target, sir." The little man was slowly regaining his ability to string more words together. "Cartwright said he was on a bomber headed to Stuttgart when he was shot down. Well, something was bothering me about what he said, only I couldn't put my finger on it.

"I finally did, sir, while I was looking at the maps. Stuttgart is too far in the wrong direction—four hundred kilometers too far. Indeed, right now we're further south than Stuttgart is, so it would make no sense for a bomber to have a flight path that veers this far south just to come back up around to its target." Krauss made a giant V shape with his hand, indicating how far out of a straight line a plane would have to fly based on what Cartwright had claimed. "That's assuming they could even carry that much fuel. But I simply didn't realize it until it was right there in front of me on the maps."

"You couldn't read a map to get us through Dijon. What makes you think you can read one now?" Eppler cracked.

Tiedemann waved him to be silent. "Well then, Krauss, he's lying about his mission. What does it mean?"

"It means that the Englishman wasn't on a bombing run. If he truly was shot down, he was on a flight that certainly wasn't headed toward Germany."

"Or maybe," Eppler countered, "he's telling the truth about Stuttgart, and he's simply being smuggled to Spain so he can get back home."

"No, Cartwright hasn't been on the ground long enough to travel that far by foot."

Eppler was clearly falling into the clique of all the other officers arraigned against Krauss. "If you think he's a liar, why do you believe him when he says how many days ago he was shot down?"

"No, you're not listening to me. My point is—"

"And why would you believe *anything* an enemy combatant might say?" Eppler continued. "If I were captured, I'd do everything I could to give bad information."

The arguing continued, yet another sign of the work Tiedemann had yet to do in rebuilding discipline in his replacement officer corps. It was ridiculous that this could take place in front of a commanding officer. Did other Waffen SS divisions aside from *Totenkopf* have these issues? Tiedemann pinched the bridge of his nose and closed his eyes. The headache was coming back.

So, what did he know? What did he think? Tiedemann fought to review the facts in his head.

Tiedemann could easily guess that Hoffmann went to the cellar for alcohol. Did he surprise someone, or was he followed? What else might be in the cellar that was worth the risk of discovery?

Hoffmann and the murder's paths crossed in the cellar, where Hoffmann was killed presumably out of self-defense.

Why would self-defense be necessary?

The only unobtrusive way to access the cellar without the notice of the sentries was from the outside entrance. Tiedemann did not like the other theories.

Did Cartwright come in from the outside?

Was the Englishman truly lying about how he got to the Conti estate?

Tiedemann tuned out all the noise and thought hard.

There *had* to be more going on here than a simple murder in self-defense.

Footsteps echoed from the bottom of the spiral staircase. A moment later, Springer's head popped up. His face looked bleak.

"Springer?"

The blond lieutenant shook his head with disappointment. "You won't believe this, but the Englishman's feet are the cleanest part of his body. No mud whatsoever."

Tiedemann frowned. It was time for a new approach.

"Herr Springer," he said quietly. "Go get Sturmscharführer Gohler."

Springer blinked in surprise, but it only stopped him for an instant. "*Jawohl*, Herr Hauptsturmführer," he said before exiting the kitchen.

The two remaining lieutenants wisely remained silent. Tiedemann paced for a minute, then walked over to the back door and stared out into the courtyard at the rain. If only they had not detoured to this damnable place in the French countryside in the first place. That cursed rain.

Minutes later, Springer and Gohler both marched into the kitchen. Gohler stood at attention.

The mere presence of the tough sergeant changed the intensity in the room. Gohler had been in *Totenkopf* throughout its existence: working the concentration camps, the invasion of Poland and France, fighting while surrounded by Russians in the Demyansk pocket. He was the product of harsh, unyielding discipline, which is what Tiedemann desperately needed in his investigation right now.

The wicked, silvery scar that traced the sergeant's jaw served as a visual reminder of how hard he was. So much the better.

"Sturmscharführer, I recall that you were an interrogator on the Eastern front," Tiedemann said. "Is that correct?"

"Yes, Herr Hauptsturmführer."

"Were you any good?"

"Yes, Herr Hauptsturmführer."

"You don't speak English, do you?"

"No, sir, just Russian."

"Very well." Tiedemann leaned next to the sergeant's ear. The clues weren't lining up, the clock was ticking... he needed all of this *done*. He felt his lip twisting. "I want you to get us answers from the Englishman downstairs. Krauss will translate, but you lead. If he is withholding information, get through the resistance. I want nothing but the absolute truth from our prisoner. I am tired of being behind schedule. Do you understand me?"

"Perfectly."

Krauss shifted uneasily from the side of the room.

"Herr Hauptsturmführer, permission to speak?"

Tiedemann turned his head. "Yes, Krauss."

"Sir," the small man said. His voice was uncertain. "The Englishman is not *ein Untermensch*. He is a prisoner of war. The rules of engagement must be followed—"

The icy gaze Tiedemann gave his lieutenant was all it took to end the conversation.

18

Cartwright guessed that it was evening based on how many guard changes there had been. Every few hours a new German came to relieve the soldier on duty, with nary so much as a glance in his direction. The entire episode made for an aching, chilly, hungry, and quite boring captivity.

A clutter of jackboots outside in the corridor signaled that that might be about to change.

A stream of Germans filed into the cellar, including two soldiers wielding machine pistols and the conniving little man Cartwright had nicknamed The Rat. Next was the German captain, followed by the blond-haired officer that had escorted Gabrielle out of the cellar earlier. Then another, deeply-tanned German whom Cartwright did not recognize entered and took a place quietly against the far wall.

Last was Gohler, the sergeant with the scar on his face. Cartwright's stomach did involuntary flip flops. There had already been too much contact with that fellow. Literally.

For some reason, the captain took a long glance at Cartwright's shoes. Then he barked instructions at the two infantrymen. They forcefully grabbed him by his armpits and hauled him clear of the wine racks until he was kneeling in the middle of the room.

This didn't seem good.

The Rat was standing off to the right and had pulled out his little notebook once again. Cartwright thought he looked oddly uneasy. Why was that?

Without warning, pain shot through Cartwright's side from his kidney. Cartwright jerked forward as his body tried to instinctively writhe away from the blow. The pain came again, wave after searing wave, heavy hands holding him down and making it impossible to wiggle away. Breath left his lungs. Light left his eyes. Cartwright's ears were filled with a deafening void of sound. It went on and on for what seemed like forever.

Gradually a sense of reality returned to Cartwright's brain. He was lying on his side in a pool of sweat and vomit. Not that he could see it—his eyes were still closed—but his nose knew what it smelled. Somehow Cartwright didn't care. He was just thankful that the beating had ended.

"Setzen Sie ihn auf."

The voice was vaguely familiar, yet somehow not. Not the captain's.

Cartwright was pulled upright until he was kneeling again. Somehow he kept his balance and managed to not fall back over. He again became aware of his body's existence: breathing, sweating, shaking. Hurting.

The strange voice spoke in German. *"Fragen Sie ihn, wie er hierher gekommen ist?"*

"How did you come to be at the Conti's estate?" the Rat asked in English.

"I to—" Cartwright froze, the agony of trying to make words paralyzing him. He stopped, took a careful breath, composed himself. "I told you all that already."

The Rat translated. Almost immediately another fist landed on Cartwright's side. He crumpled to the ground on his side.

"We don't believe you," the Rat said, following the voice in German.

Cartwright forced his eyes open. Who was talking before the translation?

He found he couldn't lift his head off the ground, which meant that all he saw was a pair of black boots pacing a few feet away. But gradually Cartwright tilted his eyes upward and Gohler came into focus. The sergeant had stripped to his undershirt and had steam coming off his shoulders. It dawned on Cartwright that there was very little blood on that shirt. All the punishment he was dishing out was focused on body work. They intended to leave his face alone. *So he could speak.*

"Do you want more? If so, keep lying. Otherwise tell us how you came to be here."

"I said, I told you everything."

"Er sagte, dass er uns alles bereits erklärte," the Rat told Gohler.

A boot to the crotch. Cartwright doubled over until his knees were near his cheeks. His attempt to puke met with failure, as there was nothing left in his stomach.

Gohler paced, a shark toying with his prey. Again, he refrained from asking questions. The silence was terrifying.

Cartwright struggled to maintain his will. Why were they doing this to him? What had happened to the Geneva Convention? What would he have to tell them to get them to stop?

A new voice broke the silence. The German captain asked Gohler a question, conversing briefly before finally giving more instructions to the Rat.

The Rat nodded, then cleared his throat almost reluctantly. "You see, Herr Cartwright, we know you weren't shot down from a bombing mission over Stuttgart. We're too far for that to be your target. No bomber has that sort of fuel capacity.

"Add to that the fact that we've spent all day interrogating the Conti family, and you should know that we have a quite a fair idea of what's happened here. We know what your involvement is. Make things easy on yourself and give us what we want. We want to hear it from you. Simply tell us what you're really doing here."

Cartwright looked up at the bespectacled translator. Was The Rat lying? Cartwright sure hoped so—particularly about the Contis giving up too much information. But until he was sure, it was irrelevant whether or not the Germans had managed to piece things together. All he knew was that if he changed his story now he was a dead man. And the Contis would be dead along with him.

"I'm telling you the truth," he rasped. "We were headed to Stuttgart. We never quite got there... maybe our pilot got lost, I don't know. All I know is that it was the middle of the night and we were intercepted by fighters. It was dark, we got shot up, and I bailed out. That's all I can tell you because that's all that happened."

Cartwright stole a glance at Gohler. The sergeant was slowly turning red as he listened to the translation. He obviously was not convinced. Then, as if suddenly remembering where he might have misplaced a long-lost item, Gohler turned briskly away and walked over to his pack against the wall. He quickly rummaged through his belongings and turned around holding a knife that seemed like it was a good twelve inches long. The German studiously examined the point of the blade as he crept back to Cartwright's huddled form.

Cartwright snapped frantically at The Rat. "What's all this business, you Kraut bastard? I'm a prisoner of war. You can't do this!"

The Rat blinked uneasily. But instead of saying anything he just turned his head away, as if a doctor was about to put a needle in a vein and watching might make him nauseous.

Gohler directed the two soldiers to flip Cartwright over and hold his back down against the ground. A genuine panic seized the Englishman at the same time as did the Nazis' gloved hands.

"What are you going to do?"

No reply.

He looked again to The Rat. The German was not making eye contact.

"Stop! Please!"

Cartwright frantically tried to squirm his way out of the grip of the two infantrymen. But with each of them using their entire bodyweight on his arms it was too much.

Gohler knelt down until they were face to face.

"Warum töteten Sie einen unserer Offiziere?"

"Why did you kill one of our officers?" the Rat repeated in English.

"I-I don't understand. I don't know what you're talking about. I didn't kill anyone."

Gohler peered hard into his eyes for a long moment. Cartwright could hear his pulse beating in his ears.

The sergeant smirked as if to say, *typical.*

In a sudden jerk, Gohler swiveled until his knee was down hard across Cartwright's thigh.

A sharp, blinding pain shot through the center of Cartwright's leg, so intense that he couldn't muster enough focus to even scream. He shook violently in an effort to get free from the hurt. The hold of the Germans was far stronger. All of Cartwright's conscious thought was soaked in an agony he had never known in his life. He wanted to shout, he wanted to beg, to whimper, to do whatever it would take to end the pain and blood that gushed from his knee like lava erupting from a volcano, the agony that was soaking his thigh with fire. Waves of tears poured out of his eyes and flowed freely down his cheeks until the taste of salt lined his lips. If the German captain had asked him then and there to convert to the Nazi cause, Cartwright would have done it on the spot if it meant that it would end the suffering.

An eternity passed. Gradually Cartwright became aware again of the men surrounding him. The hands that had once held him down were instead now the only thing keeping him upright. Vaguely he sensed the acrid smell of urine. The intense pain in Cartwright's leg had dropped to a numb thumping that displaced any normal sense of feeling.

Slowly, Gohler turned around until he was facing Cartwright nose to nose. He held something small and gray between two blood-soaked fingertips and theatrically inspected it up close.

It was his kneecap.

"Sehr schön, ja?"

A wave of nausea swept over him. Oh, God, how he hurt.

"Und wir sind erst am Anfang."

Cartwright started weeping.

"Let's try again," the Rat prompted suddenly. "Tell us how you really came to be here. Tell us the truth or you will have a very long, painful, unpleasant death."

Gohler sat on Cartwright's leg awaiting an answer. His eyes were terrifying. They shone with the simple gaze of a man going to work, only in this case the profession was to break a man's will. And he understood how to use a knife.

Cartwright knew he would break. It might be an hour, it might be a few minutes, but it would happen, and if the Nazis hadn't bought off on what he had previously told him, then there was no way in Hell that he could come up with a new lie now that would convince them.

It was no use. The human body was simply too frail.

"W-we w-weren't on a b-bombing mission," Cartwright stammered out.

"Go on."

"W-we were flying an air drop. A c-cargo drop."

Oh, God, he was going to tell them. Cartwright couldn't believe the words were coming from his lips, but it was started now, and there was no stopping the momentum.

"How many others are here with you?"

"No one. W-we were shot down after making the drop. I w-was the only one who made it out of the p-plane."

"What sort of cargo?"

Cartwright tried to stop talking.

"*What kind of cargo?*" The Rat screamed.

"Ordnance. Explosives." *God help him.*

The Rat leaned over the sergeant and the Englishman. "And if *you* are here at the Conti estate, Herr Cartwright, then where are these arms?"

Cartwright paused ever so briefly as he contemplated what to say.

A scrape along his cheek made his heart jump.

Gohler pulled away the piece of bone he had extracted from Cartwright's knee and fingered it as if it were a sacred family heirloom. When their eyes met, Cartwright knew what anything other than the truth would get him.

He knew he was going to tell the Germans everything. As much as he didn't want to, as much as he had sworn he wouldn't, to not do so would simply mean that the Nazis would carve it out of him piece by agonizing piece. He had to talk. God help them all.

The Briton drew in a shaky, ragged breath.

"It's here. All of it is here."

"Where?"

Cartwright shut his eyes in agony.

"*Where?*"

The Englishman slowly, so ever slowly, shifted his gaze toward the far wall of the cellar.

19

The wine racks were the first to go. Nazi goons threw them aside and trashed countless bottles of Burgundy along with them until the floor was stained a deep crimson. Next came out the entrenching tools as the Germans hacked away at the south wall. Chunk by chunk, limestone and mortar flew in every direction to the accompaniment of a sustained chorus of slashing. Minutes later the first breakthrough was made. A foot-long portion of the false wall fell in on itself and revealed open space behind it. The soldiers now started smashing the wall with boot kicks in an effort to make the hole bigger.

Cartwright watched helplessly underneath a German's iron grip. The hole quickly grew to a man-sized opening and one of the soldiers, an older, lanky man with a gaunt face and narrow eyes, threw down his shovel to wriggle his way through. Once he got to the other side, he stuck his hand back through and someone gave him flashlight. There was an urgent conversation before a second German grabbed a pry bar and twisted through the opening. The sound of creaking metal soon snapped through the cold air of the cellar. The SS captain hovered near the hole and alternated shouting questions and commands to the other side.

While he didn't understand German, Cartwright already knew what was happening.

They were assessing the size of the weapons cache. Cylindrical airdrop canisters containing portable two-way radios. Another canister of Sten guns. Thousands of rounds of ammo. But the most damning part would be the containers of explosives, detonators, and everything an underground movement would need to disrupt an occupying force. God help them if the Nazis had also found the ammonium nitrate in the wine barn. Cartwright knew any given cell of the Resistance would only have limited information about another in order to contain the damage if discovered. But the Contis were making explosives for the region. If that supply was disrupted, any subversive operations would take a serious blow.

Even the parachutes were there, rolled up in neat bundles and piled against the wall. All of it was there for the inspection of the Nazis.

Gohler was eyeing him from just a few feet away, fingering Cartwright's kneecap.

Cartwright tried to ignore the dull, throbbing pain. He felt sick. The thought of the knife tearing through tendons and ligaments, with the blade sliding under the kneecap and twisting until the bone popped out... Cartwright was afraid to look. All he knew was that Gohler was pure evil. So he did what little he was capable of at the moment and avoided eye contact with everyone, instead just looking off into the far corner of the room. To do any more than that would cause him to lose what little nerve he had left.

It didn't matter anyway. The entire mission was compromised. Donner, Simon, the others—they had died for nothing, and Cartwright would undoubtedly soon join them.

The conversations by the hole grew loud and animated. Clearly the Germans were not happy with what they were finding.

"Herr Cartwright," the Rat asked. "Who is all of this for?"

"Resistance fighters, I suppose," Cartwright whispered. A desperate thought flashed across his mind. "The Contis are just caught up in all of this through happenstance."

"Where was this going to be delivered then? And when?"

"I don't know."

"Not acceptable. *Where and when*?" the Rat repeated. "Who were your contacts?"

"God's truth, I don't know any more than that. I was never told how it was going to be used, or where it was supposed to go. We were just supposed to air drop the stuff and return to England."

Gohler listened to the translation and picked up his knife from the ground. He inspected the blade as if he was sorry he had prematurely cleaned it of blood.

"Oh, please, I told you everything I know!" Cartwright pleaded. "We were just supposed to deliver the weapons. We were never supposed to even be on the ground but we got shot down! Please!"

"Herr Gohler, eine Minute bitte," said the captain.

The sergeant's eyes slid reluctantly up from the knife blade. But he didn't put it down.

Slowly, the SS captain turned away from the false wall and back towards his prisoner. There were a lot of munitions in that cache. Weapons that were meant to kill Germans. Yet the captain seemed somehow detached from that reality as he stared thoughtfully into space for a moment, as if he were a professor at University pondering the theories of his field. He held his hand on his chin, his arms close to his chest, and seemed completely lost in thought.

Then he looked at Cartwright with such stunning intensity that Cartwright physically flinched. God, what had he done?

"Come inside," the Contis had told him when he had shown up, soaking wet, on their front door.

"My family will help you," Marc had said when they realized he was an Allied airman shot down behind enemy lines.

"Mon ami," *Robert had called him, when he told the Frenchman about the airdropped weapons that needed to be hidden.*

Now he had betrayed them as well.

Carving up his knee had been nothing. Like a weak fool, the Briton had now involved Marc, Robert, Claudette, and their entire family. And the daughter. Oh God, that poor, beautiful girl. One look into the SS captain's eyes was all it took to know with certainty that the Germans were going to kill them all.

* * *

Gabrielle slowed her pace as she returned under guard from the toilet. She had had to beg and plead for a trip out of the bedroom where she was being held. Now she was nearing the door to the other room Papa had discussed with her. Another opportunity would not be forthcoming for some time.

"Warum werden Sie langsamer?" the German soldier asked. Why are you slowing down?

"It's cold in our room," Gabrielle replied. "Can I go in here and get something to keep me warm?"

The soldier didn't understand French but attempted to follow her words nonetheless. Gabrielle knew there were advantages to being pretty. She crossed her arms in front of her chest and shivered theatrically, maximizing the effect of shaking her breasts in front of the young soldier. "You know, cold. It's cold. Can I get a blanket from the bedroom here? A blanket?"

The German seemed to piece together her pantomime and pointed inquisitively to the oaken door. *"Sie möchten da hinein gehen?"* Do you want to go in there?

"*Oui.*"

Gabrielle watched him closely. He was young, maybe her age. She did her best to look demure and non-threatening. After all, there couldn't be anything wrong with indulging a simple request from such a pretty young woman, could there? She almost feared she had overdone it when the soldier's expression changed and she was sure he had bought it. He gave a quick nod and motioned for Gabrielle to proceed.

She gingerly took hold of the door latch with one hand, pushed the door wide open, and without waiting another second swept into the bedroom before the German changed his mind.

The aged armoire stood alone against the wall as the only piece of furniture in the room. It was one of those family heirlooms that would never be gotten rid of, but was in poor enough condition that it would not be displayed proudly either. Gabrielle brushed her fingers across the scratches down the oak front before she pulled the doors open. It contained linens that hadn't been used in years by anyone other than her Uncle Yves, who had not visited from Paris since the war began.

The red blanket was folded neatly underneath a stack of bed sheets.

Gabrielle used her left hand to hold the other things in place as she pulled the blanket out. It was so faded that it almost appeared pink. For a moment, Gabrielle wasn't even sure she had the right one. A wave of panic fought to spill out from inside of her and she had to freeze to keep her hands from shaking. Please, let this be the right one.

The guard was watching her from just a few feet away.

"Oh, my," Gabrielle said. She feigned a quick inspection. "This blanket looks so dirty. Do you mind if I hang it out the window while I get out another one?"

The German shook his head in puzzlement. "*Was?*"

"*Schmutzig,*" Gabrielle replied. That was the right word, wasn't it?

A look of comprehension, followed by an obvious expression that he really didn't care. That was perfect as far as Gabrielle was concerned.

Shouting was coming from another part of the house. Gabrielle decided she had better hurry.

With as much nonchalance as she could manage, she quickly walked to the window that overlooked the dark French countryside. What weak light there had been earlier in the day was gone. She unlatched the window. The shouting was getting closer. Fighting to stay calm, Gabrielle ignored the rain pooled on the windowsill and unfolded the blanket. Then she quickly laid it halfway out the window frame and closed the panes. Dark splotches of red formed where the water soaked through the fabric. They reminded Gabrielle of pooling blood.

Snapping to, Gabrielle quickly went back to the armoire and pulled out another blanket. She clutched it to her chest and waddled to the bedroom door. Mere seconds passed before a squad of soldiers appeared in the corridor, led by the sergeant with the long, silvery scar on his face.

The sergeant blinked in surprise but was clearly not pleased at finding one of their prisoners out of their room.

"*Komm hieraus, Fraulein.*"

He grabbed her arm and nearly pulled it out of its socket as he led her down the hall. Gabrielle defiantly refused to wince at the pain. They could take her wherever they wanted, they could keep her a prisoner forever, but after what that blond German monster had done to her, she was determined to fight her captors. That much, at least, she could control.

The detachment stopped outside her father's room. The SS sergeant opened the door and shoved Gabrielle in with such force than she lost her footing and spilled onto the floor on top of the blanket.

"Gabrielle!"

She heard her father stand up from the bed and prayed that he stay put until the Germans left. *Don't make any sudden moves*, he had told her. *Don't look threatening*. That was exactly what he might risk if he went to her aid. Luckily, Papa seemed to be taking his own advice and remained still. Gabrielle heard some orders barked in German and then the squeak of the hinges as the door was pulled shut.

She started to pick herself back up. "Papa, I did what you asked. The blanket—"

"Shh," her father said abruptly, softly. Dangerously.

Gabrielle slowly turned and saw why. A soldier was guarding them from inside the room. This one did not look friendly. In fact, he looked angry.

As if to punctuate the message, he gently stroked his machine pistol hanging from the strap around his shoulder.

She couldn't be sure what exactly, but Gabrielle sensed from the guard's demeanor something important had happened. Something bad. The fine hairs on the back of Gabrielle's neck instantly stood on end.

20

Consciousness came and went for Cartwright. One minute the room was spinning and the lights seemed very bright. The next, there was only darkness and strange voices speaking an unknown language. Through it all Cartwright felt very cold. The only other sensation he could acknowledge with any consistency was the dull thrumming in his leg.

That was the way the entire night passed, in a blurry fog through which Cartwright had sporadic recollections. He remembered how the German soldiers finished knocking down the rest of the wall. He remembered their many trips back and forth carrying the supply canisters from his plane. He recalled how the soldiers altogether ignored him, leaving him adrift in and out of awareness and shock. Time seemed both fleeting and infinite. The only reality he had was the vague feeling that he was going to die soon. And even then, he didn't care.

Blackness.

At one point, in a fleeting moment of lucidity that brought the Englishman out of his exhausted slumber, Cartwright caught himself watching two SS officers conversing by the far wall. One was the blond German. The other had dark hair and a very deep tan from many days in the sun. The tanned one seemed unusually interested in him and kept glancing at Cartwright sitting in his puddle of various fluids. Cartwright didn't understand why. Perhaps it wasn't every day one saw such a disgusting pile of abused filth. But before he had a chance for any insight, Cartwright's awareness of the material world around him would slip away.

Floating.

Another start at the realization he was in the real world. Now there was only a guard with a machine pistol standing in the doorway. He was clearly bored, and did not take the same interest in the prisoner as had the two officers. It was still cold. Cartwright took note of the texture of the limestone brick in the cellar.

Aching.

A person was standing over him. "*Scheisse*," a voice whispered.

Cartwright tried to focus. Another set of eyes was right in front of him and staring back.

The Englishman jumped—as much as his body would allow him. The German officer with the suntan was back, kneeling in front of him with a disgusted grimace on his face. Cartwright watched as the German's eyes swept over his uniform, down past his injured knee, across the piss and vomit on the floor, and back to his face. Their eyes met again, and all Cartwright could do was stare into the intensity that was focused back on him.

The repugnance was still there, no doubt from the smell. Cartwright knew he reeked. He just no longer had energy to care. But something else shone in the man's eyes, softer and more human than the Englishman would have expected. Not a look of remorse. Not malice, despite their positions on different sides of the war. Perhaps... pity? Acknowledgment of these piss poor circumstances into which Cartwright had fallen?

"*Sie haben kein Glück gehabt,*" the German said.

Sounded like *no luck*. That was the truth.

The officer stood back up and regarded Cartwright one last time before turning on his heels. Now there was only that lone guard who couldn't be bothered to even glance at his prisoner. Just as well.

Cartwright tried to take a deep breath and immediately regretted it. Pain hit his lungs like knives. It almost took his mind off of the bloody gash where his knee used to be.

Almost.

Somewhere a little voice was telling him he needed to be working out some kind of plan, but all Cartwright had the energy to do was stare at the same nothing that the German soldier was focused on not ten feet away.

* * *

Morning brought the first sunshine Tiedemann had seen in days.

They were making progress. Gohler's men had freed the truck and gotten it back onto the dirt road at last. The contraband explosives and weapons were now loaded onboard and ready to be hauled with them to Perpignan. And Tiedemann felt they had made a breakthrough in the events leading up to Hoffman's murder. Completion of all these efforts meant he had netted about four hours of sleep which, an amazingly recuperative rest when no alcohol was involved.

Unsettled with hunger, Tiedemann made his way to the kitchen to scrounge for leftovers. Krauss had unmercifully joined him with his notebook. Even now he was nosing into the decision process about how to handle the prisoners.

"So now what do we do, Herr Hauptsturmführer? Those weapons. Some sort of organized resistance must be nearby for the British to airdrop cargo like that."

Tiedemann was only partially listening as he rummaged through the storage cabinets. How could there be no food here? He would take anything--fruit, a bit of bread, or a random something that might let him avoid field rations. He had found some bits of cheese that had barely lasted longer than the time it had taken to shove them in his mouth. Otherwise, it seemed the Contis subsisted on thin air. He pulled open the next cabinet and saw some pans and crockery stored on various shelves. Nothing. Undeterred, Tiedemann moved on.

"Herr Hauptsturmführer?"

"What, Krauss?"

"Sir, my question." Krauss's voice was betraying his exasperation. "The clock is ticking. We should decide on a course of action. If the intended recipients of these armaments realize we intercepted them, they could scramble off into the countryside before we have a chance to go after them. They could be gone forever from our grasp."

Tiedemann's eyes lit up when he opened a small wooden box on the countertop. It contained a basket of apples cleverly covered with a canvas bag to obscure someone who was hungry. Tiedemann pulled out a fat, green piece of fruit and took a large bite that sprayed juice into the air. It tasted so delicious that he immediately confiscated the entire basket.

"Sir!"

"Oh, Krauss, enough already. Leaving the family alone for another hour or two won't hurt anything."

Krauss blinked in silence, his mind unable to process the lack of urgency.

Tiedemann took another few bites and watched him. For all his book smarts, his lieutenant still had trouble with the obvious.

"Look, Krauss. We found *weapons*. Weapons to be used against *us*. There's only one course of action."

"And what is that?"

"We have to execute them. All of them." Tiedemann bit into his apple again.

"Sir! We'll be missing a golden opportunity! You can't do that!"

Tiedemann stiffened. "You forget yourself, Obersturmführer."

Krauss slouched apologetically. It took a moment to regain his backbone. "Permission to speak, sir."

Sigh. "Yes."

"Sir, the Contis are farmers. There are women here, and a child. Two of the men are either elderly or infirm. They got at us once when we let our guard down. Now, we control the house and are on the alert, and have them separated and controlled. They are prisoners. They are not an immediate threat. Do you agree?"

"Yes."

Krauss straightened up. "So, if we just eliminated all of them for subversive activity, what would the ultimate outcome be? Strategically, I mean? They'd be replaced by someone else. The threat to German forces would still be here.

"The Contis are obviously just a single link in a very long chain. They're simply providing a place to store contraband. To kill them outright would squander the opportunity to lure out the real threat. The *Maquis.* Resistance fighters hiding in the countryside. They're the real opportunity. They're the fighters who blow up railways or harass supply movements. The real enemy is not sitting upstairs."

"Do you mean to lecture me now, Krauss?"

The lieutenant flushed. "No, sir."

"I know all of this, Krauss. And I don't disagree. But we are not the SD. We fight on the front lines, not conduct counterinsurgent operations. And we don't have the luxury of spending any more time here."

"But sir!"

"Believe me when I tell you, Krauss, I wish there was an option other than mass execution. I don't look forward to killing a little boy. I don't want to kill women. It's probably just Robert Conti and Marc Rimbault who've orchestrated this arms underground. But we don't know that for sure and we can't take any chances. We need to exterminate the entire node. We need to set an *example*."

"By shooting a ten year old—"

"Whose death will spare the lives of countless other ten year olds when their parents think twice about helping the *Maquis*."

Krauss dropped his eyes to the floor.

Tiedemann let out a sigh. "Krauss, look. On a personal level, I'd love to focus retribution on a single culprit. If it was just Conti who killed Hoffman and was singlehandedly responsible for supplying arms to the enemy, I could rationalize just taking him out by himself. But with the discovery of those weapons, and without any conclusive outcome from our murder investigation, I have no other choice. Our time is gone. We're overdue in Perpignan and the Allies could invade any day. We must move on."

"What about the Englishman? He is a prisoner of war."

"We could treat him as a spy. His end would be a foregone conclusion."

Krauss looked uncomfortable.

Tiedemann thought again to the lack of mud on Cartwright's boots. While the theory changed by the hour, right now it seemed he was just a soldier caught up in circumstance. At least, thinking of him that way gave Tiedemann a sliver of much needed humanity. "Relax, Krauss. We'll turn him over to the local police. He'll be in a Stalag camp in a week."

Krauss began to scribble in his little notebook as if he needed to capture his thoughts in writing. Tiedemann wondered what on earth he might have said that was worthy of putting down on paper. No doubt Krauss would commit all his words to memory, yet still lose the intent of what any of it actually meant.

Another bite of the apple finished it off. Tiedemann tossed the core nonchalantly onto the countertop and wiped his fingers with a nearby towel. He admitted to himself he hated the position he was in. He was a soldier who fought wars. This discussion made him feel nothing of the sort.

"It seems a shame, sir," Krauss said. He finished writing and closed his notebook. "To not deal a blow to the Resistance here. Before we carry out your directive, is there nothing left for us to try? I'm not saying we start hunting partisans in the hills. But if we only had time to get more information, it could save German lives."

"We have an hour or two before we mobilize," Tiedemann replied. "If you have some ideas, be my guest."

"I fear an hour isn't enough time," Krauss said.

"You're probably right. War is hell."

* * *

In the green bedroom upstairs, a room that had once been the guest quarters for visitors, Marc Rimbault sat back on his heels and pondered. Things were getting much worse, very rapidly.

The old man stared at the large floor rug. It covered the loose floorboards and crawlspace where they had scrambled to hide the Englishman just two nights ago. The crawlspace was directly over the kitchen. The Germans' voices had carried and Marc had heard it all.

Marc had lived a full life, had fought the Germans once before in the Great War. He knew the German language almost as well as Robert. His body might be frail but his mind was not. And he had to save his family.

Time was running out.

21

The guard at the door continued to glare at Gabrielle and her father. Silence was all he got in return since he had forcibly prevented Gabrielle and her father from speaking. Now they were sitting in opposite corners of the room. For a while, Papa had tried to communicate with her through hand gestures when the soldier's attention wandered. But there was only so much one could get across without speech, and it proved to be not much of a dialogue.

It was just as well. Gabrielle didn't feel like talking. She wanted to let her mind be free of thoughts, be numb, be forgetful of what had happened to her in the wine cave. Springer's attack on her made her want to crawl into the corner alone and cry and now she had an opportunity to do so.

She had never felt this helpless before. To have someone take control over her and do what he pleased was so overwhelming it was almost too difficult to comprehend how it could have actually happened. She hadn't been able to defend herself, nor had any of her family been able to protect her. Her whole identity had been debased so that she felt like an animal, dirty and used. The only way out of the darkness that she could find was to not think at all. The rare reconnection she tried to make with the real world was the occasional stolen glance at Papa, who before long was also staring at the floor lost in his own thoughts. Gabrielle wondered if he was reconsidering his definition of French patriotism.

Time seemed to stand still and they sat, father and daughter, on the floor in their corners. Gabrielle swung between mental emptiness and unwelcome flashbacks to being raped humiliatingly in the dirt. When more boot steps sounded out in the hall, Gabrielle surprised herself by not even blinking at this noise.

A pair of soldiers entered the room, pointed at her, and spoke with urgency to the guard on duty. *"Wir sind gekommen, das Mädchen zu holen."*

Papa cleared his throat to get Gabrielle's attention. When she looked over, he pointed first at the German, then her, then the door. They had come for her. But why?

The guard stationed in their room seemed reluctant to relinquish her. A short debate ensued, and Gabrielle thought for a moment that maybe she would be left alone. Then, finally, the guard snapped a salute and stood back against the wall. No such luck.

The soldiers went to Gabrielle in two giant strides and hauled her up by her arms. If she had been her normal self, Gabrielle probably would have screamed out in indignation. Right now it was too easy to remain detached. *Merde*, Springer could have her again for all she cared. The Germans couldn't hurt her if her nurturing, caring soul was locked up far and away.

The soldiers dragged her out the doorway and carried her at such a pace that her feet barely touched the floor long enough to take a step herself. Off they went down the grand staircase, through the kitchen, down the spiral staircase to the cellar corridors. Why were they going down here? She stumbled past broken plaster and cobwebs until they entered the wine cellar. Once upon a time she had loved to play hide and seek with Philippe, with one of her favorite hiding places found in this very cellar among the racks that held her family's personal collection of bottles. That seemed like such a long time ago. The reality of what was to be found here now was much different.

The Germans let go of her arms and she had to take an extra step to not fall forward. Springer stepped in front of her. There was no acknowledgement visible that he had done anything wrong to her. Gabrielle found him repugnant.

"I understand from your mother you've had some medical training?"

Why would this monster be asking her or her mother such a question? Yes, she had spent two months training as a nurse's aide when it had become apparent hostilities were coming between France and Germany. Her country's participation in the war had not lasted long enough for her skills to be needed.

"*Do you have medical training?*" Springer shouted.

"*Oui*," she replied.

"Then get to work in patching up your guest."

Springer grabbed Gabrielle's shoulder and shoved her to the right, making her stutter step yet again. As she regained her balance she saw a man propped up against the far wall. His legs were straight out in front of him and his chin slumped down. He looked like he was dead.

It took a moment before she realized she was looking at the Englishman. Gabrielle rushed over so fast that she ended up tripping on the floor after all.

Cartwright was filthy. His pale face was covered with bruises and he stunk to high heaven. Gabrielle knelt beside him and patted his cheeks with growing forcefulness. When no reaction came, she grabbed his sweat-soaked hair and pulled his head upright. His jaw was slack, his eyes closed. The realization hit her that the floor was very wet where she was kneeling. What had happened here? Some of the wetness had gotten on her skirt and provided a dull, rusty color. Blood? No, there was too much of it. Spilled wine? She thought that must be it until her eyes fell onto his knee.

Gabrielle shuddered. It looked as if someone had cut away nearly all of the flesh around the joint. Skin and sinew hung out from a gaping wound as if it had exploded from within, and there seemed to be parts... missing. Gabrielle was squatting down in a puddle of Cartwright's own blood. How long had he been left like this? All night? What a naïve fool she was. Panic welled up inside of her at the thought of this poor man dying on their basement floor.

But the panic lasted only for a moment. Adrenaline took over and Gabrielle quickly assessed the damage to Cartwright's knee. He was undoubtedly in shock. The wound wasn't bleeding much, which meant all of the major arteries and veins were probably intact. Whoever had done this must have known—sickeningly—what they were doing.

"I need some bandages," Gabrielle announced, standing up as straight as she could for maximum presence. She was still a quarter of a meter shorter than any of the Germans in the room. "This knee... I need to wrap it up immediately."

"Make do with what you have here," Springer said. "Use his shirt for a bandage if you need to."

"No, it has to be clean."

"Then use *your* shirt," the Nazi said. He folded his arms across his chest and smirked.

Gabrielle fought to keep her hands from trembling. Humiliation was replaced with anger. She would have loved to punch this *Boche* in the face or otherwise claw his eyes out. But she knew better. She thought to the blanket she had set out the window upstairs. The fight to be had was not here in the basement.

"Monsieur, you brought me down here to keep this man from dying. I'm sure that must be an order from your leader. Are you going to cause me to fail? Will the captain be pleased with that?"

Springer narrowed his eyes. Gabrielle hoped she had touched the right nerve.

"Very well. Get what you need. You have one minute."

Without delay, Gabrielle dashed out of the cellar until she was almost back to the pantry at the base of the spiral staircase. She knew there was a supply of kitchen cloths and linens stored there, from a time when her family entertained visitors as guests rather than thugs. She had to find some material clean and soft enough to be used as packing for Cartwright's wound.

The pantry's natural coolness from being underground made an ideal location for storing food and other related supplies, though since the day France had fallen there seemed to be less to go around for her family to put there. Gabrielle took a quick visual inventory of what remained. The shelves were mostly bare, though there were actually still a few cans of vegetables that had miraculously escaped the Germans' gorging. A small wooden chest containing their good silver for special occasions that had long since ceased. Three round wicker baskets pushed into the corner to store table cloths, linen napkins, and spare dishrags. That was what she needed.

Gabrielle stepped forward to rummage through the baskets and paused. Her eyes focused inadvertently on the spot on the floor where she had found the letter.

The paper had been wadded up and tossed away unwanted by one of the soldiers. It was written in German, so she hadn't understood it, but judging from the handwriting it looked as if a woman had penned it. It bore the lines of having been folded and unfolded, read and reread many, many times. The letter was odd enough that Gabrielle had picked it up to investigate later and perhaps ask her father to translate it. For a German soldier many miles from home, she was sure something like this would be treasured by its owner, not casually tossed away in the corner of a basement. But Springer had confiscated it and the opportunity was gone.

The passing thought of Springer alone with her made Gabrielle shudder.

Gabrielle snapped back to the present and quickly rummaged through the baskets. She pulled out dishrags and linens into a pile at her feet and tried to think through how she would create the bandage needed. The softer cloth would pack the wound, while she could use the stronger, stiffer linen napkins to tie the dressing in place and keep pressure against the gash. Assuming Stefan survived, the bandages would need to be changed periodically to prevent infection. But that was getting ahead of herself.

She made a small bundle of cloth and picked it up. As she turned to leave the pantry, her eyes fell on the stairs to the kitchen.

I could climb that staircase. Exit out into the courtyard, and run away into the night. Find shelter with Monsieur Dubois, or some other neighbors on the road to Dijon. The Nazis would never find me. They might not even bother to look. All I have to do is leave and I'd be safe. The more distance between me and the Germans, the better.

She froze. The thought was so tempting, to run away from danger, hide and be safe. To run from Springer.

But then her family would die.

Gabrielle shook her head to snap out of it. While Papa might have told her to jump at the chance, there was no way she was going to abandon her family. And she would be damned if she let that beast Springer gloat over Stefan's body as he died slowly on the cold, stone floor. Instead, she turned one last time and opened the small wooden chest that held the silver serving ware. Forks and spoons lay nestled in the red velvet. So did the long carving knife. Gabrielle stared at it, at the wide, flat blade used to filet wild game on special occasions. And she reached out and slipped it under her dress and into the waistband of her underwear.

Springer was waiting impatiently near Stefan's unconscious body when she walked back into the cellar.

"What are you doing, girl? Can you be any slower? I'm glad you're not tending to German soldiers!"

The other SS guards snorted and laughed caustically. Gabrielle quickly dropped to her knees and began ripping off what remained of the poor man's trouser leg. Once the skin was bare, she took one of the dishrags and gently patted the insides of the wound to soak up the blood. It was an ugly, gaping hole where the Englishman's knee had once been, and it was very bloody and swollen.

The good thing about bleeding, Gabrielle knew, was that it helped clean the wounded area of germs and debris. As long as the blood was then washed or padded away it was almost as good as flushing an infection with water. She went through three dishtowels in that very activity and left them in a red-soaked pile to her left. Once the joint was relatively dry Gabrielle took another rag, wadded it up, and packed it into the hole, then began dressing the Englishman's knee with the linens by wrapping them around his leg and tying them tightly in place. Stefan let out a soft moan and shifted his head slightly against the wall while she worked. The poor man. No one deserved to be tortured in such a way. Except, perhaps, the monsters who had done this.

After finishing with the leg, Gabrielle tried to wipe some of the sweat and filth from the Englishman's face. Stefan remained out cold but he subconsciously moved his head away from her touch. Gabrielle found herself gently shushing him as she dabbed the cloth against his skin. If only she had had some sort of painkiller she could slip him without the Nazis watching, if only there was something that she could *really* do to take the suffering away. What pain he must have endured for him to pass out. It was a fearsome thought that filled her with loathing for anyone and anything German.

"Stand up," Springer said.

Gabrielle stiffened. Slowly, she put down her cloth and turned to face her captor.

"My dear, it seems it's time for you to be somewhere else. I have instructions to send you to the courtyard this very moment."

Gabrielle saw another German, presumably a messenger, standing in the archway entrance. He was glaring at her with a very hard look. She had not even heard him enter the room.

"The courtyard?"

"That's what I said."

The randomness of the location seemed too unusual to make sense out of it. She had to think of a way to stay and tend to Stefan. "This man's condition is very serious. He looks to be in deep shock and requires close attention. It would be best if I remained here with him to look after him."

Springer glanced over the Englishman's body. "You've done what I've asked of you. That's that. Let's go, my pretty one."

"Herr Springer, look at him! Why would you have gone to fetch me if you didn't think his condition was dire? Please, let me stay with him!"

For a split second, the blond German's eyes actually seemed to soften. The narrow glimpse of humanity was so foreign that Gabrielle's skin ran cold.

"It seems we've progressed beyond that now." His voice was no longer harsh. "Let's go."

Gabrielle squirmed in the grasp of the SS trooper who grabbed her arm but his grip was too strong. She couldn't even resist being pulled towards the corridor. Gabrielle fought to keep the panic down. Apparently she had an unavoidable date with the courtyard, though as to why, she had no idea.

22

The door swung open and two large SS soldiers swept into the room. Robert didn't even have time to react. The men grabbed him by the arms and hauled him from his chair so roughly that the explosion of agony in his ribcage left him in tatters.

"To the courtyard, with the others," a third soldier standing out in the hallway said in German.

Robert was forcibly carried through the house until they exited the back kitchen door. His head was spinning with such a degree of suffering he barely noticed it had stopped raining. The soldiers dragged him to the middle of the courtyard between the house and the wine barn before throwing him down onto the flagstones. He caught a brief glimpse of Girard, Philippe, and his father-in-law Marc before he smacked face first into the wet stone.

"On your knees," one of the soldiers barked.

Slowly, Robert sat back on his heels. The sky was very dark. The aftermath of the storm was everywhere in the form of standing water pooled between the flagstones. He could see out of the corner of his eye his family kneeling in a line. A soldier's boots echoed behind him so Robert dared not turn his head to see more.

The captain, Tiedemann, was standing stone-faced several meters in front of them. His three lieutenants were also nearby, as were two soldiers with heavy trench coats and machine pistols. Robert's heart sank. The way the Germans were watching, the way his family was being set down... he could tell what this sort of arrangement must mean. But Philippe was here too, and surely that must mean something different?

A few minutes passed. Claudette and Gabrielle were ushered out as well. Robert silently suffered the indignity of watching the two most important women in his life get manhandled like herd animals. Gabrielle seemed to fall especially hard when the Germans threw her down. He clenched his teeth even tighter. As bad as the Vichy government had been before the occupation, at least it had been civilized. He couldn't say the same for a nation that allowed the *Boches* to behave so brutally.

Tiedemann began pacing as if he was rehearsing lines for a theatrical performance. His boots echoed eerily across the courtyard.

But the first person to talk was not a German.

"Monsieur, if it pleases you may I make a statement on the behalf of my family?"

Just as it had been in the Great Room the previous morning, it was Marc, speaking in French.

At first Tiedemann looked offended that his big pronouncement had been interrupted, but his expression softened when Springer finished the translation. Amazingly, Robert could see that the captain was going to defer to Marc and listen to what he had to say. Perhaps it was simple curiosity, or maybe Tiedemann was in a generous mood that afternoon. A glimmer of hope found its way to Robert's heart.

"*Was?*" Tiedemann said.

Marc opened his hands in front of him. "I killed your officer. It was me."

All of the blood flushed from Robert's face. Surely he had misheard.

Springer translated. Tiedemann even looked surprised. He crossed his arms in front of his chest and glared at Marc.

"*Erklaeren Sie.*" Explain.

Robert's brain was spinning. He was staring—*everyone* was staring—at the frail old man crumpled into a pile out on the bare ground.

Marc drew a shaky breath and continued. "From the looks of things you've figured out most of it. Your officer, what was his name? Hoffmann? We crossed paths in one of the corridors as he was on his way to the cellar. He made me go with him. He ordered me to select some of the best bottles.

"Your man started looking too closely at the masonry of my false wall. I had to stop him. You see, there's a large supply of ordnance hidden in our wine cellar. Your officer was too suspicious and I had to stop him."

What did he just say?

Abject terror flowed through Robert. He thought he would feint. *Oh my God! What in God's name are you doing! Don't tell them about the cellar, you old fool!*

His father-in-law continued. "When Herr Hoffman started scraping away at the mortar, I panicked. Without thinking, I struck him on the head with the bottle I happened to be holding. He crumpled to the floor and I ran away, afraid."

Robert couldn't believe what he was hearing. How could the old man have told them about the cache of weapons? Had the pressure of captivity caused him to go insane? Marc hated the Germans. What would compel him to seal their fate by offering them up the explosives stockpile for the local Resistance cell? They were all going to die now!

"Is that it?" Tiedemann asked.

"More or less. You see, monsieur, my hidden weapons were the reason I was fighting with my son-in-law the night you arrived. He's..." Marc twisted his face sourly. "He's a sympathizer. He didn't see what the big deal was for your men to stay with us. He didn't know what I was really doing. Robert didn't think twice about opening up our cellars and inviting you to be comfortable."

The captain stared at Marc for a long time before finally clearing his throat. "Why are you telling me this?"

"It's pretty clear what's about to happen, monsieur. There's no need. I'm the one you want. The rest of the family? They're all innocents. Look at the little boy. Look at the teenage girl. Look at all of them. They don't know anything. They're sympathetic to you. I'm not, nor will I ever be. I fought your country and its evil twenty-five years ago. It's been a great hardship for me to live with them and put up with their collaborative *merde*. So, I thought you should know. You should know before you go ahead and shoot everyone indiscriminately, and prove out every reason for why I oppose you and why the Maquis will *cut your throat*."

Dead silence hung over the courtyard save for a lonely rumble of thunder in the distance.

Robert was dumbfounded. But as he tried to make sense of it all, Marc turned his head slightly and their eyes met. For a brief instant Robert saw a sad, knowing smile on the old man's lips and a glint in his eye. He recognized the look. It was the same way he himself appeared when one of the children got into trouble and he was going to clear it up. Exasperation, resignation... and love. And the he understood.

The Germans had already found the explosives in the cellar. It had been a hasty masonry job anyway after Cartwright had led the Contis back to the airdrop site. They had found the explosives and were going to execute all of them as partisans. Marc was offering a red herring and trying to deflect the danger.

Yes, Robert understood. And in his own eyes he hoped he was conveying his love and thanks.

Tiedemann was conversing with one of his lieutenants who was becoming increasingly animated. The man with the small round glasses gestured alternately between Marc and the house, seemingly in some sort of debate about this new revelation. Tiedemann seemed to be shaking his head no. After a full minute, Tiedemann finally appeared to have enough and hissed a rebuke at the smaller man. The lieutenant stepped back and flipped shut the little black notebook he had had open during the interrogations.

Tiedemann stepped forward and pointed at Marc. "Shoot him."

Claudette did not know German, but anyone in that courtyard would have understood the purpose of Tiedemann's command. Robert's wife began to shriek and stood to run towards her father. Robert tried to stop her but a Nazi soldier beat him to it, shoving his rifle into her chest and knocking her to the ground. Philippe started crying. Girard gritted his teeth and knelt helplessly, his bad leg propped awkwardly to the side.

One of the soldiers was hauling Marc to the side while another was unslinging his machine pistol.

Robert intended to keep his eyes on his father in law as long as he could in order to savor the last few moments of his life. The confession had been risky but it appeared to have worked. Tiedemann was not going to shoot them all. Marc was going to take the hit. The fate of the rest of the family was still uncertain but they still had a chance, all thanks to the quick and clever thinking of this old codger.

The sound of the bolt being pulled back echoed off of the flagstones. The soldier with the gun was walking behind Marc's back.

Robert finally dropped his gaze to the ground. He couldn't watch. Their estate had been in the Conti family for three generations, and there had never been anything but happy memories of love and life that had filled it. The thought that the courtyard could become an execution ground was unfathomable.

Claudette was screaming hysterically. Robert said a silent prayer to the Almighty for both Marc and the rest of them, so that they might have the strength to continue the fight and not let the old man's sacrifice be in vain.

Then a loud, staccato burst of gunfire deafened his ears, and Robert cried.

23

The world revolved in a blur. Gabrielle couldn't focus on anything other than the thought of her grandfather collapsing under a spray of bullets until the blood pooled around his body. Why had he done that? *Why*? A tiny voice told her he had sacrificed himself somehow, that his false confession had narrowly saved the rest of their lives. But her ability to rationally process events was in tatters after witnessing such a cold murder.

She was only dimly aware of the present and of where she was being told to go by the shouting SS soldiers. They were trekking back into the manor. Germans pushed them up the stairs until they were all corralled back into the green bedroom on the second floor. At least they were together. As the door slammed shut, Gabrielle shuffled across the room until she was pressed against her father's back. Her mother was already in Papa's huddled embrace and they were fighting not to weep.

No one spoke for a long time. Alone with her thoughts, Gabrielle replayed the horrific scene of the execution again and again. The crack of the gunfire. Her grandpere's legs exploding and him falling to the cobblestones. His struggle with the pain as the soldier with the machine gun pumped more bullets into his limbs and let him lay awash in the agony. Then the final burst to the head. The way his arm fell limply to his right, palm up and fingers open. His empty eyes gazing up to the heavens, perhaps wondering how God could have abandoned them. The only outside feeling that Gabrielle could feel was the salty taste of her tears as they ran down her cheeks and past the corners of her lips.

Only gradually did she become aware of what her father was doing. Papa had quietly rolled up the edge of the large rug. The floorboards were long and thin, a modern remodel versus the heavy beams and planks of some of the other rooms. He was kneeling on the floor and staring at them as if he was unsure about committing himself to the next action.

Everyone else in the room was watching silently. Still sniffling, Gabrielle walked over and slowly crouched down beside him.

"Papa?"

Her father did not answer. His fingers gently swept across the floorboards, caressing the wood of some planks that were visibly brighter than the rest of the floor.

"Papa?" Gabrielle whispered again.

He turned to look at her. His eyes were red, shining with emotion and hurt. They overflowed with great love for her and the rest of the family. But Gabrielle also saw that her father had crossed over some imaginary line in making a decision that they would no longer allow fate to just happen to them, and that there was no turning back.

Papa began to slowly and quietly pull the loose planks up one-by-one, awkwardly using only his right arm, carefully placing them on the edge of the rug so as to keep the noise down. In just a few minutes he had opened up the hole into which they had hastily stuffed Stefan upon the Nazis' arrival, the small nook between floors where he had whiled away the hours concealed from the Germans. Gabrielle could see the planks laid across the tops of the beams of the lowered ceiling below. Dim light was coming from past the end of the crawlspace. The kitchen.

"So what are we going to do?" Mama asked, tightening her grip around Philippe. "Hide? If we just disappear, they'll tear the house apart to find us."

Papa didn't take his eyes off of the dark hole in the floor. "We are not going to hide."

The room waited in silence for what seemed like forever. Gabrielle reached out and took hold of her father's arm, both to offer solidarity and to bring him back to answering what his intentions were.

"The edge, there," Papa said at last. He pointed at the gap where the light was filtering up. "That's right above the cupboard in the kitchen. Cartwright must have fallen down or climbed out there when he was hiding, and slipped into the cabinet when the Nazis came."

Gabrielle drew a sharp breath. "Are you saying...?"

"We have to get out of here. *Now*."

Mama started crying. Gabrielle felt the hairs on her neck stand on end. Despite everything that had just happened, the thought of actually sneaking away from armed men who would shoot them on sight was still paralyzing.

Girard gave a low hiss and put his finger to his lips. Then he pointed to the hole in the floor. Gabrielle understood, and scanned the others to make sure they did as well. The thin subfloor meant that anyone in the bedroom could hear noises from the kitchen, and vice versa. Too much noise would attract the attention of anyone underneath.

"How should we do this?" Gabrielle asked.

"Keep it simple. The kitchen door opens into the courtyard. The vineyards are a hundred meters away. We run for it and hope that the *Boches* don't notice for the next half hour," her father replied.

"What if there are guards watching?" Mama said. She clutched Philippe again. "He's *ten*, Robert."

"And Girard's leg," Gabrielle added.

"We have no other choice. You saw what just happened. Now they've thrown us all in one room together. They're done questioning us here." Papa scanned the room. His expression was set. "The next step has got to be either imprisonment or a follow-on firing squad. We need to take advantage of the lull that God has provided us."

Gabrielle thought in the quiet moments that followed. She knew in her heart that her father was right. How hard it must have been for him to come to that conclusion, after his steadfast support of governmental change and the welcome of the German occupation. Now he had seen what was in store for their country, what the Nazis truly were. Their captors had clearly shown what sort of treatment would await them. The Contis would be considered criminals, torn away from their home, tried as partisans and then either imprisoned or executed. The remaining question was not if, but how.

Gabrielle studied her father and despite his words saw a lingering uncertainty that remained. To say they needed to escape was one thing, but to actually risk it, with the stakes no less than the lives of their entire family, was another entirely.

She felt her own resolve harden.

"Papa," Gabrielle said, "Mama's right. Look at us. We won't be able to move undetected. Even in this room, we need to whisper so that no soldiers in the kitchen hear us. We need a distraction."

"A distraction?" Papa said. He seemed to twist the idea around in his head until his eyes became focused again. The confidence in his voice rose. "Yes. A distraction."

Everyone in the room waited in anticipation but Papa did not speak. After nearly a minute Gabrielle shook his arm with the grip on his sleeve that she found she had never released. She started to become afraid of what her father had in mind. Why wasn't he letting them in on the secret?

Papa looked around the room at each of them. "I'll slip out first. The rest of you, wait here for fifteen minutes, then go through the hole one-by-one. Drop into the kitchen and get out to the courtyard. Run as fast as you can to the vineyard, away from the wine barn. *Away* from it. Then stay low and make your way down the hill to the road north of here. Maybe we can regroup, maybe not, but try to get to Monsieur Dubois' estate. It's about ten kilometers, so it's far, but doable. I'll make sure there are no Germans watching that side of the house. All right?"

The lack of specifics was worrisome. Gabrielle took a deep breath.

"What are you going to do, Robert?" Girard asked. The words held a great weight coming from a man who rarely spoke.

"Something long overdue. Give them a good fight."

Girard nodded, a small smile on his lips.

Mama was crying again. "Robert! No! You must come with us!"

Robert shook his head. "No, no. This is the only way. If something doesn't keep the soldiers' attention elsewhere, it's too dangerous for all. It must be done."

"Papa?" Gabrielle asked.

"Yes, my dear?"

"What about Stefan?"

"I don't know where they're keeping him, sweetheart. We don't have time to help him."

"He's in the cellar."

Her father's face betrayed his curiosity. "Can he fight?"

"Papa, the Germans... hurt him. They cut open his leg in some kind of torture session. He can't walk."

"That's unfortunate." Robert thought for a moment and sighed heavily. "We'll have to leave him."

"No, Papa."

Her father frowned at her. Gabrielle could see that his mind was unchanged. But that wasn't enough for her, not now. She had already lost her grandfather, her innocence, her honor, and very soon potentially her life. She wouldn't entertain the thought of leaving another human being with these Nazi monsters, especially when he was a soldier committed to fighting on the other side.

"I'll help him, then," Gabrielle said.

Papa emphatically shook his head.

"It is my decision, Papa. Stefan risked his life to get weapons in the hands of the Resistance. We know what we're up against now with the Germans. We're not going to just leave him here."

Now her mother was really bawling. Girard hobbled over to her to first shush, then muffle her sobs as Gabrielle and her father stared each other down.

"No. It's unfortunate, Gabrielle, but if he's hurt he'll just put everything at risk. This isn't a game where we can take that chance."

"If you don't agree, I'm going to do it on my own. I'll follow you to the cellar and get him myself. It's that simple. Don't test me, Papa. You know me too well."

A long, hard look was her reply. Papa didn't say anything and it was clear that he wanted resolution quickly; with the rug rolled back and floorboards removed, they were sitting ducks if a guard decided to poke his head into the room to check on them. Finally, after a long minute and with no small amount of reluctance, he capitulated.

"You are your father's daughter, it seems."

"Yes. I am." She smiled grimly.

"Very well, you come with me, Gabrielle. The rest of you, please listen. You must wait long enough for me to get into place. Girard, do you still have your watch?"

"*Oui*, monsieur."

"Fifteen minutes. Then all of you slip into the kitchen and run north toward the Dubois estate. Get over the hill as fast as you can and you'll be out of line of sight. Don't bunch up, but try not to lose track of each other, either."

Between stifled sobs Gabrielle's mother asked, "What about you, Robert?"

"Don't worry about me. I'll join you later."

Who knew if that would be true, Gabrielle thought.

Her mother and father regard each other for a moment. Papa finally stood up and they embraced, rocking slowly back and forth under the tension of their arms.

Gabrielle quickly inserted herself into their grasp, immediately followed by Philippe and Girard. For a brief, simple moment they were entwined in each other's arms as a single organism. Muffled cries and free-flowing tears became lost in the huddle. It was the first time since the Germans had arrived that the family had been able to truly hold one another. It had been even longer since Gabrielle had really thought about how much all of these people meant to her.

And then it was over. The huddle broke, Papa looked at Girard and tapped his wristwatch, and then silently lowered himself into the hole in the floorboards.

24

Cartwright sat awake and would have killed for a cigarette. He imagined taking a drag to savor the taste of smoke in his mouth for a few moments before exhaling with a long, slow breath. Then he'd watch the thin trail of smoke as it twisted around up into the air. There it would join the haze that had already collected along the ceiling from the previous ones he would have smoked until all of it gradually faded into the darkness. He sat and imagined and ached.

It almost would have been better if he had remained unconscious. But somehow, apparently due to some past transgression against the Almighty, Cartwright found himself awake and alert of both his surroundings and the pain that very much still numbed his leg.

The bandage around his knee indicated that apparently someone had taken pity on him. But Cartwright still had a grim idea of what his treatment indicated might be in store for him. Surely the Nazis weren't interested in transporting a butchered enemy to the local hospital? Nor would he last in a prison camp if he was an incapacitated cripple. The most probable fate was as clear as the Death's Head emblem on the collar of the guard.

Soon even the imaginary cigarettes was gone, mere stubs of paper and tobacco that his mind found difficult to hold any longer. There was nothing left to watch, nothing left to do but sit idly and try not to think about the throbbing in his knee. He stared at the bottles in their racks, the rubble remaining from the Nazi's excavation of the south wall, the worn leather of his boots on the other end of his numb feet. Everything seemed worth watching when one was living on borrowed time.

On the other hand, the SS guard had moved out into the corridor and was now pacing back and forth. Perhaps he had grown tired of the smell of blood, urine, and vomit that still covered the cellar floor. Cartwright wouldn't have minded being out in that corridor as well.

A voice spoke in the corridor and Cartwright tilted his head to listen. The pitch sounded odd, far different than all of the barking the Goons had been doing earlier. But the sound did not carry and he couldn't quite catch the nature of the strangeness. He sat and listened, wondering if this was the pronouncement of his end.

Suddenly Cartwright realized what was so strange. The voice was female.

As if on cue, the Frenchman's daughter appeared in the doorway and walked towards Cartwright. She was carrying a bundle of bandages and a small carafe of water. Comprehension fought its way into the Englishman's muddled brain. Of course the Germans wouldn't have bandaged him up. It was the Contis. And now it was time to change the dressing? There was still too much pain to get a clear thought through, but when Cartwright looked down at the linen already wrapped around his knee he thought that it still looked pretty clean. Perhaps the padding underneath the wrap was bloody enough to need a change. Or maybe the girl was bringing cigarettes. Cartwright chuckled, sending him into an extraordinary hell of pain.

The guard dutifully followed her into the room. It was obvious from the look on his face that he found the stench quite unpleasant. The girl knelt down and began unwrapping the bandage on Cartwright's knee slowly, carefully, with the soldier standing right behind her and observing everything. The German was so intent, in fact, on watching the girl's body as much as the medical treatment she was providing that he never noticed the shadowy figure skulking up behind him.

A quick gleam of metal flashed across the guard's throat in a violent spray of crimson.

Cartwright inadvertently jumped. The guard fell heavily to the ground with to reveal Robert Conti standing in his place, holding a bloody knife in his hand. The girl glanced at her father and instantly started to rewrap Cartwright's knee more tightly than it had originally been. Cartwright was at a loss.

"How... what in the name of Christ is going on?" Cartwright gasped.

Robert held his finger to his lips in an indication to be silent. He shuffled lightly back to cellar archway to listen for a few moments before finally deciding the coast was clear. Only then did he turn back around to give the Englishman his due.

"It is time to get you out of here, monsieur," Robert said with an accent so heavy that is was difficult to follow. "Your knee looks very poor. Can you walk?"

To Cartwright, hearing English spoken by someone other than an interrogator was like a salve applied directly to his wounded knee. All the feelings he had abandoned the night before—pride, hope, and the prayers that he might continue to live—came flooding back into his empty heart. It was almost enough to make him think he could do anything, even walk.

Almost.

Pain warped his face as he tried to push off the floor. "No, I don't think so. How did you get down here? Haven't you been prisoners like myself?"

Robert knelt down and used his thumb to probe how much damage the Nazis had done to the Englishman. The examination was nearly unbearable. Cartwright gritted his teeth to keep from crying out.

"We are still prisoners, at least the Germans think so," Robert whispered. "They put all of us together in the green bedroom."

Cartwright wrinkled his forehead. It was so difficult to follow with the accent. "The one at the top of the stairs? With the hole in the floor where you hid me?"

"Yes. We slipped out through the hole."

"Is it safe? Where are the Germans?"

"They are all around, so we must hurry." Robert paused with his hand around the bottom of Cartwright's thigh. "I think you can still put weight on this leg, but it will need some support. We need a splint."

The Frenchman stood up strangely and looked around the cellar before his eyes settled on some scrap piled in the corner. He rummaged about until he returned holding a two foot length of angle iron.

"We use this to build wine racks. It should make a good support for your leg." Robert turned to his daughter. "*Gabrielle, aidez-moi à placer cet appui contre sa jambe et à l'envelopper dans des bandages.*"

He knelt down and held the angle iron against the outside of Cartwright's leg. The girl began to tear long strips from her bundle of cloth and tied them around his leg and the metal to make a single, stiff limb. Each knot made Cartwright wince at the growing tightness and accompanying discomfort. But it was a small price to pay for a chance at freedom.

"Good," Robert said at last. "How does that feel?"

Cartwright tried to turn sideways and push himself up. Again, the pain was nearly overwhelming. But he gritted his teeth and was able to get up to a kneeling position, keeping his newly splinted leg rigid and immobile. "It's... okay."

Robert and the girl looked hard at each other. Their expressions were grim.

"What's the plan?" Cartwright asked.

"We are splitting up to make our escape. Gabrielle here will help you. She knows the area and obviously she speaks French. You'll go out through the wine cave, out the barn and into the countryside. Once you're over the hill, follow the main road north until you come to the next estate, *Domaine Dubois*. We have friends there."

Cartwright looked at the pretty girl kneeling beside him and managed a smile when he caught her eye. So that was his angel. Finally they had had an introduction.

"So, you're Gabby, are you? I'm very pleased to make your acquaintance."

She smiled back.

"What about you?" Cartwright asked, turning back to Robert.

Deep resignation wore on his voice. "I'm going to buy everyone some time."

"Oh? And how is it that you're going to do that?"

Robert stood wearily and hobbled over to the guard's body. Cartwright saw how he hunched to his left, his posture crumpled into a vision of frailty. The Frenchman took great effort to squat down and untangle the strap of the machine gun with his one good arm. When he stood again, he awkwardly held the weapon and attempted to prop the barrel on an elbow that seemed welded to his ribs.

"Robert—no. You're not serious?"

"I—this is something I should have committed to long ago."

"Maybe so, but you pull that trigger and it'll knock you over onto your arse. You can barely stand."

Robert's eyes narrowed. "What would you have me do, Stefan? This is the only way to buy time for the others."

Cartwright turned to Gabrielle. She looked a lot like her father—same chin, same nose, same eyes. Definitely the same eyes. They contained an identical level of determination and grit.

He thought back to Simon, Donner, McCoy. Their Dakota had gone down on one wing, a fireball in the night. There had been no time to go back into the plane. Nothing he could have done would have saved them.

Maybe here was a chance to make up for it.

"Let me take care of your distraction, Robert. I've got just the idea for the job."

"What?"

"The Germans found the explosives from the air drop, didn't they? But they don't seem to have found the domestic vintage."

Robert stared hard at him. Then understanding flashed into his eyes, and he actually smiled.

"It's even on the way," Cartwright added.

"You can't walk well."

"Gabby will be helping me."

The Frenchman's frown returned. "That was the plan when you were running away from the distraction."

Cartwright forced himself upward until he was on one knee and not in danger of tipping over. "Robert, it's the best way. We're wasting time debating it. Get back upstairs and get your family out. I'll get the Goons off the trail and we'll meet you at your friend's place." He turned his head to Gabby. "I'll take good care of her. I owe you."

Robert looked like he might throw up, but he allowed for a pale nod. He quickly explained the change in plans to his daughter. To Cartwright's relief, she didn't flinch but actually looked even more motivated.

They finished doctoring his leg. With Gabrielle's help, Cartwright hoisted himself into a standing position and tested his weight on his leg. The vertigo was immediate. After a moment of stabilizing himself, however, his head cleared and he tried again. The angle iron did its job and allowed for a basic, if minimal, level of locomotion.

"All right, it is time," Conti concluded.

Cartwright took the machine pistol from his host and stuck his head underneath the strap. He hoped to God he wouldn't have to use it.

"Robert."

The Frenchman paused awkwardly. "*Oui?*"

"I know you didn't want me here. I know Monsieur Rimbault forced it upon you. I—"

Robert waited.

"Thank you."

Robert smiled. "What is important now is to get you away from this house, you and Gabrielle. Take care of her. Please."

"I will."

Robert clasped Cartwright's shoulder before turning and hobbling back through the arch. Cartwright put his arm over Gabrielle and leaned heavily on her. She took the weight and put her own arm around his back. Cartwright grunted and thanked God he had this chance.

25

The three former prisoners stepped carefully and quietly through the ancient corridor, always listening for the sounds of boot steps or other signs that the Germans were coming. Mercifully there were none. Yet. Robert went with them as far as the entrance to the wine cave. Then he grabbed Cartwright and Gabrielle by their arms and brought them close.

"I'm headed back to the kitchen. That's where the others are coming out. Please, whatever you do, you've got to hurry. There's no telling when we'll be out of time."

"If you've got to run, then run," Cartwright replied. "A late diversion's better than none."

Robert turned to Gabrielle and said some soft words of encouragement that Cartwright could neither hear nor understand. She stared him in the eye and nodded as he spoke. Cartwright realized she was crying. Hell, he probably should be, too. Robert kissed his daughter on each cheek and her forehead, turned to give Cartwright one last glance.

"Take care of her. For God's sake, keep her safe."

"I will do everything I can, Robert."

And Conti turned and hobbled back toward the house.

"Into the cave, then, shall we?" Cartwright prompted, eager to get as far away from his cell as possible.

Gabrielle looked back at him with a blank face, uncomprehending.

"You don't speak English, do you?"

"*Non.*"

Cartwright studied the girl's face for a moment. Now that she was this close to him, standing under his arm, he couldn't get over how gorgeous she was. She seemed like the prettiest thing he had ever laid eyes on. Somehow, despite the absurdity of a crippled man trying to escape from armed soldiers, he felt empowered to make a go at it simply because she was there to help him.

"That's all right, love, we'll figure it out. Let's go. That way," Cartwright said. He started shuffling into the barrel cave.

The air temperature instantly dropped as they entered the cave. Rows of great oaken casks stacked three high formed long walls to partition the great open space. Here was the lifetime work of the Conti family, years of labor and carefully cultivated product combined through secret processes that produced some of the best wine in Burgundy. Cartwright grimaced. Sometime in the future, their wine would be sitting in a glass at some fine restaurant to be enjoyed by some absolute wanker.

Gabrielle pulled his arm tightly over her shoulder and helped him hobble past the barrels. Cartwright barely noticed his surroundings because of the overriding pain that shot through his leg. His knee pushed mercilessly against the tightly wrapped bandages, and while the splint kept him from being unable to use his injured leg it left his gait far from graceful. Yet Cartwright became aware of how strong the girl was in being able to support his weight. For a petite girl, she was as steady as a rock. Perhaps her strength came from years growing up on a farm.

They managed to make it ten meters or so before Cartwright could go no further. "Wait, wait," he gasped. Gabrielle leaned him against one of the barrels and watched expectantly, urgently.

Panting, Cartwright tried to let his eyes adjust to the dim light. The sporadic light bulbs wired in at various intervals along the walls didn't do much to illuminate anything, but they were enough to reveal an enormity of the place that was overwhelming. How could such a giant cave exist under the house? He didn't know much about limestone but apparently this could happen. Great pockets of open space trapped in the earth. Amazing.

"Looks different than I remember," Cartwright said. "Didn't seem so dark when we dragged those drop canisters down from the barn. But I suppose this time darkness is our friend, right?"

Gabby stared at him. He had forgotten she only spoke French. She was so pretty that he wondered if it even really mattered.

"I could gawk at you all day, but we should keep moving."

Cartwright's push off of the nearest barrel sent bits of dust and dirt falling from the top. Gabrielle staggered for a second and then continued to help him along. Each barrel was a good three feet in diameter and rested on a metal frame to square up the curves so that they would remain stable when stacked. It was very difficult if not impossible to see through to the other side of a given stack. The barrels formed long rows perhaps sixty to seventy feet long before there came any sort of lateral break through which one might move to another lane.

They continued hurriedly until Cartwright again had to stop. If Gabrielle hadn't remained under his arm he knew he'd fall over. The pain throbbed through his leg so strongly that his knee was surely going to explode any moment and shower them all with blood and guts.

Gabby continued to prop him up as he regained his composure. Their faces were close. Cartwright watched her eyes as he gritted his teeth.

"Gabrielle."

"*Oui?*" the girl whispered back.

"Do you know what ammonal is?"

"*Je ne comprends pas.*"

"Ammonal. It's an explosive. You can make it from things you use in farming. Your grandfather's been busy helping out the local hooligans."

"*Je ne comprends pas, Stefan.*"

He thought of a different way to explain.

"We're going to give old Adolf's men a little surprise. *Le Boom*," Cartwright said in a parody of a French accent.

"*Le Boom*?"

"That's right."

Cartwright had no idea if that was a French word, but the smile Gabby flashed him indicated she seemed to understand. Which was good, because if the level of pain he was dealing with got worse, or even remained the same, he was going to need some assistance.

With another heave, Cartwright stood himself up and leaned heavily on his female companion. His mind was starting to click, to think through what he had to do. The focus on his upcoming task helped him push out the pain a little. On the other side of this vast storeroom was a ramp that led up into the barn. They would climb up the ramp—that would hurt—and find the boxes of bottles that contained not wine but the homemade explosive the Conti's had been brewing up. The blasting caps were in the glass cabinet full of chemistry equipment. A quick setup and the barn would be smashed into smithereens, drawing every Goon from miles to investigate while the Contis and Cartwright went in the other direction.

Crack.

Cartwright and Gabrielle froze. Was that a gunshot?

Had their chances ended already?

Without waiting to find out more, the Englishman started hobbling towards the end of the row of barrels with renewed vigor, half dragging Gabrielle with him, half pushing off of her to provide locomotion in the absence of one of his legs. The lane they were in right now had full visibility back to the corridor leading underneath the house and to the cellar. They had to get to the end of that row of barrels. They had to find something behind which to hide.

26

Tiedemann was feeling good.

He finally had some closure. Hoffman's murderer had confessed and received a just punishment. His men had captured an enemy supply of ordnance for covert use against the Reich. And while he didn't necessarily buy the line that the rest of the family's hands were clean, Tiedemann felt it was plausible enough that he had decided not to shoot them all on the spot. He'd simply turn them over to the SD for interrogation; with vengeance enacted and a pile of explosives confiscated, what could have been an embarrassment would instead be a coup.

When all was said and done, Tiedemann would still be behind schedule by a good two days, but now things could progress again and the limits had been established as to how much this side journey would impact the Reich's timetables. All they needed was for the rain to hold off a little longer. With a little luck, Tiedemann might actually receive a commendation instead of a reprimand.

Tiedemann sat at the table in the library that had become his de facto center of operations during the investigation. His officers were arrayed around the room, each of them now joking around in a moment's respite from the difficulties of war. Eppler was standing with his hands on one of the chair backrests and rocking it back and forth, eyeing what was left of the small bowl of fruit Tiedemann had found in the kitchen. Krauss had his nose buried in his little leather-bound notebook. Springer was telling war stories as he sat across the table from Tiedemann and next to Gohler, whom he periodically tried to get to drink more from the open wine bottles on the table. More wine, even now. What an evil bastard.

Tiedemann contented himself with following the small talk. Once they reached southern France the day would be consumed with fortifying, planning, and training, and this would likely be the last chance they'd have to simply relax. The maps of the region were arranged on the top of the table, a forgotten sprawl left to be resolved later.

Springer was far more interesting.

"It was freezing, and the snow made it difficult to see anything," he said, his blond hair falling into his eyes. The story was about a troop movement Springer had been involved in back in Poland, shortly after Germany had blitzkrieged its way to victory. "We were marching about twenty meters behind the panzer and men were slipping in the ice on the road if they weren't careful, falling flat on their asses. Sometimes they would take out the man next to him as well and both would go down."

"Sounds like outside here," Tiedemann noted. All the rain.

"Not far off, but the frozen ground hurt worse when you fell. Here, the mud feels a lot softer," Springer shot back with a smile.

Gohler looked puzzled. "Wasn't anyone riding on the tank?"

"Of course. But that wasn't any better. Either you became frozen solid sitting on that mound of metal, high up off the ground where the wind got you, or you kept yourself moving on foot and hopefully stayed active. There wasn't any escape from the conditions.

"So anyway, we're all miserable, the wind is blowing straight into our faces, and we can't see very well. And we get to edge of the downward slope of this hill, and all of a sudden the panzer is just gone."

Eppler snorted. "What do you mean, just gone?" He was digging through the fruit bowl, looking for the best piece.

"I mean, *whoosh*, gone, disappeared," Springer replied. "I ran with Von Braun to the edge to see what had happened. And all we could make out were all of these soldiers jumping off as fast as they could while the panzer turned around sideways and slid down the hill. People were diving off all over the place, rolling off the side of the road if they were lucky, or down the hill behind the tank if they weren't. So we stopped the column behind us and started rushing down the hill as fast as we could, trying to catch up to the tank.

"It's snowing like crazy, and I'm dodging all these bodies underneath my feet running on this sheet of ice down the hill with Von Braun right behind me. Half the time we're falling on the ground ourselves. And we get to the bottom of the hill and see that the panzer has crashed straight through the side of this stone farmhouse. Knocked a holed in the side so that all we see is this rear end of a tank sticking out of a building."

"Was the crew injured?" Gohler asked.

"Well, we didn't know yet. But that's what we needed to find out, if the driver and commander got banged up or not, so we're looking for the door to this farmhouse to get inside because the turret and the hatch are on the other side of the wall."

Tiedemann listened to the story and watched the starving Eppler fidget with the fruit. He pulled out a bright green apple with his heavily tanned hand. Juice and saliva sprayed over the table when he bit into it.

"So we find the front door and Von Braun knocks it in with a couple kicks," Springer said, fighting to keep a straight face. "And we rush in and just burst out laughing. Von Braun even fell over backwards. Because the whole front of the panzer had gone through the wall and come up right to the edge of the kitchen table where this Polish family had just sat down to eat supper, and they were absolutely motionless with shock. I mean, they had forks and spoons half raised to their mouths, you name it, and they were just frozen solid looking at this tank that had just came crashing into their home."

The guffaws were starting to build in the room as Tiedemann and his men reflected on the thought of such a rude interruption. It wasn't every day that a Polish farmer would have seen a tank. Especially one so up close and personal.

"And wait, I haven't told you the best part yet. The gun barrel of the turret was right over the kitchen table, perfectly aligned down the center. It was hanging right over their bowls of porridge and loaves of bread and whatever else they were eating, and the farmer's wife was looking up at it like this." Springer demonstrated the old woman's expression and it was hilarious, with a pretend spoon halfway raised to his mouth and wide, disbelieving eyes staring up at an imaginary tank barrel.

Everyone was laughing now at the idea of an old country woman struggling to comprehend why there would be such a thing suddenly invited to supper. Even Krauss looked up from his little notebook and was chuckling. Springer went on to explain that the panzer captain was quite apologetic about the uninvited entry, though he immediately inquired in a very polite tone about whether there might be any food the family would be willing to share with him, given that it appeared they had lost their appetite. Gohler and Eppler traded some cracks about what an appropriate reply might be, all of them quite rude.

Tiedemann shook his head with a smile, tipped forward in his chair, and placed both elbows on the table to bury his face in his hands in response to such buffoonery. What a bunch of characters. Gohler was laughing so hard now that his face was turning bright red.

The apple went again to Eppler's mouth with a loud crunch. Tiedemann glanced over at the *Afrika Korps* veteran. It was so remarkable, here in the wet and dreary countryside, how bronzed the man's skin was. That spoke of long, idle hours spent in the desert waiting for an engagement with an enemy that often did not come. Tiedemann wondered if Perpignan would be like that. What if the Americans *didn't* mean to invade the south of France? What if they intended to hit Tunisia and Libya? Would Tiedemann and his men end up whiling away the days on the coast, waiting for an invasion that would never come? That might not be such a bad proposition. Tiedemann could work on a tan of his own in the hot Mediterranean sun.

Deep down, however, he knew that such hopes were fleeting. Once it was more apparent what the Allied forces were going to do, if an invasion into Europe was not likely then *Totenkopf* would undoubtedly be sent back to the East to fight the Russians. That was the life of a professional soldier, to go where the conflict was found. At least Tiedemann would be commanding a *Kompanie* of men that were strong, tough, and ready to drive out the enemy no matter how much resistance was met.

Eppler was holding the apple core against the backrest of the chair while he joked with Springer. Tiedemann studied the dark and rough hands, the bruised thumbnail that stood out in blackened splendor more than even the pale band of skin that remained untanned around Eppler's fourth finger. White skin that had once been shielded from the North African sun by a ring.

A ring.

Tiedemann blinked. Where was the ring?

Had Eppler ever worn a ring?

It was the ring finger of his left hand.

It was not there now.

Tiedemann wrinkled his forehead in thought as the others continued to laugh and joke. This was very odd. Quickly, frantically, Tiedemann relayed through his head everything that had happened over the past two days. What did it mean?

No...

As Tiedemann came to his conclusion, the smile slid off his face despite the joking of his comrades. All he felt now was a knot in his stomach.

The German captain slowly pulled his elbows off the table until his hands were out of view.

27

Eppler was holding the apple core and trying to decide what to do with it before he just settled on flinging it into the corner. Satisfied, he glanced about the room to see with whom he should plug himself back into conversation. As luck would have it, he settled on his captain.

"Herr Hauptsturmführer?"

Tiedemann blinked in the realization that he had been staring at Eppler. "Yes?"

"You look troubled. Is something the matter?"

Tiedemann took a deep breath. "Nothing. A random thought. But it doesn't matter now."

Eppler nodded and began to switch his attention to his peers.

"Ah, I almost forgot," Tiedemann said. "I think I found something of yours. It was outside in the dirt. Quite lucky I noticed it." He pulled out the gold wedding ring from his coat pocket and tossed it across the table. It spiraled around in a circle before finally coming to rest near Eppler.

Eppler looked surprised at the ring. "You found...?"

"Yes, by the front door to the estate," Tiedemann said. He was watching his lieutenant carefully. "Almost didn't see it, but there was a break in the rain and somehow it caught the light just the right way."

Eppler was staring at him uncertainly.

"It is yours, isn't it? Something had to cause that tan line on your finger. Why don't you try it on?"

Tiedemann's voice had cut through the other conversations and all eyes were focused now on them. Eppler seemed to be fighting a subconscious urge to cover up his hands, that somehow the question of the ring made him uncomfortable. Not the normal, gratified reaction one would expect upon the return of lost property.

"I'm sorry, sir," Eppler said at last. "You must be mistaken. I lost my wedding band back in Tunisia. That's not mine."

"Then perhaps you need a replacement. Put it on."

"Herr Hauptsturmführer, with all due respect, that wouldn't be proper."

Tiedemann's voice was cold. "Put it on."

Eppler looked down at the ring as if it were a ticking hand grenade. Then, after resigning himself to the inevitable, he tried as casually as possible to pick up the ring and slide it on his finger.

It fit perfectly.

With one smooth motion, Tiedemann stood up and pointed his Luger at his subordinate.

"Herr Obersturmführer!" Springer cried. He stood up, alarmed.

It was as if a bomb had gone off. The jovial atmosphere had stopped so abruptly that there was a deafening silence in the room. Krauss's eyes flicked between Tiedemann and Eppler with growing alarm as it dawned on him what was happening. Only Gohler remained inconspicuously frozen, watching. Tiedemann could feel the sergeant's eyes burning into them.

He understood everything now, and the reality of it was beyond hurtful. It was shameful. He was disappointed in himself that he hadn't seen it before, but the fact of the matter was that he never should have had to see any of it at all.

"All this time. *All this time*!" Tiedemann hissed. He was finding it difficult to control his anger. "I thought the ring I found in the cellar was Hoffman's. No wonder it didn't fit. It was yours. *You* are the killer."

Eppler looked shocked at the accusation. "Sir, with all due respect, what are you talking about? How could you think such a thing?"

It was a good act. Perhaps the delivery was enhanced by Eppler looking at the end of a pistol pointed at him. But Tiedemann didn't buy it. The logic fit perfectly now and there was no escaping the conclusion that it laid out.

Tiedemann struggled to keep his voice steady. "You know, there was something about all this that didn't seem quite right. I think it was the confession. It just didn't make sense somehow. The old man said he had killed Hoffman when he got too close to the wall hiding the ordnance. I think his words were, 'I panicked, and struck him on the head without thinking, and he fell to the floor and I ran away'. Yet we found Hoffman's body on the opposite side of the cellar. Not exactly next to the cache of weapons, yes? Difficult to justify the old man's explanation, given what we were told, yes?

"And then, while sitting here, it just came to me. The ring. Such a simple thing, in front of my eyes the whole time. The wedding ring from the struggle fits you, not the victim. The ring is yours. The *murder* is yours."

Eppler stood frozen. His face was all innocence but his breathing was rapid and shallow, and Tiedemann could sense that the lieutenant's mind was racing for a way out of the accusation. Tiedemann also knew enough about people to recognize guilt. Again, he silently cursed himself for not seeing it all earlier.

"Sir... this is not..."

"I wonder, Herr Eppler, was the wine stain on your uniform yesterday an accident? Or was it to cover up bloodstains on your tunic after you killed my officer?"

The room was silent. Springer and the others made no motions to distract attention. Tiedemann could feel their uncertainty. He felt it important that they believe him. Even though they would do whatever he told them simply because he was their commanding officer, right down to placing Eppler under arrest, it was still vitally important right now to build the trust and comradeship that they would need when they would all be on the front lines together.

Eppler felt the uncertainty as well, and acted upon it.

"Herr Tiedemann. This ring isn't mine. Why would I kill Herr Hoffman? I'd never met him before a few days ago. What possible motive would I have to take a fellow comrade's life?"

All eyes turned back to Tiedemann.

"That's right," the SS captain conceded. His eyes narrowed thoughtfully. "I *do* believe you didn't know Hoffman personally before joining this unit.

"But your wife did."

For a brief moment, Eppler stared back in puzzlement. But only for a moment. When the color drained from his face, Tiedemann knew he had him.

"Ah, yes," Tiedemann continued. "Herr Hoffman was quite the womanizer, wasn't he? A good number of exploits from what I understand from Herr Gohler. Especially when he was stationed at the work camp at Bad Tölz. You can't blame him, really. He was a good-looking fellow. A strong build, a noble, Aryan face.

"And it's tedious, boring work, watching prisoners is. Understandable that a man's attention might wander in the off hours, perhaps to a poor, lonely *hausfrau* whose husband has gone off to war. A woman has needs, too, yes? She might have herself an affair and become involved with another man who is there for her in these trying times, physically, emotionally. Sexually."

Tiedemann reached into his tunic pocket and pulled out the letter Springer had confiscated from the Conti girl. He shook it open without taking his aim off of Eppler's chest. "Such a woman might even be foolish enough to fall for her lover to the point where she decides to end her marriage with her husband. A bit cold, to do so in a letter, but I suppose there really wouldn't be another way if her husband was deployed to Africa, now, would there?"

Eppler's eyes went down to the letter on the oak table. Tiny droplets of sweat beaded on his forehead even though the air was cool. Tiedemann watched the physiological reactions carefully, calculating his next words.

Suddenly, Tiedemann leaned forward and spoke to his captive. "Why, Herr Eppler! *You're* from Bad Tölz as well, aren't you?"

Eppler's eyes were locked on Tiedemann and his expression had become impassive.

"And what was your wife's name again, Herr Eppler? You've told me before, but please refresh my memory."

There was a long pause. "Greta."

"Greta," Tiedemann repeated. He looked down at the signature on the letter. "Greta. Signs her name with *G*."

Tiedemann was rolling through his exposition now. "What an odd thing this letter was, to find in a French chateaux. I thought it was from the French girl, meant for a lover in the German army. What was her name? Ah, yes. Gabrielle. Springer found the letter on her and confiscated it. Once I read it I thought, what good taste she must have, even if she is hasn't yet mailed the letter to break off the relationship. But things didn't make sense. The paper was much too worn for something yet unsent. It's been read many times, folded again and again, as if by someone who can't quite bring himself to believe what the words are telling him. Someone who keeps looking at it to see if his eyes are being deceived by the desert heat. Someone who can only feel outrage at being betrayed at home while he is stuck in North Africa, nobly fighting for the Fatherland. Someone who would go so far as to join the SS and orchestrate his transfer in order to track down and take revenge against his wife's lover."

He walked around the table, his Luger level.

"The thing is, Herr Eppler, I can't say I don't feel your pain in losing your marriage. But you've done something far worse than cheat on a spouse. You betrayed your fellow soldiers. You found out who stole your wife, you transferred to the same unit, then you murdered in cold blood a man who would have, without question, given his own life to protect yours on the field of battle. You turned your back on all of us. You joined the SS only to desecrate it."

Tiedemann felt the pistol grip shift from the sweat of his palms. How easy it would be to put this swine of a traitor on the floor with a neat bullet hole to the chest. Just the faintest squeeze of the finger and justice would be served. The temptation was so overwhelming that Tiedemann could scarcely believe that his pistol hadn't already gone off, that there was no wisp of smoke already rising in a twirling spiral from the end of the barrel. That such a person could infiltrate the ranks of the Waffen-SS and insidiously gain the confidence of his companions was so disgusting that Tiedemann wanted to puke his guts out. The whole concept of loyalty and honor had been swept away by such an outrageous disregard for the essence of a soldier. The betrayal was complete. The pain was unbearable.

The wind outside howled faintly against the window. Tiedemann suddenly became aware of how still the room was, his loyal officers still waiting for an order. It was time to give them one.

"Herr Gohler," Tiedemann said.

"*Jawohl!*"

"Place this... *person* under arrest and put him with the Englishman. We'll be taking both of them to Perpignan with us. Our superiors will want to see if the airman has any more intelligence to provide, and *I* will want to watch this piece of shit here crawl and beg for mercy before he's executed. That's something that should be shared with those whom he betrayed."

The Sturmscharführer walked carefully over to Eppler and removed the lieutenant's pistol from its holster.

Eppler stiffened. "Herr Hauptsturmführer, I assure you, I don't know what you're talking about. These accusations you're making are simply not true."

Tiedemann refused to acknowledge the words. "Take him away."

Gohler gave Eppler a sharp push. The lieutenant stumbled before moving reluctantly, his eyes still on Tiedemann. There was still the look of disbelief, or perhaps incredulity, that he had been caught in his crime. And then they were gone.

Normally Tiedemann would have found great satisfaction in ferreting out the truth. But not this time. As the two men disappeared, Tiedemann placed both hands on the tabletop to support his weariness. He hung his head and cursed the day that he and his men had ever come to France.

28

Wilhelm Eppler marched out of the study with Gohler holding him at gunpoint. He couldn't believe what had just happened. Did he malign the gods in a previous life? How was it that he found himself a prisoner of his own unit?

The circumstances had been perfect. A one-night layover at an unfamiliar location. Plenty of alcohol to dull the senses. A variety of scapegoats nearby, including an enemy soldier hiding contraband ordnance. A private cellar where he could accost Hoffmann. Eppler couldn't have asked for a better situation to take his revenge, which was why he had seized the opportunity instead of continuing with his original plan. And yet now it had all backfired. He had been accused of murder and was surely headed towards a firing squad. How had that happened?

As they headed to the kitchen, a wave of memories and emotion flooded into Eppler's mind. He thought back to Bad Tölz and the SS men that streamed through the work camp there as they rotated back from the Front. He thought of Greta, the love of his life whom he had known since grammar school. *How lonely she must have been, with me gone for so long.* The temptation was easy to imagine, particularly with a good-looking fellow like Hoffmann. How cruel that this man had drawn a duty station near his home? Did their relationship begin innocently, a random meeting at some club? Or had it been lusty and banal from the start? Her parents were gone. Eppler was far away. She was lonely. She had needs.

But what about him? Hadn't he been just as lonely huddling behind sandbags while under British shellfire? Hadn't he been through his share of suffering as his *Kompanie* struggled with supply lines stretched perilously across the desert? Where was *his* comfort? He hadn't asked for the life thrust upon him. And while he could perhaps reconcile a temporary refuge in the arms of another, he could *never* condone the complete and utter abandonment Greta had sent him in that fateful letter.

I am leaving you.

I am in love with him.

It is not your fault.

No, it wasn't his fault. It was Hoffmann's.

What Hoffmann hadn't counted on, however, was being found out by one of Eppler's friends. The administrator of the SS camp in Bad Tölz could write letters too—ones that not only supplied the identity of the cuckold, but also the names of allies who could orchestrate a transfer to that same Waffen-SS unit. It paid off to have friends in high places.

Unfortunately, the tables had now turned. One of Hoffman's was holding the gun.

"Be careful, Sturmscharführer. That pistol was given to me by General Rommel himself." Eppler spoke carefully as they walked. "You'd best take care of it until this mess gets fixed and my name is cleared. I'll be wanting it back."

"Quiet. Keep moving," Gohler replied, unimpressed.

The kitchen was deserted, with copper pots and pans strewn all across the oak countertops. Gohler motioned to the iron staircase for Eppler to climb down. Eppler slowed his pace, testing his escort to see what he would do. A heavy shove was the answer. Gohler was being careful in his control of his prisoner, not getting too close and keeping his Luger out of arm's reach. Any sudden moves to grapple would undoubtedly be disastrous. Eppler grabbed the handrail and descended around the helix of the rickety stairs towards the cellar.

The well-maintained corridors of the manor gave way to cracked plaster and exposed brick of the underground. Eppler again walked slowly and continued his probing.

"Do you really believe that concocted explanation, Herr Sturmscharführer? I realize you have orders, of course, but I want to know on a personal level. Man to man. Do you really think I would do such a terrible thing?"

Silence.

"It seems to me," Eppler continued, "that Herr Tiedemann is discounting the obvious, here. A downed Allied airman overseeing a cache of weapons for the Maquis? A murder in the same room as where the contraband was hidden? How do you feel that stacks up against an absurd accusation of lost love and jealousy?"

Another shove was the response. The two men continued walking. Maybe he was just obeying orders, or maybe he was busy sorting through a torrent of emotions around discovering his friend's killer, but Gohler wasn't letting on.

Eppler walked slowly through the brick archway of the wine cellar and stopped abruptly.

"Where's the Englishman?" he said.

There was no sign of Cartwright except for a dried puddle of blood. Still keeping his hands out to his side, Eppler started to scan the room. Both of them saw the body in the far corner at the same time. The uniform was the charcoal gray of the Waffen-SS, not the brown of the Royal Air Force.

"Peterson! *Scheisse!*"

Gohler dashed across the room and knelt by the motionless body. Eppler followed slowly behind, temporarily forgotten by his captor. As he got closer he saw that the body was indeed that of *SS-Schütze* Peterson, who if not for wartime would have been an athletic, good-looking young lad of eighteen. Now he was a corpse. The body was deathly pale, with a bright red gash cut horizontally across his throat and blood all over his uniform. Had Cartwright done it, perhaps surprised him from behind?

Attacked from behind.

Gohler was down low next to the body, his fingers pressed against the boy's neck for a pulse. Eppler quietly pulled a dusty wine bottle from the iron rack nearby. In one smooth motion, he brought it down with as much force as he could muster against the sergeant's neck. There was a muffled thud as the bottle connected. Gohler lurched forward across Peterson's shoulder and onto the hard floor. Almost simultaneously there was a loud *crack* as Gohler's pistol fired from a last, semi-conscious jerk of nerves. The bullet flew into the limestone and showered the air with thick yellow dust that quickly covered Eppler, Gohler, and the corpse.

Eppler stood over the bodies and stared curiously at the heavy bottle he was holding. It was fully intact. Not the outcome he had expected. The one he had clubbed Hoffman with had exploded into a thousand shards of green glass and showered them both with wine. Perhaps this one would have broken if he had aimed at Gohler's skull instead of his neck? No matter. Eppler had temporarily bought his freedom with it. And since he was now inexorably committed to a path of desertion, he would need a weapon more lethal than a bottle. Eppler let it slip to the limestone floor and retrieved the pistol from the sergeant's motionless fist.

There was no reaction from Gohler. Eppler didn't bother to check whether the sergeant was alive. He turned and walked to the archway, pressed tightly against the red brick, and listened. He heard only silence.

Most of the troops would be outside near the vehicles in preparation for moving out. If any of the officers had heard that gunshot, they'd be running down to see what had happened and their footsteps would announce them. But there was nothing—at least, not yet. Perhaps the earth that surrounded the room had muffled the sound.

Time was of the essence now. Eppler had to get as far away from the manor as possible before anyone discovered his escape. He didn't know where he would go, or what he would do once he got there, but he was a fugitive now just as surely as that downed airman from across the Channel. And it was even odds whom Tiedemann would try to hunt down first.

Without dwelling any more on his future, Eppler walked around the corner and headed to the cave with the barrels.

29

Krauss stopped the reassurances of his navigation skills in mid-sentence. "What was that?"

Tiedemann leaned forward in his chair and held up his hand for silence. The noise had been very faint. But it certainly sounded like a gunshot.

Springer was looking at him. Tiedemann saw his junior officer was thinking the same thing.

"*Scheisse,*" Springer muttered.

Without further hesitation, Tiedemann flung himself out of his chair and pulled his pistol out on his way to the door. He yelled for the others to come with him and then was out in the corridor making a mad dash for the front foyer.

At the grand staircase in the manor's entryway, Tiedemann skidded to a halt and paused to listen again. "Where did the shot come from?"

Two young soldiers appeared at the top of the stairs, the ones who had been guarding the Contis.

"*Achtung!* Did you hear that?" Tiedemann said.

"*Jawohl,* Herr Hauptsturmführer. It sounded like it came from down there."

Down there. The cellar? Surely Eppler had not been able to overpower someone like Gohler.

"Are the prisoners secure?"

"Yes, sir. We haven't had any trouble with them."

"*Are you sure?*" Tiedemann shouted.

The soldiers got the message and disappeared into the hallway. The SS captain stroked his thumb against the knurled pommel of his Luger while he waited. After a few moments, urgent footsteps thundered back at the top of the stairs.

One of the men reappeared. "Sir, they're gone!"

Tiedemann heard the words but struggled to accept them. "What do you mean, *gone*?"

"The prisoners aren't in their room! The floorboards are torn up inside... they must have snuck out through the floor... we didn't...." The soldier panicked at the realization of having failed in his duty.

Tiedemann was at a loss. His mind raced to process all the information and come up with orders to give his men. The entire family had disappeared from under the noses of a double guard? With a cripple, and a little boy? Somehow they had managed it. How far had they gotten? And did they have a weapon?

He realized he was squeezing the grip of his pistol so tightly that his knuckles had turned bright white.

Follow the gunfire.

Tiedemann barked out his orders. "Krauss, get the men loading the truck. Bring them up here with rifles ready. Put sentries around the grounds and fan out—the courtyard, the wine barn, everything. Then come down with the rest through the ramp in the barn to seal off any escape."

"Yes, sir," Krauss said. He was a buzz with nervousness.

Tiedemann put his hand on the man's shoulder. "No one gets out. If anyone sees Eppler, shoot him on sight. Got it?"

"Yes."

"Springer," he said, then gestured upstairs. "And the two of you up there. You come with me."

"*Jawohl,* Herr Hauptsturmführer!" all men shouted in unison.

Krauss disappeared out the front door while the two infantrymen came down the stairs to join Tiedemann and Springer. The foursome hurried through the adjoining corridor and into the kitchen. As they neared the spiral staircase, Tiedemann held up his hand to slow his comrades down and be silent. He couldn't hear anything out of the ordinary from where they stood.

A stray image worked its way into Tiedemann's memory, one of moving from house to house in the abandoned streets of Russian towns, wondering where the next ambush would come from. There was one place in particular—a nameless village that had been shelled to rubble—through which as an *Obersturmführer* himself he had led his troops looking for partisans. Tiedemann remembered coming to a crumbling wall at the edge of a city block with an exposed staircase much like the one he looked at now. There had been death around that corner; Soviet snipers had cost him half his squad. He had had to withdraw and call in artillery. Now he wondered what waited for him and his men here. Another ambush? Should he withdraw, burn the entire manor to the ground, and shoot anyone trying to escape the flaming deathtrap?

Not this time. Tiedemann was not going to leave anything to chance.

The heard a tiny click behind him as Springer flipped his safety off.

Tiedemann put his foot on the top of the staircase and took a first careful step. The iron creaked with his weight, then that of Springer and the others following several meters behind. They reached the bottom landing with weapons drawn. The small space between the pantry and the corridor was very dim and in all assessment made a favorable place for an ambush. None came. Tiedemann proceeded slowly down the hall, brushing the back of his shoulders against the cracked plaster and brick so that he made the narrowest target possible.

The squad of men approached the outside of the archway forming the entrance to the wine cellar. To the right the tunnel continued on to the large barrel cave. Tiedemann remained pressed against the wall and used hand signals to direct the infantrymen to the opposite side. The men carefully crept up until they flanked the archway. Springer held his pistol down low, Tiedemann up high, while the soldiers had their Mausers shouldered and ready to bring up. Finally, on a silent count of three, Tiedemann waved his troops into the cellar before following himself, ready to shoot anything that was not made of glass and grapes.

What Tiedemann saw made him catch his breath. No Englishman. No Eppler.

All that remained was a dark stain of blood where the Englishman had been sitting during his interrogation. *The blood... the knee.* Tiedemann was sure Cartwright couldn't be walking on his own. From what the guards had reported, he'd been borderline conscious for most of the night.

"Herr Hauptsturmführer! Look!" Springer rushed to the far corner. Two bodies wearing SS uniforms lay piled atop one another. A blood trail stretched back to Cartwright's corner.

"Who are they? Are they alive?"

Springer pushed the motionless forms around with his free hand. "Gohler. And Peterson, on the bottom. Peterson looks like his throat was cut."

Kneeling down next to Springer, Tiedemann could see the ugly gash that separated the young infantryman's neck. There was no such wound on his sergeant, however. Tiedemann reached over and felt for a pulse.

"By God, he's still alive. Gohler!" Tiedemann hissed, gently but firmly batting the man's cheeks. "Gohler! Can you hear me? Get up!"

No response. Tiedemann rolled the sergeant over to his back. He couldn't find any wounds, but it was clear Gohler wouldn't be much help in tracking the prisoners.

And his Luger was missing.

"Peterson's weapon is gone, too," Springer said. He was watching from over Tiedemann's shoulder.

"What did he carry?"

"MP40." A machine pistol. Eppler—or the Contis?—would be well armed.

Tiedemann remained kneeling and thought. How had this happened? Eppler had been under armed escort by a careful and seasoned warrior. Cartwright was severely wounded and under guard. To find the tables turned seemed fantastical.

"Sir?" Springer said with urgency.

Tiedemann's joints popped as he stood upright. He didn't like this. Four soldiers might seem like an effective tracking force against a lone renegade or a crippled enemy, but none of his men had automatic weapons. They'd be following Eppler into the maze-like, ambush-ready expanse of the barrel cave, the only logical place that he could have fled. And as for Cartwright, who had helped him? Surely not the Contis from all the way upstairs? Was there some new element in play? The *Maquis*?

If he waited Krauss arrived with more armed troops, they could encircle and destroy the fugitives. But there was another factor Tiedemann knew was also vital for battle, and that was initiative. It was rapidly diminishing. Every moment that he and Springer delayed was another second that Eppler had to run through the cave and escape through the barn. Krauss might take five minutes to arrive with his SS. That was time that they did not have.

"It's up to the four of us, Herr Springer. We're going into that cave with the barrels. It's the only logical place Eppler or anyone else could have gone." He looked at each of his men. "Be careful."

"*Jawohl*," the two soldiers replied. Their voices betrayed a measure of trepidation.

Springer took over the tactical. "Knappe, Kohl. Just like Russia. Keep to cover and shoot first."

Tiedemann readied his pistol again. "Let's go."

The four SS soldiers proceeded out the archway towards the barrel cave.

30

Only two or three minutes had passed since Cartwright and Gabrielle heard the *bang* and dove for cover at the end of the row of barrels. Cartwright felt like they'd been hiding for an eternity. If his own movement hadn't been so clumsy and noisy, hiding wouldn't have even been an option—they'd have kept on running, as fast and as far as possible from what was obviously a gunshot. But with his wounded leg it was a miracle they had even reached the end of this particular row of barrels, and even that had been accomplished only in a continuous stumble.

Now they both were leaning against the edge of a dusty barrel, trying to see the passage back to the wine cellar while simultaneously staying out of sight. Cartwright had his shoulder propped up and the German machine gun ready in both hands.

They heard running. But instead of a crowd of troops streaming into the cave behind them, Cartwright saw a lone silhouette moving briskly down the corridor until it reached the cave. Then the figure turned left and continued without interruption. Not the behavior one would expect from someone conducting a search for fugitives.

"Well, that's odd," Cartwright whispered.

"*Oui*," Gabrielle replied. He looked at her, and her expression showed she understood.

"Let's get going, shall we, Gabby?" Cartwright said. "No telling where that bloke went, but it won't help matters just sitting here and letting him stumble across us. Are you up to helping me a bit more?"

Gabrielle had had her hands against the back of his shoulders before Cartwright began talking, and now she was leaning forward with her face close to his. Cartwright could feel the brush of her hair on his neck, the warmness of her breath. What a beautiful creature God had chosen for his guardian angel.

"*Je ne comprends pas, Stefan.*"

Cartwright frowned. "Right." Thinking for a second, he pointed first to her, then himself, made a walking gesture with his fingers, and finally jerked his finger out into the blackness of the cave. "Yes?"

She understood. Nodding her head, Gabrielle wrapped her arms tightly under his shoulder and hauled him up to his feet with surprising strength. Pain shot through his bandaged knee and he shoved his knuckle into his mouth to keep from groaning. Desperately trying to think of anything to distract himself, Cartwright concentrated on the feeling of Gabrielle's breasts pressed against his arm.

* * *

With a soldier in front of him and Springer close behind, Tiedemann kept pressed against the limestone wall of the corridor until they reached the barrel cave. The space before him was enormously dark and vast, filled with enough stacks of wine barrels that it could take a squad of men the better part of an afternoon to find someone who didn't want to be discovered. Tiedemann cursed silently to himself. What were they up against? Was he doing the right thing, pushing a poor position into battle? A small enemy number could pin them down in a place such as this, or possibly ambush and kill them all. What were they rushing into?

They were pursuing a traitor and an escaped prisoner, Tiedemann reminded himself. Time was of the essence before they slipped away. There wasn't any alternative.

Tiedemann waved Springer close with his empty hand.

"*Ja,* Herr Hauptsturmführer?"

"I'm going to shout out to Eppler. I want you to take Kohl, head that way, to the right, and loop around. Don't put too much distance between us but stay out of sight. I'm going to try to get him to move towards Knappe and myself. I want you to flank him and kill him."

"Sir, are you sure you want to give your position away? You'll make yourself a target."

"We'll never find him in here, Springer," Tiedemann said. "He has a head start and a lot of cover."

"What if there are others in the cave?"

"We'll accept those risks." Tiedemann looked levelly at his lieutenant. "But if you see someone else, shoot them, too."

"*Jawohl.*"

Tiedemann pointed his finger and directed Springer to go. Then he turned and explained the plan to Knappe. The soldier understood and indicated he was ready to follow any order he was given. Finally, Tiedemann himself darted out into the openness of the cave and proceeded to the left. After he had walked past several rows of barrels, he stopped and took cover. He heard Knappe slinking up quietly behind him and cleared his voice to make sure he would be heard.

"Eppler, you cowardly pig! I have men waiting to shoot you at the exit of the cave! You are surrounded and cut off from escape. If you really want us to believe you're innocent, give yourself up and step into the open!"

Then he waited. There would be no reply, of course, at least, not right away. But that wasn't the goal. All Tiedemann needed was to put enough doubt in Eppler's mind that he would be distracted from escape. Then Krauss would arrive with ten more SS troops and the game would be over.

* * *

The oak barrels were stacked three high, with curved supports in between so that they didn't teeter from the instability inherent in their rounded shape. Cartwright could feel their weight and how solid they were with his left side. Even had they been empty the barrels would have been formidable. Behind him was Gabrielle, who helped hold him in place as he kept the machine gun ready.

A minute passed before the voice shouted out again. "*Kommen Sie heraus, Eppler! Wir haben den ganzen Zug hier im Kellar. Sie koennen ein Mann sein und sich stellen oder abschlachten lassen wie ein Tier. Kommen sie heraus!*"

"What the hell is that bastard saying?" Cartwright muttered under his breath. *Kommen heraus* sounded like it was an invitation to give themselves up. Not bloody likely.

He considered which direction to go. Straight ahead was the first, obvious choice. That route led all the way to the ramp underneath the barn. The problem, however, was that that route was a straight shot from the other entrance to the cave. The visibility back to the cellar corridor was too good, even in the dim light. It was too risky despite the promise of being the quickest way out of the cave.

The machine pistol shifted slightly in Cartwright's sweaty palm. He realized he was gripping it so tightly that his fingers were beginning to ache. As he forced himself to relax his hands, the weight of the heavy weapon seemed to pull his arms into the ground.

"Gabby," he whispered. Cartwright waited until she was looking at him before he jerked his head to the side. "Time to take a little detour."

The girl's expression made it seem as if she understood. She presented herself to him so that she could shoulder his weight again, and he wrapped his left arm behind her neck. Together they turned away from the giant wine barrel and stumbled towards one of the other aisles farther away from the center row of the cave.

* * *

The electric bulbs wired into the ceiling were underpowered and spaced far apart, so they did very little to illuminate the aisles formed by the towering rows of barrels. It was amazing that the vineyard even had electricity this far out in the country. But Tiedemann's eyes were well adjusted now to the dim light and he could finally see, more or less, down the long rows of the barrel maze.

Each cask had a year stamped on the end to identify which harvest it contained. Tiedemann subconsciously glanced at the nearest one and noted it had been sealed in 1940. He didn't know how long wine was aged in barrels rather than bottles, but two years seemed like it ought to be about the limit. Most were dirty from long periods of storage. What a place to find connections to the Resistance, he thought. War turns even the most normal and innocuous settings into a bed of conflict.

Out of the corner of his eye Tiedemann saw movement. He snapped his head around but didn't see anything out of the ordinary. Had it been imagined? He looked back at Knappe but the soldier didn't acknowledge any threat. Tiedemann turned back, dashed to the other side of the row, and listened. There was only silence. Slowly he stalked around the corner and raised his pistol, ready to shoot.

He was now in a four-way intersection of barrels, with the cross path about four or five meters wide and extending out of sight in either direction. If the movement he had seen had been a person, he or she could have run in any direction. Tiedemann heard Knappe raising his rifle to provide cover as he flanked to the side. Again Tiedemann listened for a clue. There was nothing. With no leads to go on, Tiedemann walked two rows over and crossed the cross path to enter another aisle formed by the rows of wine.

Another long, empty corridor. Tiedemann automatically pressed his back against the wood to minimize his profile. The wine barrels were providing too many spots for an ambush, and he reminded himself his prey was armed. Butterflies fluttered in the pit of his stomach as he crept forward. Tiedemann wasn't scared at the prospect of danger, he was far too much the old soldier for that and had the matter-of-factness about death that one developed after seeing many people die. But he was not pleased about the odds he was subjecting himself to in order to catch Eppler.

Another flash of movement some distance down the aisle. Tiedemann leveled his pistol and came within a hair of pulling the trigger tight enough to release a bullet even though he had no target. No one was visible. He looked back at Knappe and got a quick, knowing glance in return. The soldier's cheek was plastered against the stock of his raised rifle. So they both had seen it. Was it Eppler darting to a new hiding place and preparing an ambush? Tiedemann crept slowly forward.

A meter above him, a cat walked nonchalantly from barrel to barrel, following them. A damn cat.

A few seconds passed before Tiedemann felt his heart beat again. He lowered his pistol. The animal above him sat down and watched him curiously. Tiedemann wanted to shoot it.

* * *

Cartwright's head was starting to spin as the aching in his leg became more demanding. *The pain.* It had grown from a dull thumping to sudden, massive convulsions which washed up from his toes to his stomach. The flashes of torture threatened to incapacitate him completely. He had already lost his bearings now that they were no longer able to see the dim light from the wine cellar corridor behind them. It was up to Gabrielle now to guide them where they needed to go. For all Cartwright knew, they could have been headed back towards his former cell rather than the unguarded exit of the wine barn.

After another forced stagger he could take no more. Cartwright's legs buckled and he very nearly brought Gabrielle down to the hard ground with him, except that she managed to ungraciously shrug him off of her shoulder before it was too late. The impact made a loud *smack* and left the Englishman's cheek pressed against the back of his hand on the floor.

"*Eppler! Wo sind Sie?*" the German voice shouted again. This time it was much closer.

Cartwright felt his shoulder being pulled in short, forceful jerks. He twisted his head to see Gabrielle trying to get him back on his feet, but she wasn't able to do much more than rock him back and forth where he lay. He could see the furrows of fear on the girl's forehead, and in his own mind he knew he should be running. But somehow he didn't think he knew *how*. Behind her Cartwright saw a wall of barrels that all looked the same, great barriers of rounded oak with wooded blocks interspersed in the matrix. They extended another fifteen feet or so until the next crossing where the edge cut sharply into blackness.

Or was it blackness? Maybe it was just a trick being played on his eyes from the pain, but

Cartwright thought that it was lighter here than what he remembered from traveling so far through the cave. There seemed to be more brightness that made the planks in the barrels a little bit more detailed, the contours of the ceiling a shade sharper.

"Partons!" Gabrielle hissed. She was still trying to pull him into a sitting position. He looked at her and she pointed past her shoulder to the edge of the barrels. *"La sortie est exacte là. Regard! Partons!"*

Partons... that sounded like "parting." Did she mean the exit was near? Was that what she was yelling at him in words a poor lad from Birmingham had no chance of understanding?

Almost there. If there was anything that Cartwright could latch on to that would get him through another bout of wracking convulsions, perhaps it was the knowledge that they were very nearly at the edge of freedom.

"Stefan. Stefan..."

Summoning up all the strength he had left, Cartwright forced his upper body off of the ground and into Gabrielle's waiting arms. She squatted near his back and hauled him vertically up until he was standing. The pain in Cartwright's leg was like shooting knives slicing flesh off of the bone and he very nearly toppled over into the wine barrels in front of him. Gabrielle's arms remained tightly around him, but the Englishman knew instantly that his legs would bear no weight and that he would crumple back to the ground.

Yet he didn't fall. Gabrielle held him firmly and pushed him forward until he was within arm's reach of the wine barrels, at which point he could stretch out his arms and try walking his hands along the wood and maybe help with their progress. Slowly they moved toward the end of the barrel wall. There was definitely more light here, Cartwright was sure of it. Hope began to resurge and gave him the strength to fight the pain down to where it could be tolerated. They were getting closer to the edge of the wall. If they could just keep this going a little while longer, Cartwright dared to think they might have a chance.

The brightness dimmed suddenly. Cartwright turned his head to see the dark shape of an SS officer standing not five feet away staring back. He had a pistol pointed at them.

31

Cartwright froze.

They were dead. The only thing that he could think of to do in his injured condition was to not make any sudden moves that might provoke a shot a few milliseconds earlier than when it would come anyway. He gritted his teeth and waited for the bullet.

Gabrielle tugged one more time on his arm before noticing the enforced stillness. Desperate, she turned to her right and saw the SS man for the first time. Cartwright felt her terror through her hands as she jumped a half step away from the German before freezing herself.

And yet, the shot did not come.

The German had a wide stance, with his right arm extending straight from his body so that his pistol was well aimed. He clearly looked as if he had jumped around the corner with the intent of killing the person he found on the other side. But the man's savage expression changed to one of surprise, then chagrin. Were they to become prisoners again? Or was the German dreaming up elaborate schemes of torture to punish one who dared escape from their captivity?

"Wieder kein Glück, meine Freunde," the German muttered.

Cartwright recognized him now. He was the deeply tanned soldier who had taunted him during the previous night. Or was it that morning? The soldier had the same smirk as when they had been in the wine cellar.

Without warning and still keeping his pistol aimed at the two of them, the German started shouting at the top of his lungs. *"Herr Hauptsturmführer! Hier bin ich! Hier können Sie mich finden! Hier, hier!"*

And then he turned and ran.

"Gabby," Cartwright said. "Run."

She looked back at him with wide eyes. If she understood, she was clearly horrified at the thought.

"Get out of here. They're coming. Hurry. *Go!*"

He pushed her away and pleaded with his eyes for her to save herself. She stared hard at him. Then, mercifully, she turned and disappeared into the cave.

"At least one of us will make it," he muttered.

He still didn't understand what had happened with the German. Why had he run away? The "recapture" didn't make any sense.

In any event, he had to get ready. It took an eternity to crawl back to the edge of the barrels. Another minute to prop himself up into a sitting position. He didn't dare check the ammunition in the machine pistol because he knew if he did, with his luck the enemy would pop around the corner as soon as he had the magazine removed. Instead he thumbed off the safety and tried to take aim. If this was where he was going down, he was going to do it with a fight and buy Gabrielle as much time as he could. Maybe the Goons wouldn't even realize there were two of them.

He waited as patiently as he could with the lightning bolts of pain in his leg. Time had seemed to slow. Cartwright couldn't tell if seconds, minutes, or even hours had gone by. His arms started wavering as he held the machine pistol.

"*Halt!*"

The *crack* of a gunshot sounded loudly behind him, followed by the *pop* of a double geyser of wine flowing out of the nearby barrel that had received the bullet hole.

Cartwright froze. He had been flanked.

It was no use. He barely had the strength to hold his weapon. Turning around and trying to take a shot at a person behind him was ludicrous. Cartwright raised his right hand and the gun tumbled to the earthen floor. Angry footsteps approached and someone grabbed him roughly by the shoulder to spin him around. He looked up and saw the imposing figure of the SS captain towering above him, pistol in hand.

* * *

Tiedemann stared incredulously at the Englishman before him. He looked pitiful. With a quick step he walked over to Cartwright and kicked the MP40 away from his reach.

"Springer," Tiedemann hissed.

"Here."

"I've got the Englishman."

A crouching figure slunk out of the shadows with pistol drawn. Knappe and Kohl stood nearby, scanning for more enemy.

"Did you hear Eppler's shouting?" Springer said. "It was from right around here."

Tiedemann understood. They were being baited. The fugitive Eppler must still be very close.

"You and Kohl keep going. He's got to be headed to the barn."

"*Jawohl.*"

The two men left. With Krauss coming in from the surface, Eppler would be caught between two sides and killed.

Tiedemann heard nothing but his own breathing, the splash of wine from the wounded barrel, and the panting from the Englishman.

A few seconds ticked by as he thought of what to do next. Had Eppler freed the Englishman as an unwitting distraction? Possibly, though that meant he still would have had to overpower Gohler. He should just shoot the bastard now and tie off one of the variables. Look at the man, he wasn't going to survive anyway! Shooting him would be merciful.

Something told Tiedemann that there was still an important but missing piece to the puzzle, something that he needed to figure out before it as too late—

A thunderous explosion from above shook the universe around them. Knappe let out a brief scream that was cut off sharply before a series of thuds. A moment later all Tiedemann knew was that the floor had suddenly rushed up to meet him.

* * *

Gabrielle coughed, and a cloud of limestone dust rolled into the air in front of her. Her ears were ringing church bells. As she gradually pieced together her senses she realized she was back down in the barrel cave. She looked behind her and the ramp that had led up to the barn was gone.

Another person rustled in the wreckage of the barrels nearby.

"Come on, monsieur!"

Gabrielle crawled back to her feet. Where had she left Stefan?

She darted recklessly back into the cave. The barrels nearest the ramp had toppled off of their stands and now formed a haphazard array that was practically impassable. Gabrielle had to push off of each of the casks to keep her balance after such a great concussion from above. As she worked her way around to the aisles that were still intact, she heard the person following her close behind.

"Come on! Quicker!"

Gabrielle began to jog back to where she thought she had left the Englishman. It took a turn or two to get past more upset barrels. A great number had tumbled from their neat stacks and several had splintered open, bathing the ground in puddles of half-aged Burgundy. A few moments later she saw a crumpled figure on the ground. She instantly broke into a sprint and rushed to the huddled form.

"Stefan! Are you hurt?"

The Englishman stared at her without comprehension. He started mumbling a foggy question.

Gabrielle gave him a quick kiss. He was covered in dust. "*Le boom*," she said.

"*Le boom*?"

"Yes." She smiled.

Understanding slowly dawned on his face. He started to smirk. Then his jaw went slack and he turned his head over his shoulder to look down the aisle. Gabrielle followed his eyes and then she saw him too.

Tiedemann was on his knees about ten feet away. With one arm he was steadying himself on the ground. With the other he held a pistol. And he was pointing it at them.

As she looked into his eyes she could see the confusion as the German tried to piece together what had happened. Gabrielle supposed she wouldn't have understood either. When her father explained to her what ammonal was and how he and her Grandpere had been stuffing wine bottles full of it for the past few months, the idea of their winery becoming a bomb factory belonged in a fairy tale. Never in a million years would she have thought of the Contis supplying explosives to the local *Maquis* fighters. Yet that is what they had been doing, led by her grandfather's nationalism and balanced by Papa's reluctant participation. The wine barn had cases of the stuff ready for delivery, and the quick application of a few blasting caps had been all it took to set it off.

Of course, Gabrielle didn't really know how to use a blasting cap. She had been lucky she had help.

Tiedemann's eyes raised up to look past her. He raised his pistol.

Crack-crack-crack.

Gabrielle dove to the ground and tried to cover Stefan. The sound of gunfire would have been deafening if their hearing had returned from the explosion, which it still hadn't. A few seconds ticked by until she dared open her eyes.

Monsieur Dubois stood a few feet behind her. He lowered the Sten gun he had just fired. "Come on, Gabrielle. We have to get moving."

32

"He's badly hurt," Dubois said. "You'll have to help me carry him."

"Yes, of course." Gabrielle hoisted one arm over his shoulder while the stout man who lived down the road handled the other. "I still don't understand how you knew to come help us."

"There was a red blanket out the window."

Gabrielle blinked as they dragged the stunned Englishman. "The blanket—"

"An old signal for help, girl. We can't exactly use the shortwave to talk to each other, can we? Someone might hear."

They kept moving carefully back toward the wine cellar, toward the house. Every so often Dubois would stop them to listen. Listening was hard. Gabrielle still had the ringing in her ears from the deafening noise of hundreds of pounds of homemade explosives detonating.

"Did you see Papa?"

"I did."

Gabrielle turned her attention sharply. "You did? Where is he? Mama? Philippe—"

"Settle down, girl. Charles has your mother and brother. We stumbled across them in the vineyard and he's taking them to our house. Your father and Girard are helping me."

"Helping? How?"

"Do you ever stop with the questions? Why don't we worry about getting out of here first?"

They proceeded slowly until they were back in the corridor under the house. Dubois left Gabrielle to hold Stefan while he crept forward with his Sten. The Englishman was more lucid now and watching silently as this helpful, armed stranger scouted ahead. Gabrielle stole a few glances at him and on the third one he looked back at her and smiled grimly. Then he winked.

All she cared about was staying alive and escaping to safety. And she wanted Stefan with her. Despite his condition she somehow felt safe with him. If she could have those two things, she could live the rest of her life without feeling that her grandfather had died for nothing.

Dubois came back. “Come on.”

They continued through the corridor, past the wine cellar, and up the rickety staircase until they were above ground in the kitchen. The sweet noontime sun was streaming through the dirty windows. Dubois peered out the glass before apparently being satisfied that danger was not lurking outside. He opened the kitchen door and motioned for them to step out of the line of sight from the courtyard while he scanned again.

Gabrielle snuck a peek across the courtyard at the obliterated wine barn. She had spent many, many hours in there as part of her childhood. Now all that remained was the memories. It was absolutely and totally gone. Shards of wooden planks covered their estate from the massive explosion. By the far edge where the cobblestones would have ended, Gabrielle noticed two crumpled bodies dressed in gray. One of them was oriented toward her, and while the face wasn't visible from the way the head was turned, the shock of blond hair was unmistakable. Springer.

Gabrielle felt a faint smile creep across her lips at the satisfaction of knowing there was still some justice in the universe.

She gradually became aware of Stefan studying her. He glanced across the courtyard at where she was looking and saw the bodies. Then he looked back at her.

"*Mon ami,*" he said softly.

"Not bad. You're pronunciation stinks."

He smirked. Gabrielle didn't know if he understood what she had said, but he acted like it. And he seemed to find it funny.

Dubois made rapid motions with his hand for them to step forward. "Come on, come on, let's go, *now!*"

He grabbed Stefan's other arm and the three of them dashed out the door. The Englishman grimaced as he dangled between them. They were out in the courtyard now and Gabrielle felt suddenly very exposed and vulnerable. There was no cover or protection. Were more SS watching them? Were they ready to pop out from around the corner and gun them down as they fled across open ground? It was all motivation to run as fast as possible and hope that three sets of feet didn't stumble over each other. Her heartbeat quickened, the hairs on the back of her neck stood out, and she found herself running as fast as she could. They had to get to safety. They had to.

33

The fugitives stumbled through the vineyard between rows of trellises that stretched out on either side of them. Red and yellow grape leaves covered the ground after having just recently dropped from the skeletal vines still hanging over the wires. They made wet crackling noises with each step. The ground sloped away down the side of the great hill on which the Conti estate had been built. A small blessing that the escape would be downhill, Cartwright thought. He would have been delirious from everything that had just happened if not for the overpowering feel and smell of the outdoors hitting his senses square on. It was the feel and smell of freedom.

"Vite, vite! Vous ne venez pas assez rapidement!" the Frenchman in the lead whispered harshly.

Instantly Cartwright was being dragged faster than before, to the point that he thought he was the only one keeping Gabrielle on her feet rather than the other way around. The only way they could have gone faster was to tuck their knees and roll down the hill.

As they put more distance between them and the manor house, Gabrielle began to start pulling back on her pace. It only took the arrival of the inevitable bad step to make Cartwright stumble and curse loudly as he forced them to a stop. The heavy-set man egging them on was not pleased.

"Que faites-vous? Quel est le problème avec vous? Partons!"

Cartwright thought of the rest of the Contis and prayed they were okay. He felt a sudden pang from having abandoned his mates once before, hurdling down from fifteen thousand feet and making the brutal choice between selfishly saving his own hide rather than remaining behind to die nobly together. He had chosen the former. It was not desertion. It was the grim reality of discretion.

Gabrielle turned her body back into Cartwright's torso and shouldered his weight again. Cartwright caught her eye in one long, lingering moment before they started moving again. He could see the determination that had gotten them out of the barrel cave, but also the same worry and fear that he felt. He didn't know the fate of the others. Not knowing what else to do, he extracted his arm from Dubois's grasp and reached up so that he could gently stroke Gabrielle's cheek with the back of his fingers. Her eyes locked with his. Cartwright ignored his own pain and, language barrier or not, tried to will her into knowing that he was grateful and would take care of her the best that he could. He owed them all his life. He owed *her*.

The foursome continued down the hill, occasionally ducking under the rows of trellises and working their way parallel to the direction from which they had come. Finally they came around the edge of a deep furrow in the ground to see a horse and wagon waiting patiently by a large, leafless tree.

"The getaway car?" Cartwright noted dryly.

Dubois glanced at him without comprehension, which was just as well, then motioned for he and Gabrielle to get in the back of the wagon. It appeared to be full of barrels standing on end, but once they closed the distance, Cartwright could see that there was space in the center for them to conceal themselves. They hoisted the wounded Englishman over the rear cross-board while Gabrielle clamored in behind him. The force of the girl's body on top of his made Cartwright wince. He was starting to think that death was preferable to the continual need to vomit.

Dubois covered them in burlap sacks and climbed up front to take the reins. Gabrielle turned one last time to the stout Frenchman and tugged on his sleeve until he turned to face her.

"Monsieur Dubois, que ferons-nous avec Stefan une fois que nous obtenons à votre maison? Il a besoin d'un docteur."

"Yes," Cartwright said in agreement. He would indeed need a doctor.

The Frenchman went back and forth with Gabby in hushed, quick tones, then turned his attention back to the reigns. The cart lurched forward. Cartwright could see the anxiety on the girl's face—the worry about the others in her family, the loss of their home, what the future would hold as the shadow of war darkened around them. He lifted his arm and took hold of

Gabrielle's elbow to offer what small amount of assurance he could. He knew it was difficult to leave people and comfort behind. He knew it firsthand, from the moment his unexpected journey into Occupied France had begun by bailing out of a mortally wounded plane. But since then Cartwright had also found hope. Hope for life, for himself and for others. For Gabrielle. Perhaps, God willing, her life might be with him.

Somehow, the meaning of Cartwright's touch made it through the language barrier. She gave him a smile. As she slipped down onto the bed of the wagon with him, Cartwright saw that her eyes did not leave his for a moment. And for that little moment in time they shared a sliver of hope that the future would turn out for the better.

*   *   *

SS-Sturmscharführer Rudolph Gohler stumbled unsteadily up the spiral staircase until he was standing in the kitchen. His thoughts were still unfocused and he lost his balance every couple of moments. As he extended a hand against a small wooden table, he surveyed the surrounding picture out the open back door. While his thinking was still not clear, he knew he did not like what he saw.

The courtyard was in shambles. Debris littered every square meter in a jagged symphony. Presumably it had all come from the wine barn, which was now... gone, replaced only by smoking fires and splintered wood. Bodies were strewn about wearing the charred uniforms of the SS. All of them were dead.

Gohler put down the wine bottle he had procured as a weapon and leaned even more heavily against the door. He saw the body of Springer and his unmistakable blond hair out in the wreckage. Part of him wanted to run. There obviously had been some sort of explosion, and only a fool would stay in a hot zone without a weapon, cover, or support. But another part of him sensed that for whatever altercation had taken place here, it was now over, and that safety, however relative, had returned to the battle zone.

And the battle apparently had been lost.

Gohler furrowed his brow. The thought of the traitor Eppler escaping was bad enough. Add the loss of his superior officers and infantrymen and it was sickening. How had he missed it all? Granted, in retrospect he had been foolish in rushing to Peterson's body when he saw him in the cellar. He had been escorting a prisoner and should have kept his priorities straight. Perhaps he had let his guard down because he had wanted to believe Eppler's story, that it all was a big misunderstanding and it would be cleared up once they reached Perpignan. But blame didn't really figure into the grand equation of war. There was only life and death. And sometimes, the only difference between the two was a random roll of the dice.

A lone man stumbled from behind a stone pillar that had miraculously remained standing. Krauss. He appeared hurt and now staggered in a circle, lost.

With a determined sigh, Gohler pushed off of the kitchen door and headed out into the courtyard for whatever fate had next in store for him.

* * *

Although they had come late to the spectacle, another set of eyes got to watch the smoke billow forth from the wine barn. German eyes.

Observing from high upon a neighboring hill, sitting among some scant brush that provided what little cover was available, Wilhelm Eppler stroked his chin with his fingers as he watched the remnants of the wine barn burn. What he saw made him snort in amusement. Krauss looked shell shocked and eventually just sat down in the dirt after turning around multiple times. A man in a sergeant's uniform—Gohler? Yes, it was him—was exiting the back of the manor carrying a wine bottle. Amazing that the bastard was alive after the clubbing Eppler had given him. Another soldier was creeping up on the carnage, his rifle lowered in disbelief. There was no sign of Tiedemann or the other officers.

What had happened? Eppler didn't care. He had no love for these SS men, these ideological mutants who marched in lockstep unison to the Führer's wishes. He had been sickened by their arrogance when he had seen them in Bad Tölz. His wife had been seduced by one of their leaders. Eppler had no use for them and was glad they were all dead. His country was dead to him after Greta had left. He did wonder about the girl and the Englishman, though. Cartwright. That man was a survivor. All the abuse that had been heaped upon him and he still had managed to almost get out. Maybe he had.

But what about himself? Where would he go?

Eppler's eyes swept past the manor over to the road far down the hill. The Opel was out of the ditch and Tiedemann's staff car sat motionless just in front. A lone soldier was leaning against the bumper.

The staff car. Eppler smiled, stood up, and walked carefully down the hill.

As he approached, the soldier gave him a snappy salute at the sight of the warrior who had fought on the battle lines of the legendary Rommel. Eppler waved him at ease, then regarded the truck disapprovingly. Finally he turned his attention to the staff car.

"There's been a terrible accident. The Hauptsturmführer needs us to get aid. We're taking his car into town to find help."

"*Jawohl, Herr Obersturmführer!*" the soldier barked.

Eppler and his driver climbed in and pulled away from the silent transport truck. As they passed the bottom of the footpath that led to the house, there were no people in sight. Perhaps this idea would work after all.

"Herr Obersturmführer," the driver said simply, asking for permission to speak.

"Yes?"

"That explosion. What happened?"

"I told you. An accident."

"Yes, sir."

Eppler paused thoughtfully. "What's your name, soldier?"

"Thomsen, sir."

"Well, Thomsen, head back to Dijon. All these little villages no doubt have only horses and carts. We need real help—an ambulance at minimum. That means Dijon."

"Jawohl."

"When we get there I'm going to drop you off at the fire station. Hitch a ride with them back to the Conti estate immediately. While you're doing that I'm going to head to the police. We don't know if there is subversive activity in this region and if many of our men are injured, we might need their help to secure the manor. Understand?"

"Yes, Herr Obersturmführer."

Of course, Eppler's drive to the police station might detour through Spain. There was no life for him in Germany now.

Gazing out the window, Eppler took a deep breath as the countryside glided by. It had been a long journey from North Africa to southern France, a journey that had taken him from one armed service to another, through lies and deception as he came to grips with betrayal by his life partner. He had known early on that embarking on a path of revenge could lead to being a fugitive. Or worse. Even now, with his reprisal complete, he felt empty and alone inside. But he didn't care.

Tiedemann had said more than he knew when he had talked of why men fought through the horrors of war. It would begin, of course, with patriotism and ideals, but the glue that kept it going was individual loyalty to each other. Continuing to push when there was no reason to keep going, all for the sake of keeping your comrades alive. Eppler had that trust broken and responded in kind. Now he didn't care about the Reich or the Allies or any grand political implications of the world war. He didn't care about anything other than living to the next day.

In that particular respect, he was still no different than any other soldier.

Author's Note

Thank you for reading The Hazards of War. I truly hope you enjoyed the story. If you did—please leave a review online! A little encouragement goes a long way in continuing the effort with new tales.

There is a ton of work involved in putting a story together. The characters and plot do not spontaneously assemble; the research (especially for a novel such as this) does not present itself wrapped up in a bow; and it is all too easy to botch the dialogue, editing, or any number of details. So I would be remiss if I did not offer my thanks to my wife for supporting my writing hobby; my beta readers—especially Chris, Scott, and Brian for their unvarnished and sometimes critical feedback to try and make the end result better; and all of my friends and family who continue to offer words of encouragement and support.

I got into writing as a simple mental escape. I quickly found it to be a great vehicle for indulging my curiosity and performing research in the name of "the story." My interests vary quite a bit and are reflected in my choice of topics. Please consider looking at my other works published online and in print.

Did you see the headline around the latest credit card hack? For a thrilling tale of cybercrime, international intrigue, military adventure, and a bit of geeky online role playing (how could these things possibly be related?), check out my novel **Armchair Safari**—one of IndieReader's Best Books of 2014 and an Amazon best seller. All proceeds go to The Sgt. Byron W. Norwood Memorial Scholarship Fund.

Need a pick-me-up? Be glad you're not Nate Merritt—he lost his job, his aunt, and his girlfriend all in one day. But when he inherits his aunt's dilapidated mansion, Nate decides he'll flip it for a quick profit. There's just one problem: he doesn't know anything about remodeling. And the ghost that haunts the house doesn't appreciate a newbie making all this racket. Pre-order **The House That Jack Built** for a humorous spin on a not-so-typical haunted house story. (Release date Spring 2016.)

Follow me on social media for updates on new releases.

http://www.jonathanpaulisaacs.com
Facebook page at
http://www.facebook.com/armchairsafari
Email me at jpisaacsauthor@gmail.com
Follow me on Twitter at @jpisaacsauthor

CPSIA information can be obtained
at www.ICGtesting.com
Printed in the USA
BVOW03s0229230817
492838BV00001B/77/P

9 781517 65008